Repo Girl

A Novel

By Jane Fenton

This is a work of fiction. References to real people, events, establishments, organizations or locales are intended only to provide a sense of authenticity and are used fictitiously. All other characters, incidents, and dialogue are drawn from the author's imagination and are not to be construed as real.

ISBN: 978-1-7321165-1-1
Paperback Edition

For my loving, crazy, fun, wonderful family.

Chapter One

Why did it have to be a church?

Andrea Sloan already felt guilty about taking the 1965 canary yellow Mustang convertible on their wedding day but stealing the car from a church? Sister Kathleen's stern face popped into her head. She cringed. Now was not the time for post-traumatic stress disorder from her Catholic education. Focus on the job. Even though she wasn't invited to this ceremony, she'd learned over the last two weeks that if she acted like she belonged, she blended in much better.

With the Mustang car key in her hand and her purse slung over her shoulder, she squared her shoulders and walked with purpose across the parking lot, right up to the convertible parked at the curb in front of the church. It was covered in white streamers and balloons with "Just-Married" written in white glass chalk marker across the trunk and there were about a dozen empty beer cans tied to the bumper. *Great.* This wasn't going to be a quiet get-away. She took a deep breath and held it as she opened the car door and sat down like it was her car, waiting for something bad to happen. *Nothing.* No car alarm went off. No one came running and screaming at her to get out of the car. No lightning strike from the heavens. *Okay.* It was going to be alright. She breathed a sigh of relief, smiled and inserted the key into the ignition.

The doors to the church flew open and all at once, 50 people poured out of the church tossing confetti at the bride and groom as they were laughing and walking down the church steps. The groom looked at his precious car and saw a woman he didn't know in the driver's seat.

"Who the hell are..." was all Andi heard him yell before she turned the key and the roar of the engine drowned out the rest of his question.

"Congratulations," Andi yelled at them as she bit her lower lip and pressed down on the accelerator, speeding away from the church, cans rattling behind her. Thank goodness this car had good pickup. She took a quick glance in the rearview mirror and saw the groom, who had run after her, was now two blocks away. He couldn't outrun the car's v-8 engine.

She made a right onto Elm Street and saw a large woman wearing white capri pants and a bright orange top who grinned and yelled, "You go runaway bride! You don't need no man to make you happy!" Andi smiled and waved at her—she agreed completely. She merged onto I-581 where cars honked at her and people waved at her. She just smiled and cranked up the stereo, singing along to a song on the radio.

About fifteen minutes later, Andi pulled into The Repo Doctor parking lot, drove around back, punched in a code and the fenced gate slid open. She pulled the Mustang in and the gate closed behind her. She grabbed her purse, checked the glove box and under the seats for personal items. *Nothing.* Then she popped the trunk. *Oh man.* The newlywed's suitcases were there. The couple was not off to a very good start to wedded bliss. She hauled the heavy suitcases out of the trunk one at a time and then wheeled them both in through the back door of the office.

"What the hell, Andi? Are you moving into the office?" Jerry grumbled, sitting at his desk in front of piles of papers neatly stacked on the surface.

"Oh, that's okay. You just sit there at your desk, Jer," Andi said as she struggled to get both suitcases through the door. Once she was finally inside, she dropped into the nearest seat and heaved a sigh. "I've got these. No problem."

"How many times do I have to tell you, Andi, you are supposed to leave the owner's valuables securely behind." Jerry just shook his head. "Rookies."

"Oh, and just how was I supposed to do that? This was my only chance to get the Mustang. It's been locked up in the groom's parent's garage until this morning. I snagged it the first moment no one was around."

"Well that's just great," Jerry complained. "Now *I* get to call the groom and let him know he can come by the office to get his luggage." Jerry wrote a note on the pad of paper on his desk, then looked at her with a grimace. "You know I hate dealing with the skips face-to-face."

"That's why you get paid the big bucks, being the owner and everything," she waved away his objection.

Then his expression changed. His eyes widened and a big smile spread across his face.

"Wait, did you say the *Mustang*? Are you talking about the '65 Mustang convertible? It's out back?" Jerry asked. He didn't wait for her to answer. He was already getting up from his chair.

"Oh, sure, now you jump up. Where was that energy when I was struggling with the suitcases?"

Jerry ignored her and said, "You know, before we turn the Mustang over to the lender, I'd better take it for a test drive just to make sure the engine still runs well."

Andi snorted. "Whatever. I don't remember you doing that with any other cars I've delivered."

Jerry walked over to her chair, still grinning like a big kid, and held out his hand. "Don't be a smart ass," he said and wiggled his fingers. "Hand over the key, Squirt."

He was the only person who ever dared to call her *Squirt*—a ridiculous nickname he'd been using with affection since they were kids. They grew up in the same neighborhood, and since he was 6 years her senior, he was kind of like an older brother or maybe an annoying, overprotective cousin.

She dropped the key in his hand and rolled her eyes. "Be careful with the car, *old man*. I'm counting on my nice, big, fat check from this job."

"Don't worry. I'll write you that check as soon as I get back from my drive. You make an okay repo agent, Andrea Sloan." Jerry ruffled her hair and then walked out the back door, whistling.

Yes! Andi pumped her fist in the air. This check would give her a little breathing room. Things were always so tight financially. She'd been one mortgage payment away from foreclosure with her former waitress job at Star City Bar and Grill. This repo gig was bringing in decent cash. She smiled. Time to celebrate. She pulled out her phone and sent a text to her two best friends.

Ben, Maggie: `Indian takeout & Avengers`
                    `2night—my place & my treat`

***

Later that night, Andi grabbed a handful of organic popcorn from the bowl on her coffee table and popped several pieces in her mouth. She loved just hanging out on her comfy sofa in her childhood home with her two best friends in the entire world. Leaning forward, she took a sip from her can of Cherry Coke and placed it back on the coffee table.

"Okay, which of these amazing superheroes would represent your ideal guy? Maggy, you go first," Andi said. They were watching *The Avengers* movie, but they'd seen it so many times, they sometimes said the dialogue along with the characters.

"Duh," Maggy replied, "Bruce Banner, *obviously*. He's a scientist, for starters, which I find incredibly sexy. Plus, no one messes with him because they don't want to make him angry and deal with The Hulk."

Andi laughed, "Ha! We both know that you like him because he's literally green and you love green food and smoothies, being a vegan and all."

Maggy smiled and swung a sofa pillow at Andi, who laughed and managed to dodge it just in time.

"Now me," Andi pointed to herself and tucked her feet under herself, "I'm Team Thor all the way. You've got to agree with me, right Ben?" She turned to look at Ben. "Those amazing muscles, hair, that intense blue gaze, all completely melt-worthy, right?" she asked Ben.

"Thor is tempting, but I'll have to go with Tony Stark—Iron Man."

Ben leaned back in the chair and took a swig of his beer out of the long neck, brown bottle.

"What? How can you say that with a straight face?" Andi asked.

"Well, he's got the super suit that allows him to fly *and* shoot people. Plus, he's obscenely rich, dresses fabulously, and has the best gadgets."

Ben set his bottle down on the coffee table, reached forward and grabbed a handful of popcorn from the bowl.

"Okay, I'll give you that. Having loads of money and being able to fly would be cool superpowers," Andi said.

"Of course, what do you need with Tony Stark when you're dating Daniel, the super sexy drummer?"

Ben smiled and his entire face lit up.

"Oh, and he's completely smitten," Andi grinned as she elbowed Maggy. "Just look at that face." She turned serious and said, "I'm really happy for you, Ben. You're an amazing guy, and you deserve someone absolutely wonderful to love you. I just hope for his sake that he's as worthy as you claim because if he breaks your heart," Andi made a fist with her right hand and punched it into her open left hand, "then he'll have to answer to me. Remember, I'm really good at finding people."

"Well," Ben said, "you can both meet him tomorrow night and judge for yourselves. He and his band, Riot Act, are going to be playing at Star City Bar & Grill. Come by, and I'll save you a seat at the bar."

"Figures. My sister's been bugging me to babysit for weeks, and I've promised to come over tomorrow night, so they can have a date night," Maggy complained. "I always miss all the fun."

"Well, I'll check him out for you, Mags. I promise to give you a full report after I meet him tomorrow night."

***

The next night, Andi headed straight for the bar and grabbed the only empty stool on the end. Ben stood looming behind the bar in front of her stool, hands on his hips, a small white towel draped over his shoulder.

"Where the hell have you been?" he asked with a scowl. "I've been chasing customers off this stool for the last hour so you'd have a seat when you finally got here."

Andi smiled at him and leaned forward, so she wouldn't have to yell over the music.

"Sorry, I'm late. I got tied up at work."

She grabbed a few peanuts from a bowl on the counter and began to shell one.

"It took me a little longer than I expected to collect the car, and then I had to go home to change," she waved a hand in front of her blouse, "I didn't want to meet your boyfriend covered in a cherry slushy."

Ben shook his head and with a slow smile, opened his mouth to speak.

She held up her hand to stop him.

"Don't even ask," Andi said then turned toward the stage to check out the band.

She spotted an extraordinarily handsome singer, with an ego to match his looks based on the way he was singing and flirting outrageously with the women in the crowd. *Gag.* Andi looked past him and noticed the gorgeous bass player with a sensual smile, who was having an equal impact on the female audience. *Being movie-star attractive must be a requirement to play in their band.* Her theory was confirmed when she saw the drummer. This heartthrob wore a sleeveless shirt that showed off amazing muscles which flexed as he pounded on the drums.

Andi turned back to Ben, rested her right elbow on the bar and pointed a finger at him.

"You lied to me," she accused. "Iron Man? I don't think so. Your boyfriend has arms more like Thor than Tony Stark."

Ben leaned forward, elbows on the bar, hands supporting his chin, "I know, right?" He looked past Andi and stared at Daniel. "I could watch him play all night."

Someone hollered for a drink. Ben rolled his eyes and stood up. "Duty calls," he said and left to wait on a customer.

That's when she noticed the guy sitting to her right, leering at her. *Great.* He leaned toward her, and she smelled the stench of cigarette smoke and whiskey on his breath.

"Hi," he said in a slurred, loud voice. He grabbed the side of the bar to steady himself. "I'm wasted, but this condom in my pocket doesn't have to be." He tapped his shirt pocket.

Andi groaned. "Pal, throw it away because you're both trashed."

She turned her back to him and watched the band. They were actually good, playing a blend of rock and alternative music. An attractive guy with a button-down shirt and tie walked up to the bar and stood next to her, waiting to order a drink.

He asked her, "Can I buy you a drink?"

"No thanks," she said without turning to look at him.

"My name's John. You look so familiar. Didn't you used to work here?" he asked.

Andi sighed sounding bored while she continued to watch the band, "Yes. Quite a few weeks ago." *Take the hint buddy. Not interested.*

"I *knew* I recognized you," he said and stepped closer. "Your name is Andi, right? Want to get a table, so we can talk? It's really loud over here at the bar, so close to the stage."

"Sorry." Andi turned to look at John and gave him her best sympathetic smile and said, "I've got a boyfriend."

He returned her smile and shook his head. "Of course. The beautiful ones always do." He shrugged, took his drink, and walked away.

Andi felt her head being shoved forward. She turned around to see Ben glaring at her.

"Liar, liar pants on fire," Ben said.

She returned Ben's glare and looked back to make sure John was gone. He seemed nice enough, and she didn't want to hurt his feelings.

"What was wrong with John? He comes in here all the time. He's a great guy and hot if you're into that corporate look."

She lifted her chin. "I *have* a boyfriend."

"Marvel comic gods don't count."

Ben whipped the towel off his shoulder and began wiping the bar in front of her.

"I'm not looking for a relationship," Andi said and folded her arms across her chest.

"Chicken," Ben said.

"I have other priorities right now. I'm focused on keeping my house and staying afloat financially."

Ben tilted his head and studied her for a minute, and then his voice turned understanding. "Aw sweetie, you're just making excuses. I know you're scared, but there are plenty of nice guys out there. It's time you took a chance with one of them."

"I'm perfectly satisfied being single. You're in the love bubble so, of course, you want to match everyone else up." She patted him on the cheek. "I really am happy for you." Andi smiled. "But I'm happy for me, too. I'm in a good place and not willing to complicate it with a man." Her smile turned cheeky. "Especially a mere mortal."

"Okay," Ben said and decided it was best not to push her.

"Can you do me a huge favor and take this tray of margaritas over to the sorority girls at table 15? They get bitchy when their drinks are late, and I can barely keep up with the bar tonight. Your next drink will be my treat," Ben said.

"If I have to deal with a sorority, you'd better make that two drinks," Andi countered.

She lifted the heavy tray with six margaritas and began to walk over to their table.

The hunky lead singer said, "I'd like to take this down a couple notches and sing a song I wrote called *Not Enough*. I hope you like it."

The man certainly knew how to command the room. The place quieted down, and she watched as he grabbed an acoustic guitar, sat on a stool in the middle of the stage, and adjusted the microphone to his sitting position. Closing his eyes, he began to strum the guitar and sing. His voice was beautiful and had such a vulnerability to it.

> *I found the note you left on the table*
> *It just said sorry; not even a real goodbye*
> *Then you were gone from my life, left no trace*
> *How could you leave me? Guess I'll never know why.*

Oh. My. God. His words stopped her in her path. She stood frozen, staring at him. It was like he pulled this right from her heart. She gazed at him, confused. *How did he know?* She'd never told anyone. Not even her closest friends. *It was not possible.* She shook her head trying to make sense. Then he opened his eyes, and he looked right at her as he sang the chorus.

> *I'm not enough for your love*
> *Not enough, no not enough*
> *There's something missing inside*
> *Not enough, no not enough*

Andi stood transfixed, barely able to hold herself together. *How could he possibly know?* Her eyes filled with tears that she blinked back. Her heart felt like it was breaking right there in the middle of the restaurant. She couldn't move. She was trapped in this stranger's gaze.

> *I wanted a normal life like others have*
> *But I guess I'm just bound to go a different way*
> *I thought you knew me and everything was fine*
> *How could you leave me? Why didn't you stay?*

This man just laid out all her deepest, darkest, most secret feelings right here in the crowded room. Andi's feelings of hurt transitioned to fury. Even if he didn't know this was her life, why was he staring at her? Was this song a glimpse into his soul? A soul so very much like her own? *No way.* She shook her head. She'd seen the way he worked the women in the crowd. He was such a player. He probably stole these lyrics from some poor schmuck whose life sucked as bad as hers did. Someone like this rock star couldn't possibly be living the kind of life this song represented. *Could he?*

> *I'm not enough for your love*
> *Not enough, no not enough*
> *There's something missing inside*
> *Not enough, no not enough*

Yes. There was something missing inside her too. She nodded completely unaware she was doing so. Andi had wondered if she was missing some sort of gene that made her lovable. A gene that made people want to stay. She bit her lower lip. The singer ended the song, and without looking away, he smiled at her with that cocky grin he'd been wearing all evening.

Oh, what an ego! She was mad and embarrassed for getting all caught up in some stupid song and refused to look at him another second. Angrily, she turned and walked right into a young woman. The heavy tray of drinks crashed against Andi and then fell to the floor, soaking them both in the fountain of tequila and limes that showered them before gravity pulled the entire tray contents to the floor, shattering the glasses. One look at the enraged, wet customer, and Andi knew she was one of the sorority sisters, and some of that tequila she was wearing, no doubt, belonged to her anyway.

In the next instant, Ben was there to sooth the drenched woman's fury with a promise of a fresh tray of complimentary margaritas. He arranged for a busboy to clean up the mess and pushed Andi towards the restroom for damage control.

She stared at her reflection in the bathroom mirror. Unfortunately, she was beyond any help. Her hair was straight where it was soaked in tequila and wavy in the dry places, and she *sparkled?* Andi peered closer into the mirror, took a tiny crystal from her hair and tasted it. Salt. *Terrific.* Her white blouse and black skirt were soaked in alcohol, and she had little nick marks of blood on her arms where the glass had cut her when it shattered. *That's it.* She was so done. She was going to head home for the night as soon as she said goodbye to Ben.

"Oh no you don't. You can't leave without meeting Daniel," Ben chided.

"You seriously want to introduce me to anyone you know, much less care about, when I look like this?" she asked exasperatedly. "What about your obligation to spread good fashion throughout the Roanoke region? I'm definitely a fashion disaster."

"Honey, he's heard all about you. He would be shocked if you appeared dry and put together," Ben teased her. At least she hoped he was teasing.

"Gee, thanks for the compliment," she replied and rolled her eyes.

"Please come meet him," Ben pleaded with a little pout expression, "You promised."

"I promised before I reeked of tequila and looked like I was caught in a rainstorm." She sighed dramatically and said, "Oh alright, take me to meet your boyfriend before I change my mind."

Ben smiled widely and then dragged her by the hand backstage where the band was taking a break between sets. The player, the one with that sexy grin that made her drop the tray of margaritas, looked up, smiled and said, "Oh good. Thanks for bringing my drink, Ben. I am so thirsty."

Oh. My. God. The man exuded sex-appeal. She was in so much trouble. He walked up to her, leaned his face close to her hair and inhaled deeply. Then, in that soft, sexy voice he murmured against her neck, "Mmm, I thought that was a tray of margaritas." He stood up straight and held out his hand. "Hello, *Margarita.* I'm Cooper."

Andi was mesmerized again. This time, not by the lyrics so much as from the guy's charm and general magnetism. He was intoxicating all on his own and clearly, she needed to stay as far from him as possible. She knew his type, and she wasn't going to fall all over him like one of those darn groupies at the bar tonight. Or maybe it wasn't him at all. She wondered if she could be slightly drunk from the alcohol that soaked into her skin. She felt like she was floating and couldn't really keep from staring at him again.

Luckily, Ben jumped in and completed the introductions since the man left her speechless.

"Cooper, this is my roommate, Andi Sloan. Andi, meet Cooper Barnett, lead singer of the hottest ticket in Roanoke, the local band *Riot Act.*" Ben looked over at Andi, his head slightly tilted, right eyebrow raised, and lips pressed together, holding in a smile.

Andi guessed he was finding her reaction amusing. What was wrong with her? She never reacted like this. She usually sent guys like him running in the opposite direction with one of her scathing looks or barbed comments before they even had a chance to say, *Hey Babe.* Ben's expression was enough to break the Cooper spell she was under. She gave him her most dangerous look, which only made Ben shake his head and chuckle.

Cooper, oblivious to their exchange, looked completely surprised.

"No way. This is Andi? When you said your roommate's name was Andi, I thought he was a dude," Cooper said as he slowly studied her from her wet black pumps to her damp hair. "You are definitely NOT a dude."

Obnoxious. So why did that intense look make her feel warm? Andi glared at Cooper, which only made him smile wider. She'd better practice that look because it was not having the effect she was going for.

Cooper couldn't help but smile at this woman, not some random waitress like he originally thought, but Ben's best friend. *Cosmic forces at work.* The woman had captivated his complete attention while he was singing the first real song he'd composed and shared with an audience. After he sang the first verse, he finally got the courage to open his eyes and look out into the crowd, and there she was, just staring at him with a shell-shock expression on her attractive face. It was like she got it, the song, which meant she got him—the real version of himself he always kept hidden. He hadn't been able to look away as he sang and her expression flashed through a rainbow of feelings—surprise, sadness, and irritation. Sort of like the expression she was wearing now. He couldn't keep the smile from spreading across his face.

"So, Andi, want to meet up for a drink after we finish," Cooper glanced at his watch, "in about 30 minutes?" He was confident her answer would be a resounding yes. Women always said yes to him.

Andi lifted her chin and stared him down, annoyed at the invitation.

"No."

Wait. What? Cooper's confident smile evaporated.

"I think six margaritas is my limit." She looked down at her wet outfit. "I just want to go home, take a hot bath and go to bed." Andi pulled the wet blouse that clung to her body away, but it just molded right back to her skin. *God, it had been such a long day.*

With a lopsided grin, Cooper said, "*Okay.* That sounds like an even better plan than my offer for a drink. Want me to just meet you at your place?"

Andi's mouth dropped open in surprise for a brief instant and then she quickly recovered, narrowed her eyes, and said in an icy tone, "Sorry, *Rock Star.* You're *not* invited."

Not the reaction he had expected. Cooper tilted his head and looked at her in confusion.

The attractive guitarist from the band stepped forward and elbowed Cooper out of the way. "Ignore him. He's the lead singer and gets way too many girls. Hi. I'm Zach, the awesome but very lonely bass player."

Wow. These gorgeous men oozed charm. Andi shook her head.

"Hi Zach," she smiled back. The guitarists were laying it on just a bit too thick, but at least Zach's flirting didn't make her stomach flutter. She could handle him easily enough.

Zach continued, "I think that crash of the drink tray was the perfect ending to that melancholy number Coop sang. We should incorporate it as a sound byte at the end of the song unless, of course, you want to join our band and drop a drink tray each night."

Zach grinned. "I've been telling the guys we should add a hot woman to the band." He looked into her eyes and in a bedroom voice said, "You'd be perfect."

Daniel stepped in-between the band boys and nudged them to each side.

"Guys. *Please.* Could you two turn down the charm decibels long enough for me to meet the famous *Andi* that Benji talks about all the time?"

He leaned toward her and stage-whispered, "He talks about you so much, that I would feel completely threatened by you if you were a guy, Andi."

Then, he simply smiled and gave a quick once-over and nodded as if she had passed some sort of test. He spoke to Ben, "You're right. She's completely adorable. Just like I pictured her," he paused, "except very, very wet." He frowned. "Damn, how many drinks were on that tray, girl?"

Andi looked down at her drenched clothes. Her blouse still clung to her body. *Oh God, they couldn't see her lace bra through her shirt, could they?* The lighting in the ladies' room was not very good. Okay, she'd met Daniel. She was out of there.

"Too many. Yes, well, I'm headed home now." She gave Ben a firm look as she pulled her blouse away from her chest. *So embarrassing.* Her obligation had officially been fulfilled. She added with a quick smile, "It was nice meeting everyone, especially you, Daniel. Hope to see you around again soon." She turned and headed quickly for the door.

"Hey, I'll walk you out," Ben said and he had to jog to catch up to her.

As soon as they stepped out into the parking lot, Ben grabbed Andi's arm and turned her to face him.

"So, what do you think of him?" Ben asked.

"I have never met anyone so completely full of himself," she said and put her fists on her hips. "Did you see the look on his face when I told him NO? It's a word I don't think he's ever heard from a woman."

Ben shook his head and laughed. "Yeah, I saw the sparks flying between you and Cooper too. You need to pursue that and see where it goes, but I was asking about *Daniel.*"

"Oh," Andi smiled at Ben and relaxed her arms back to her sides. "My first impression? You already know I approve of those muscles." She took a deep breath and then looked directly into her best friend's eyes. "I found him to be gorgeous, funny, genuine, and nice. I like him, Ben."

Ben exhaled. He hadn't realized he'd been holding his breath, waiting for Andi's verdict. She was really good at reading people, and he trusted her opinion. "Yeah, I really like him too. In fact, I'm completely in love with the man."

"You're not confessing anything to me that isn't completely obvious. I saw the way he looked at you while he was playing tonight and when we were backstage." Andi pointed a finger at his chest over his heart and said, "I think he's just as much in love with you."

Ben beamed, "You really think so? I worry that I'm projecting my own feelings for him, you know?"

She leaned in and kissed him lightly on the cheek. "He loves you. I'd bet my next repo check on it."

Ben kissed her back.

As Andi walked toward her car, she shouted over her shoulder, "He'd be a fool not to fall madly in love with you, Benny. You're amazing!"

"Night, love," Ben called out and walked back inside grinning.

Chapter Two

"You've just gotta love social media," Andi said to herself. What did repo agents do before Facebook, Twitter, and Instagram? This job was almost too easy. Her skip, Clyde Finch, had complained that he had to work the early morning shift at Lucky's Gas and Go and couldn't go hunting with his buddies this morning. The red Dodge Charger she needed to repo was parked in front of the gas station. She looked through the binoculars into the storefront glass windows and spotted Finch, a big, bald guy with tattoos on his neck and arms. He was still busy working the cash register, collecting payment for gas and breakfast burritos. She should be able to drive the car away while he was dealing with the morning rush, but she'd have to take it now.

Her stomach growled. She hadn't had a chance to get breakfast this morning, so she reached into her large purse, and yes, there was an unopened bag of Cheese Curls. She opened the bag and popped one in her mouth. Finch was busy inside, and there were a couple customers pumping gas, but if she just got in the car like she owned it, she should be able to make a clean getaway. With the key to the Dodge in her hand, her purse slung over her shoulder, she got out of her car, locked it and confidently walked across the street to the gas station.

As soon as she approached the vehicle, a dog barked at her. From *inside* the car! She looked around and noticed that a couple of the customers watching her. It was already a warm morning, and the dog was locked in the car with just the slightest crack in the window, poor guy. Was Finch planning to keep the dog here all day while he worked? The dog was big and looked pretty ferocious—a Pitt Bull maybe? Andi quickly decided Clyde Finch was an ignoramus. Everyone knew you didn't leave a dog in a car anytime, especially when it was this warm out. She reached into her purse and pulled out the bag of Cheese Curls. It wasn't a dog bone, but it was better than nothing.

"Aren't you a good boy?" Andi crooned, pretending she wasn't terrified as she talked to the beast. There was drool dripping from his mouth and smeared on the driver's side window. *Ew. Could he be rabid?* There seemed to be a lot of dog saliva. *Oh lord.* She slid a cheese curl through the narrow window opening and pulled her hand back, startled, as the dog snatched the cheese curl before it even has a chance to drop to the seat. His large tongue swept across his face to capture any stray orange dust, and then to Andi's surprise, the vicious creature sat expectantly, his long pink tongue hung out the side of his mouth, waiting for another.

Glancing over her shoulder, she noticed the customers pumping gas were no longer looking in her direction now that the barking car alarm had stopped. She took a breath and dug another Cheese Curl out of the bag, repeating the action until the bag was half empty. She carefully unlocked the car door and opened it slowly. The dog pushed his way out, and to her surprise, sat at her feet on the parking lot. She squatted next to him, cooing. "You're a good boy, aren't you?" She rubbed him on his neck then she gave him several more Cheese Curls and reached in her purse, pulled out a bottled water, untwisted the cap and poured it directly into the dog's mouth. He gulped down about half of her water. The dog sat watching her as she slid into the driver's seat and started up the car. *Jeeze,* the engine was loud. It sounded like thunder as she started the car.

Someone banged on the hood of the car, yelling "Get the fuck out of my car!"

Jesus, Mary, and Joseph! It was the large burly man, Clyde Finch. He rushed to the driver's side of the car yelling at Andi. He stopped abruptly and stared at the dog who was standing alert and growling at him.

"What the hell did you do to Dumb Ass?"

Finch took a step towards Andi, and in a flash, the dog lunged at him and grabbed hold of his crotch with his big teeth. Andi, worried for the dog, called for him.

"Here boy. Want some more Cheese Curls?" she asked and shook the bag.

The dog released his owner, jumped in the car, hopped over Andi and sat in the passenger seat, barking once as if to say "Let's blow this Popsicle stand." Andi shut the door, threw it into reverse, and tore out of the parking lot. She glanced back to see Finch doubled over on the sidewalk, holding onto himself with both hands. As she drove down the street, she looked over at the dog. He had his nose in her bag of Cheese Curls inside her purse.

"Well, they're all yours now," she said with a laugh. Dumb Ass was a terrible name from a sad excuse for a human being. She should come up with something better. Maybe Dodger, since she found him in the Dodge Charger.

"What if we change your name to Dodger, boy?" Andi asked the dog.

Dodger poked his head out of the bag of cheesy deliciousness and licked Andi on the face.

"Okay," she laughed, "Dodger it is."

After she pulled into the gated Repo lot and parked the car, Andi grabbed her purse, and Dodger followed her into the office. Jerry sat behind a desk, talking on the phone with a lender. He took one look at the dog trailing behind Andi and shook his head. He rubbed his temple with his left hand. He could feel the beginning of a headache coming on just at the sight of that dog. Andi dropped the keys in the envelope with the paperwork and put it in the completed basket and called for a taxi. By the time she turned to face Jerry, he was off the phone.

"Do you mind if I leave Dodger here while I go pick up my car? I want to avoid a run-in with his former owner."

"We have a 'no pets' office policy." He pointed with his pen to the ugly beast that was sniffing the floor.

"Since when?" she asked.

"Since that *thing* came in with you," Jerry replied making a face.

"He's not a pet. He's *family*," Andi dropped in the chair in front of Jerry's desk and lifted her feet up on the other chair, her long legs stretching between the two seats.

"Really, why don't you make yourself comfortable," Jerry said.

Andi ignored him and said, "His name is Dodger, and the skip just left him locked in the car on this hot day. I didn't have a choice. I *had* to rescue him, Jer."

Jerry sighed, and in a tone that sounded as if he was explaining a simple task to a five-year-old, he said, "You do realize that we are only paid to *collect* the cars, right? Any personal property in the car stays with the skip. You always seem to forget that part. It's important."

Andi just shook her head. "Jer, there was no way I could leave the dog. He was clearly being abused. The skip was a real *loser*. He's lucky I didn't report him to the police for leaving poor Dodger in the hot car like that."

"You know, he could waltz right in here and demand we give that thing back." He pointed to the dog that now had his head in the trash can rummaging for something. "Legally we'd have to."

"Not likely to happen. Just before I drove off with the car, Dodger was playing fetch with the skip's balls. I don't think he's going to want to see the dog ever again," Andi said and smiled at the memory.

"You're too soft, Andi. You're going to have to toughen up to make it in this business." A yellow cab pulled in front of the office. She got up from the chair, walked over to the in-box and grabbed two more folders with keys, and headed toward the front door.

"Hey, I am tough. Do soft girls walk around with ferocious looking pit-bulls? No Jerry. No, they don't. Dodger won't even fit in my purse." She winked at Jerry. "But thanks for worrying about me."

As she headed out the door, she heard him yell, "No more strays! I'm serious!"

The taxi dropped her off at her car, and she drove away without running into Finch. The jerk probably took the rest of the day off and was sitting on a bag of ice. *Karma.* Couldn't treat people or animals like that without life turning around and biting back, in Finch's case, in the balls.

Andi stopped at a pet store and picked up a few essentials for Dodger like dog food, bowls, a leash, collar, and a couple toys then headed to the City Market. It was lunchtime, she was starving, and she owed Maggy an update on Ben's boyfriend. She parked in the short-term parking lot, paid, and walked into the bustling market building.

The smells of the wide variety of delicious foods filled the air. Ironically, Maggy's *I'm Juiced* space was next to a booth called *Hot Dog Heaven*. A cute, young guy named Simon, Maggy's nemesis, owned the place. Andi walked up to Maggy's booth, and as usual, Simon and Maggy were in the middle of one of their typical arguments. She sort of had a feeling Simon liked Maggy. He especially loved to harass her about her green drinks.

"Yeah, well, the only reason you get any business at all, Mary Margaret, is because I lure customers over to your area with my amazing grilled hot dog aromas," Simon said to Maggy then turned to Andi and winked. "Hey, Andi. Haven't seen you in ages. How have you been?"

"Can't complain. How's business?" Andi asked.

"Incredible," he stared over at Maggy with a look of gratification and grinned, "Thank you for asking." He turned back to Andi, "Would you like a dog today?" he offered.

"Funny you should ask, Simon. I am the new owner of a pit-bull named Dodger that I picked up from my repo this morning. But, yes, I need three with the works. To go," Andi said. She looked at Maggy who had her hands on her hips looking irritated. "And I'd love one of your delicious healthy smoothies too."

"Yeah," Maggy said enthusiastically, "because anyone who eats at Hot Dog Heaven will be going to heaven sooner than they might like. You should have called it Hot Dog Heart Attack."

"At least they'll die happy," Simon teased and then had to turn his attention to take a customer's order.

Andi smiled at her friend and said, "I see you two are still keeping things entertaining around here. It's great for business, really. You should plan a lunchtime show."

"Oh, he's such a weiner!" Maggy said.

"Yeah, well all I'm saying is your day would be a little less lively if you didn't have Hot Dog Man to spar with," and before she could reply to that, Andi said, "I've come by for your Very Berry Shake."

"Excellent choice," she replied and began preparing the smoothie. "So, you really have a dog now?"

"Yes. The moron skip left the poor pup in his car, I guess as a security system. Anyway, I rescued him. I can't stay long. I left him with Jerry back at the office."

Maggy laughed, "Oh, I'm sure Jerry *loved* that."

Andi smiled, "Yes, let's just say he's not a fan of strays. I'm bringing Jerry a hot dog as payment for pet sitting for me."

Maggy nodded. "So," she poured the light purple mixture from the blender into a plastic cup, "what did you think of Ben's boyfriend?"

"Seems like a really nice guy," Andi rested her arms on the counter, "and he's just as enamored with Ben. They're really cute together," she snorted, "you know, if you like that syrupy sweet, hurts your teeth kind of relationship."

Maggy smiled at her friend, "Uh huh. Not the kind of thing that is appealing to you at all," she looked knowingly at Andi.

"Exactly," Andi said, oblivious to Maggy's sarcasm.

"I met the rest of the band too. All three guys are ridiculously handsome like they model full time. Oh and the lead singer? *So* obnoxious. He asked me out for a drink after they finished playing last night, and he looked completely shocked when I turned him down. Like no one has ever said no to him," Andi shook her head then muttered, "egomaniac."

Maggy nodded, put a lid on the plastic cup, pushed a straw through the top, and handed the smoothie to Andi. She paid Maggy and then put her change in the tip jar.

"I'll have to come see them play sometime," Maggy said.

"Their music is really good." Andi took a sip of the smoothie through the straw, "Mmm, so tasty. Are you sure this has spinach in it?"

Maggy laughed, "Yes Andi. Spinach is delicious."

Andi made a face, and Maggy continued, "But the berries are sweet and have a much stronger flavor, so you don't taste it. Your Grams would be proud of you for eating your vegetables."

Andi rolled her eyes, "What would she think if she could see me now? I dropped out of college. I'm working a *weird* job. I mean, I know it's completely legal, despite Jerry's history with grand theft auto, but I swear I feel like I'm stealing cars. And the crazy thing is that I'm really good at it."

"Hey, your Grams would be proud of you! You've had an awful year, losing both grandparents so suddenly plus what you went through with that loser of a boyfriend. But look at you," Maggy held her hand out toward Andi. "You are a survivor. When your old job wasn't paying enough to make ends meet, you found a job that did. You're amazing, and your grandparents would be proud. I know I am."

Andi blinked back the tears that suddenly filled her eyes. "I love you Mags!" She leaned over the counter and gave her friend a big hug. "I don't know what I'd have done this past year without you. Thanks for being such a great friend."

Maggy hugged her back hard, "Love you too, Andi"

"Three dogs with the works, ready for you Andi," Simon called out.

Andi paid for her hot dogs, said goodbye to Maggy and Simon, and headed back to the office.

When she walked through the front door, she spotted Dodger lying next to Jerry's chair. Andi smiled when she noticed Jerry absent-mindedly scratching Dodger behind the ears. It was kind of cute the way they both looked up at her. Dodger got up, pranced over to her, and sat directly in front of her, looking at her with complete adoration as he sniffed the brown paper bag of hot dogs she held in her hand. Jerry's greeting was not as welcoming.

"Took your time getting back to the office," he grumbled and then looked at the bag that had captured Dodger's attention. "If you brought me a hot dog from the City Market, I might forgive you for leaving that damn dog here. He's been nothing but trouble."

She smiled. Jerry was all bark, no bite.

"Well, then I'm forgiven," she said and walked over to his desk, Dodger on her heels. She unwrapped a hot dog for Dodger, set it in the new dish she'd bought for him, and placed it on the floor. As Dodger devoured his treat, she placed an aluminum foil wrapped hot dog in front of Jerry, and unwrapped one for herself.

She took a bite of the delicious hot dog, and a chili-mustard blob oozed out of the bun and dropped onto her shirt.

Jerry chuckled and shook his head. "You are a mess, Squirt." He turned serious and pointed at her as he said, "Make sure you never eat in the cars you repo."

"Okay, *Pops*," Andi said as she used a napkin to wipe up the mess on her top. It just seemed to smear into a brown and yellow smudge. She looked up at him and tossed the napkin in the trash. "Lucky for you, I don't have time to even think about eating when I'm bringing in a car."

Jerry reached over to the pile of papers on the corner of his desk and handed Andi a check. "Here. This is for the Dodge. Now get that damn dog out of here and get back to work. I got two more jobs just this morning."

Jerry leaned back in his chair, put his hands behind his head and smiled. "The unemployment rate just went up two point three percent from last month. Business is great when the economy sucks."

Andi shook her head and smiled. Jerry was one of a kind. *Thank goodness.*

"Thanks," Andi said as she waved her check in the air. "I'm going to see if I can track down another car." She glanced at her watch. "It's still pretty early in the day."

She drove Dodger home. As she walked in the front door, she let Dodger sniff around and called upstairs to Ben.

"I'm home, and I brought a new roommate. He's not paying us rent. I think he's going to cost me money that I don't have."

Ben came running down the stairs wearing dark denim skinny jeans, a fitted blue t-shirt that read "Fashion Police— You Are Under Arrest" and a measuring tape draped around his neck.

"What do you mean a new roommate? I'm not giving up my design studio," he said and then stopped halfway down the stairs. "What is that?" he asked, part horrified, part fascinated.

At the sound of Ben's voice, Dodger went running up the stairs and began whining and licking Ben's jeans. Ben sat on the steps and pet Dodger.

"Holy hell, what has he been eating? His breath smells like chili," Ben said.

"He just ate a hot dog from *Hot Dog Heaven,* and don't make that face at me Benjamin. I bought him real dog food, too." Andi said.

Ben started laughing as Dodger tried to lick his face. "Do I even want to know why we now have a dog?"

"I rescued him. I had to, Ben. His owner was awful," Andi said.

Dodger began chewing on the measuring tape. Ben pulled it out of his mouth and looked at him closely.

"You know, he's so ugly he's kind of cute." Ben looked over at Andi, "Okay, I like him. Especially since I don't lose my sewing room."

Ben stretched the measuring tape across the length of the dog's body.

"I'm already thinking of some designs for him. I could create an entire dog fashion line. I've got to get my sketch pad."

He stood up and started back up the stairs with Dodger following behind him.

***

An hour later, Andi pulled into Barnett Investments' parking lot and got out of her car. Her old Honda Accord seriously stood out in the sea of Mercedes and BMWs. Then she looked down at her faded skinny jeans and soft green V-neck t-shirt with a mustard/chili stain. She brushed the orange dust from her thigh. Her car wasn't the only thing that stood out. She should have dressed to blend in with the downtown business crowd, but she honestly hadn't wanted to take the time. *Oh well, too late now.* The lot was in a nice part of town and unsecured. It was those kinds of details that a repo agent really appreciated.

She scanned the lot for the car, a black Mercedes-Benz E-Class sedan and BINGO, the license plate matched her file. Andi walked toward the car, keys in hand, and stood in front of the driver's door.

"Margarita Girl?"

She automatically turned toward that sexy voice—the one belonging to the man who'd hypnotized her with his song last night. Except instead of the tight jeans, black t-shirt, and guitar draped over his chest, he was wearing an expensive gray suit, crisp cobalt blue shirt, and coordinating tie. He walked toward her and stopped just two feet in front of her. They stared at each other, and then he glanced down at her shirt and grinned. Andi narrowed her eyes, annoyed by his amusement.

"What are you doing here?" he asked still grinning.

"I'm here on business," she said, raising her chin defiantly.

"Really? Who are you consulting with?" he asked, still feeling surprised and really glad to see her again.

She wanted to say none of your darn business now go away, but instead answered with a semi-truth, "Russell Stewart." It wasn't a lie. Not really.

"His office is just down the hall from mine. I'll walk you in," he offered, still grinning and motioned toward the building, but Andi just shook her head.

"Thanks, but I'm on my way out." She gave him a nervous smile, looked quickly around the parking lot for any other surprises—like Russell Stewart—then when she saw no one else, she put the key into the car door and turned it. The alarm began to make a loud sound. *Oh no.* She quickly opened the door, slid into the driver's seat, closed the door behind her, and clicked the auto lock while looking at Cooper and his surprised expression on the other side of the glass. The situation would be funny, really, if she weren't anxious to get out of there.

"Andi, what the hell? This is Russell's car!" he said.

She put the key in the ignition, and when the engine started, the alarm stopped. But Cooper was banging on the driver's window. She smiled at him apologetically, put the car in reverse, and backed it out of the space.

Jesus. Cooper stepped back from the car before Andi drove over his foot. His heart was racing as he ran over to his car, started it up, and followed her out of the lot.

What the hell am I doing? Cooper followed her onto the highway. He should call the police. Clearly, the woman was either crazy, a car thief, or in a relationship with Russell. The latter was his least favorite option. That thought made him laugh out loud and shake his head. There was something seriously wrong with him. Dr. Martin would definitely consider his feelings toward Margarita Girl unhealthy.

It's just that he hadn't been able to stop thinking about her after last night's performance at Star City Bar & Grill. Sure, they had some sort of chemistry thing going. But the way she reacted to the song he wrote and performed—it was the first time he'd written something, real and personal—and she seemed to connect to it in a powerful way. Now he was following her to God only knew where. *A chop shop?* How the hell was he supposed to know what thieves did with stolen cars? Was he was delivering his own expensive car to the thugs as a bonus?

I'm an idiot. He gripped the steering wheel tighter and swallowed. Andi would probably get double the commission, and he'd probably end up with a couple broken ribs, if he was lucky, or killed and dropped into the Roanoke River. A sane man would take the next exit and drive back to the office, forgetting he'd ever bumped into Margarita Girl. Obviously, he was insane because he was still following Andi as she turned into…*The Repo Doctor?*

What? He watched her roll down the window and punch the keypad. The chained fence slid open, and she drove into the lot. Cooper parked his car in a space in front of the office. *Okay.* This was an option he hadn't considered. *Is Margarita a Repo Girl?* He shook his head trying to make that image fit—not that he knew anything about the repossession business. He got out of his car and stepped up onto the sidewalk as she walked toward him, purse slung over her shoulder, keys in her hand, and irritation written all over her face.

"Following me, *Rock Star?*" Andi asked.

She was adorable when she was all attitude. He smiled.

"Well, yes, actually. Russell is my co-worker, and I thought you were playing Grand Theft Auto with his Mercedes."

"Well, Russell is three months behind on his car payment, so I'm returning it to the lender," she said. She squinted her eyes and raised her voice. "It's all perfectly legal."

She was so spunky. Who knew he had a weakness for tall, spirited women with stained t-shirts? His smile grew wider.

"Hey, you could have just explained that to me back in the parking lot; then I wouldn't have had to chase you all over town." *Okay, so maybe that wasn't quite true.*

"It was none of your business," she said, dismissing him as she turned and walked into the office. Cooper followed her in.

"The Mercedes is in the yard," she said to Jerry as she dropped the keys and folder into the completed basket.

"Nice," he said without looking up from the paperwork. He finally looked up when he heard the bells alerting that someone was coming in right behind her. He assessed Cooper in about 5 seconds with a glare and pointed at Andi and said, "I was serious when I said no more strays."

She looked back at Cooper and then turned to Jerry. "Don't worry, Jer. I'm not keeping this one. He just followed me because he thought I was stealing his friend's car."

She rolled her eyes like that was the most ludicrous idea.

"I never said Russell was my friend. Just a co-worker," Cooper said.

She sighed. "Not the point, but whatever. You can go back to work now that you know I'm not a car thief."

She had dismissed him again. *What was wrong with this woman?*

She turned to Jerry and said, "I'm going to call a taxi, and pick up my car."

"Let me give you a ride," Cooper blurted without thinking.

Andi put her hands on her hips and looked at him, annoyed.

Cooper held his hands out to the side and said, "Look, it's the least I can do after chasing after you." He gave her a charming smile. "Plus, I'm going there anyway. It just makes sense."

Jerry mumbled something under his breath about strays and trouble while he shook his head.

"Alright. Let's go. See you tomorrow Jer," Andi said as she swept out of the office.

Jerry watched her leave with Cooper trailing behind her like another damn dog.

They walked out to his car, and Cooper opened the door for her.

"Wow, a Porsche. This is a pretty nice ride for a rock star that plays at the Star City Bar & Grill. If you were on tour across the US, maybe. But look at you," Andi waved at his suit, "all dressed up and everything. What kind of day job do you have exactly?" she asked as she sat down in the low sports car.

Andi watched him close her door, and *oh my.* The seats were as soft as marshmallows. She leaned her head back on the headrest. His car looked brand new. It was really clean, and it smelled so good, a combination of leather and Cooper's delicious cologne. She closed her eyes. *Heaven.*

He got in on the driver's side and closed his door. "I'm Vice President, Account Services." He glanced over at her waiting for a response. His title always impressed women, but there was no reaction from her. *Was she asleep?*

She looked so relaxed, her eyes closed, a hint of a smile on her face as she said, "Of course you are."

He started the engine and pulled out of the parking space. "What about you? I thought you were a waitress at the restaurant. Today, I learn that you repo cars. Call me surprised because I didn't see that one coming."

With her eyes closed, she said, "I used to be a waitress, but I wasn't making enough money to support myself. My neighbor helped me get the job working for her grandson, and now I'm making enough money to pay the mortgage and buy a few groceries. I've only been doing it for a couple weeks, but it pays the bills. Jerry says I'm a natural if a little too soft."

She opened her eyes and sat up in the seat suddenly awake and annoyed. "Do I look soft to you?" she asked him pointing her finger to her chest.

Cooper looked in the direction of her pointed finger, grinned and just shook his head. *Not touching that question, thank you very much.*

"Exactly," Andi continued as though he had answered. "I'm tough, darn it. I supported myself after my grandparents were killed in the car accident last fall. I dropped out of college, went to work full time as a waitress, and picked up a roommate to make ends meet. *Soft?* I don't think so. And you wouldn't believe some of the situations I've been in while working repo."

"God. I'm sorry about your grandparents. That must have been awful. I can't imagine my grandfather not being around. Weren't your parents able to help out?"

"My parents have never been in the picture. My father's an unknown, and my mother dumped me on Gram's kitchen table when I was only a couple weeks old. Haven't seen or heard from her since. She left me in the car seat with a diaper bag and a note with only one word written on it. SORRY. What kind of person does that? No explanation. Just SORRY. Anyway, my grandparents raised me. They were the only family I've ever known." She sighed. There wasn't a day that went by that she didn't still miss them.

Jesus, no wonder she reacted so strongly to his song. His gut twisted as he considered how to even respond. "Andi, I…"

"Stop." Andi interrupted him, hand raised up to stop him. "Don't you dare feel sorry for me," she said and then looked straight ahead. *Why was she telling him any of this?* What was it about this guy? She never talked about her mother. Ever. Time for a change in subject. She looked over at him studying him closely.

"So I'm trying to match the arrogant guitar player I met the other night to this Porsche driving, suit. Did you say you were a VP? No offense, but aren't you a little young to be Vice President of anything?"

He chuckled. "Well, not such a stretch to be VP when your dad owns the company. Don't get me wrong. I've got the credentials – a bachelor's from Princeton and a master's degree from Yale. I've been working at the company for the last four years and, not to brag or anything, but I've got a knack for the business." He glanced over in time to catch her eye roll and returned his attention to the road.

"What? I really am brilliant with numbers." *Damn, the woman was impossible to impress.*

"Oh, I see the similarity now. The Rock Star and the Suit are both arrogant. Thanks for clearing that up," Andi said with a playful grin.

"Very funny. I'm actually really good at both financial planning and creating music. The problem is that crunching numbers is tedious, mind-numbing work while making music is inspiring, energizing play. My fate working for Barnett Investments was pretty much sealed when I was born. I had options, of course. If I hadn't been strong in math, I could have gotten a business degree and worked in Human Resources." He shrugged. "So I simply exist at the office during the day and spend every spare moment I can writing and playing music."

Before she could reply to that bit of information, Cooper pulled into a parking spot directly in front of Nathanial's, an upscale, downtown restaurant that was a favorite of the business crowd. Too pricey for Andi's budget, but she'd heard of it.

"This isn't where my car is parked. Why are we stopping here?" Andi asked, annoyed.

He turned off the engine and twisted in his seat to face her. "Look, I'm starving. I was headed for a really late lunch when I bumped into you in the parking lot. I thought we could just pop in here, grab a quick bite to eat, and then I'll take you to your car."

"I'm not hungry, and I really don't have the time."

Her stomach growled in protest.

Cooper heard it too because he glanced down at the source of the sound and then back to her eyes, with that obnoxious, irritating smile.

She waved her hand towards the restaurant as she spoke. "This is not the type of place where you grab a quick bite to eat. If you were that hungry, we could have just gone through a drive-thru at any number of the fast food places back by the office. It would have saved a lot of time."

"First, fast food is terrible for you. Second, I never eat in my car."

He unbuckled and slid out of his seat as Andi muttered, "What a surprise," as she joined him on the sidewalk.

She looked down at her clothes and said, "Cooper, I'm not dressed for someplace this nice."

"You look perfect to me," Cooper said and winked at her.

Andi snorted and said, "*Oh my God.* Does that sort of thing really work for you? You need some new material, *Rock Star*."

Cooper just chuckled as he held the door for her then followed her inside.

Nathanial's had elegant dark stained wood walls, soft lighting, white cloth covered tables with candles in the center. This was the type of place that once you stepped inside, you had no idea what time of day it was. Andi didn't trust places where the lighting was too low to clearly see the food. What were they trying to hide, anyway?

The hostess seated them at a cozy little table and handed them each a menu. Andi glanced at the prices and bit her lip. *Holy Mary, Mother of God.* And these were the lunch prices. What the heck was lobster macaroni and cheese? The only macaroni and cheese she was familiar with came out of a blue box. She frowned.

Cooper nudged her foot under the table. She moved her foot away and lowered her menu to scowl at him.

He was smiling again and said, "Lunch is on me. Order whatever you want."

The man was so infuriating. She would buy her own darn food, *thank you very much,* if she could find something normal to eat. This place didn't even serve chili-cheese fries. What kind of freak made fries out of a sweet potato?

A beautiful waitress approached their table, introduced herself as Chelsea and was practically drooling all over Cooper. Andi rolled her eyes and sighed. It was annoying enough to watch the women swoon over him while he performed, but apparently, this happened to the man everywhere he went. No wonder he was so arrogant. She shook her head.

Cooper ordered a sweet tea and chipotle chicken sandwich with a side of sweet potato fries. Andi ordered a water with lemon and smiled at the waitress as she handed her the menu. She watched in fascination as Chelsea scrutinized Andi from her hair to her stained t-shirt, even glanced down at her shoes, and dismissed her as irrelevant before flashing a dazzling smile back at Cooper.

Andi looked over at Cooper, but he wasn't paying any attention to Chelsea. Instead, he was frowning at her.

Then he said, "She'll also have the chipotle chicken sandwich with sweet potato fries."

Chelsea sent a chilling look to Andi, then smiled back at Cooper and said, "Sure thing. I'll go put this in for you."

As soon as Chelsea left, Andi kicked Cooper's foot under the table. "Why did you order for me?"

He just smiled back at her, "Because you're obviously hungry and I didn't think the lemon in your water would be particularly filling."

She glared at him. He just grinned back at her. Normally her glare intimidated people, but for some reason, it was not having the desired effect on him. Well, then she'd take control of the conversation.

"So, I understand how you got your day job. How did you get involved with the band?"

"I met Zach and Daniel at Princeton. We belonged to the same fraternity, and when we discovered we shared a passion for music, we decided to form a band. We played cover songs at college parties. Word got around and we got a lot of gigs." Cooper shook his head and smiled. "Those were some pretty wild times."

"But what happened when you went to grad school?" Andi tried to bring him back on topic.

"Yes. So we didn't get to play very often. I was in grad school, and the guys were working on their careers, but we kept in touch and played occasionally when we could make our schedules work."

Chelsea brought the tray of food to the table, and it smelled delicious. Cooper immediately began to eat his lunch. Andi wasn't going to eat the food he'd ordered for her. She was making a point, after all, until her stomach rumbled. Maybe she'd just try one of those sweet potato fries. They were orange, which was her favorite food group.

Cooper watched Andi cautiously pick up a French fry and then sniff it before taking a bite. She looked up, and he quickly hid his smile and focused on his food.

She decided sweet potato fries were pretty good and took another bite.

"The guys and I decided that we wanted to continue playing together. We got along incredibly well, and when we played music, it flowed effortlessly."

He gently wiped his mouth with his napkin and placed it back on his lap.

"Trust me, that's a rare thing. We had the perfect timing, rhythm, texture, and harmony. It was extraordinary. Since I was the only one with a career tied to Roanoke, the guys relocated here."

"Wow. That sounds like a pretty amazing friendship as well. What do they do for a living?"

"Daniel's in real estate, and Zach's an architect. The thing is, we share the same dream of playing music full time for fan-packed stadiums around the world."

Andi smiled at him and shook her head. The guy was certainly passionate about his music. And a dreamer. And still much too good looking and arrogant for his own good, but not quite the goof-off she'd pegged him for initially. Go figure.

"What about you? What's your dream, Margarita?" Cooper asked, his eyes focused on her.

Andi snorted and pretended to give it some thought, "Hmm, my dream is to make enough money so that I can pay my bills each month."

She looked down at her plate and realized she'd eaten all the fries, so she carefully picked up the chicken sandwich, smelled it—*oh spicy*—and then took a tentative bite. She closed her eyes and slowly chewed, savoring the flavors that were having a fiesta in her mouth.

Cooper watched her with complete fascination. She was making little sounds of pleasure as she ate the sandwich, completely unaware of the effect it was having on his libido. He'd never eat a chipotle chicken sandwich again without thinking of her in this moment.

Get a grip, man. You will not be jealous of a sandwich. He nudged her foot again to get her attention. "Come on, fess up, everybody has dreams. If you could do anything, what would you do?"

She opened her eyes, narrowed them at him, and swallowed.

In a defensive tone, she said, "I *am* serious. I work really hard to make ends meet, and I'm very grateful when I can cover my expenses each month. Not all of us have time for big dreams. Some of us do the best we can just to survive."

That's what she told herself anyway. But now that she thought about it, even her closest friends had dreams. *Face it, there's something inherently wrong with you.* She was broken in some invisible way, and when you let people close enough, they can see the cracks.

Oh god. She felt sick.

What was she doing here anyway? Having lunch with some rich guy who had everything in life handed to him, and he was judging her because she didn't have a dream. She wasn't a dreamer like him. No, she was pragmatic. She was a survivor, and she would not apologize for it. She carelessly wiped her mouth with her napkin and tossed it on her plate. Then she leaned back against her chair, folded her arms under her chest and scowled at him.

What a fine opinion he had of her. First, he thought she was stealing a car, and now he was feeding her because he thought she was some charity case. She was such a fool. She should have taken the darn taxi back to her car. Instead, she was wasting time with this Rich Boy/Rock Star when she ought to be tracking down her next skip.

Cooper sat silently as he watched Andi's transformation from sex goddess to vulnerable young woman to fearless Amazon warrior in a matter of minutes. *What the hell just happened?* You'd think he poked a bear with a stick rather than asked her a simple question, but he was quickly learning there was nothing simple about Andrea Sloan.

He put his hands up defensively, "Hey, I'm not criticizing you, so don't go getting all fired up at me." He placed his palms down on the table and leaned towards her meeting her determined gaze head on and in a quiet, gentle voice said, "Actually, I think you're pretty damn amazing, Andrea Sloan, just based on the little I know about you already. I've seen plenty of people who use adversities that aren't nearly as tough as yours as excuses to whine and complain that life isn't fair. But not you. You just keep plowing ahead no matter what life throws at you. I admire that."

She had been ready to do battle with him. She just hadn't expected the last part. The anger diffused from her as quickly as air released from a balloon. Cooper Barnett confused the heck out of her. One minute he was a playboy, tossing tired lines at her or giving her a flirty grin and wink, and the next he was speaking about tried and true friendships and music with such passion and sincerity, it was enough to make her head spin.

His last statement, well, it sure didn't sound like a line, and heaven help her if it was because it chipped away at a piece of her wall. The wall that had taken her years to construct to keep her safe from people that could hurt her. "Thanks," she said quietly, and she gave him a hint of a smile. "And thanks for lunch too, it was delicious. I really should get back to work." She bit her lower lip.

Cooper swallowed. He felt more comfortable dealing with the sassy or even irritated Andi. This soft, quiet, vulnerable woman made him feel very protective. The woman sitting across the table from him made him feel all kinds of things surprising and unexpected. And *that* scared the hell out of him.

"Then I guess we'd better get you back to your car," he said, and he gave her a half smile.

Chapter Three

The next morning had been frustrating for Andi. This was one of her more challenging cases. She'd had a streak of easy repos, so she'd gotten lazy. After an unsuccessful morning of trying to get Thomas Milner's car, Andi headed home to unwind with plans to take a nap. She was exhausted, frustrated, and stressed about making ends meet and was feeling the beginning of a headache forming in her frontal lobe.

She pulled into her driveway and pressed the garage opener. It opened with the speed of an inchworm, and it was only going to be a matter of time before that stopped working too. As her door slowly rose, she began to feel the steady drumming of her headache vibrate throughout her car. *Music?* She lowered her window in order to better hear.

She peered straight ahead into her garage, first seeing pairs of jean-clad legs. Was Ben having a party in her garage? Not exactly. She blew out a sigh as a hunky guy in jeans and a black t-shirt turned toward her, hugging an electric guitar at his hips, and smiled. *Cooper.* Her stomach did a little flip, and she felt her face flush. It was so unfair that her body reacted immediately just from his smile.

She looked beyond Cooper, and there was the rest of the band. Ben, who'd been chatting with Daniel, saw Andi and came dancing toward the car. Dodger held a drumstick in his mouth while he ran circles around Ben. What in heavens were they doing in her garage? Well, since she wouldn't be parking in the garage, she put her car in Park, turned off the ignition, unbuckled, grabbed her purse and files from her front passenger seat, and stepped out of the car. As she closed the door, Ben, and Dodger reached her. She bent down to greet the dog and then stood up to face Ben. He was beaming and thumbed over his left shoulder toward the band in her garage.

"Don't they sound great?" Ben's smile lit up his entire face. The guy was so smitten.

Andi didn't know whether they sounded great, but they were loud, and her head was beginning to pound to the beat of the drums.

"Look, Ben, I've got an awful headache and just really need to go inside and sleep it off. I'm sorry, but you'll have to ask the guys to leave." Andi stepped toward the house, but Ben held his hand out to stop her.

"Sorry, but no can do. I just rented this space to them." Ben reached into his front pants pocket and pulled out bills and held them in front of her face. "How's this for easing your headache, babe? Eight Benjamin Franklins. Cooper insisted that they pay for the entire month in advance at $200/week."

Andi shook her head in disbelief. "You rented my garage? To Cooper?" Her voice cracked at the last part.

Ben continued to grin, "Pure genius, right? I'll think of a way you can repay me later. Maybe now you'll stop worrying so much about paying those damn bills and have a little fun." He lifted Andi's hand and placed the money into her palm and closed it.

Andi frowned and then glanced beyond Ben and caught Cooper watching her as he was singing before he quickly looked away. What was she going to do now? It was bad enough the man was in her dreams, now he was going to be in her house. *For a month.* She swallowed hard. She needed this money desperately, and Cooper knew it. What if this was some sort of charity? That thought made her feel ill.

It was as if Ben was reading her mind because he immediately said, "Jesus Andi, would you just relax. This is Capitalism, plain and simple. They need a space to practice, and you have a space to rent out. It's a win-win. Actually, it's a win-

win-win because this means I get extra time with my hot drummer boyfriend."

Before she could come up with a reply, Ben said, "Uh-oh. Don't look now, The *Golden Girls* are headed this way."

Andi turned around, and there they were, marching across her lawn. Individually, they were pretty sweet and manageable, but they could be quite a force to contend with unified. Andi sighed with resignation. There was no way she was getting any rest now.

Hazel Barzetti led the trio and said, "Andrea Lynn Sloan, what is going on here? What would your grandmother say, God rest her soul."

Mrs. Barzetti made the sign of the cross by touching her right hand to her forehead, then chest, then left and right shoulders respectively.

The music stopped.

"What do you mean, Mrs. Barzetti?" Andi asked with false innocence.

"You know exactly what I mean, young lady. You've got a garage full of rock musicians in your home. Are they moving in too? It's one thing to let sweet Benny move in with you," she turned and gave Ben an affectionate pat on the cheek.

"Thanks so much again, dear, for making us those dazzling bowling shirts for our team, *The Strike Queens*. The look on the Pin Pushers faces when we wore them last Tuesday night was priceless. We won too!" Mrs. Barzetti smiled at the memory and then abruptly turned and stared at Andi. "It's quite another thing to turn your Gram's home into a frat house, dear."

Andi couldn't tell if Mrs. Barzetti was horrified or excited by this prospect.

"No ma'am," a deep voice replied from behind her and startled, Andi jumped and threw her hand to her chest. She hadn't heard him come up behind her although now she could smell the slightest scent of his expensive, intoxicating cologne as he stood uncomfortably close to her. "I hope we weren't making too much noise. Please allow me to introduce myself.

My name is Cooper Barnett, and this is Daniel Moyer and Zach Jamison."

"Well, I'm Hazel Barzetti, and I live directly across the street from Andi." Mrs. Barzetti pointed to the shorter woman with curly white hair next to her. "This is Gladys Davis. She lives next door to me." Mrs. Barzetti pointed to the woman on the end with hair that was an unusual shade of red. "This is Ethel Harper, she lives two doors down from Andi."

The band members each reached out and shook hands with the neighbors.

Cooper spoke first.

"Andrea has been kind enough to let us use her garage so that we can practice our music. We're not moving in with her. You'll let us know if we're making too much noise, I hope." Then Cooper gave the ladies his high voltage, dazzling smile, and Andi noticed that women of all ages were affected by those kilowatts. Gladys giggled, and Ethel blushed and said something about polite, good-looking young men.

Mrs. Barzetti gave both of her friends a stern look which made them immediately sober and straighten their shoulders.

"Andrea, I brought you some of my homemade chocolate chip cookies." Mrs. Barzetti handed her a plate piled high with cookies and then arched her thin penciled eyebrow. "Now, mind your manners dear and invite us in, so we can get to know these boys that are going to be spending time in your garage. I'm still not sure I approve."

Andrea hid a smile. Yes, they could be overbearing sometimes, but she did love these women. They'd always looked out for her while she was growing up and even more so since her grandparents had passed. It was sweet, really.

She smiled. "Sure. Why not?" *I'm not exhausted or anything.* "Everyone come on in, and I'll get us a drink to go with these delicious cookies."

"Great, I'd love a beer!" Zach grinned, and Cooper elbowed him in the ribs. "Ow, I meant a glass of milk," Zach corrected.

***

Cooper smiled to himself as he tuned his acoustic guitar. He and the guys had been practicing for about four hours in Andi's garage. The interrogation in her kitchen with the matriarchs had gone really well. He was glad Andi had someone looking out for her. Cooper and the boys had charmed everyone, with the exception of Andi, who had managed to sneer at him whenever her adoring neighbors weren't looking. That only made him smile wider.

This morning, he'd pounced on Ben's offer to let the band practice in Andi's garage, although Cooper insisted they rent it, of course. He wasn't a complete louse. Andi desperately needed the cash, but lord she was damn prickly about money. Renting the garage was the perfect way to help her out while getting to know her better. And he wanted to get to know her better. Dr. Martin, his psychologist, might even consider his fascination with Andi an obsession, like his Rubik's cube. He worked on the cube for 9 days straight in fifth grade until he solved it. Once he'd figured out the pattern, the pieces fell easily into place, and he moved onto the next challenge. Andi was an enigma to him, just as colorful as the Rubik's cube and just as perplexing but not for long. He'd figure her out too, and that was going to be a lot of fun. He shook his head and grinned.

"Oh for the love of god, I don't know how much longer I can work under these conditions," Zach said and gave Cooper a light shove.

Cooper spun around and looked at Zach. "What conditions? Don't you like the garage? Granted, it's no studio, but there's plenty of space and decent acoustics."

"The space is fine. It's all this damn smiling that's annoying." He pointed at Daniel and then at Cooper. "Both of you, stop it."

Cooper swatted the back of Zach's head. "Hey dude, give Danny a break. The guy's in love. It's about time he met someone nice. Be happy for him."

"Ben is SO amazing," Daniel sang and played a brief, enthusiastic drum solo, raised his drumsticks above his head, looked up and smiled.

"I am happy for you, Danny, really. But both of you grinning like school girls is getting damn maddening," Zach admitted.

Cooper's mouth dropped open in disbelief, "Both? What the hell are you talking about? I'm not in love."

Zach folded his arms across his chest and raised an eyebrow.

"Okay, so I admit I've been a little distracted lately. But please, I'm not acting any different."

Zach narrowed his eyes.

"What?" Cooper stammered. He turned to Daniel for support, "Danny, tell him, I'm the same rock star genius who kicks ass on vocals."

Daniel pretended to study him closely, then burst out laughing and shook his head. "Sorry Dude, can't help you. You haven't been yourself since you met her." Daniel tilted his head, and his expression turned thoughtful. "Frankly, I don't think I've ever seen you quite like this over a woman. Interesting." Then he turned to Zach, "Shit if you aren't right, Zach. Coop doesn't even have a clue, poor sucker. Just look at him standing there, looking really pissed off." Daniel laughed again.

"You think he looks angry now, just imagine how infuriated he'll be if they actually start dating," Zach said, and he began laughing too.

"Hilarious," Cooper said. "Really, you two assholes should go on a comedy tour."

"Hey man, we're just having fun with you. Come on, let's all head over to Star City Bar & Grill. Benji's working. I'll buy the first round," Danny said.

"You guys go ahead. I'm going to hang out here and try to finish a song I've been working on," Cooper said without looking up. He continued tuning his guitar.

Danny and Zach grinned at each other.

"You know, Danny, I'm feeling left out. I need a woman. Maybe I can pick up a waitress there too, just like Coop did," Zach said. "Then maybe I'll find out later she's really a hot bounty hunter."

Cooper shook his head, grinned, reached over and grabbed his water bottle and threw it at Zach. "Asshole."

Zach and Daniel laughed as they left the garage.

***

About thirty minutes later, Andi came walking out into the garage with her purse slung over her shoulder.

She stopped and stood frozen in place when she heard Cooper playing a beautiful melody on his guitar. He looked up and smiled when he saw her.

"Oh, sorry. I thought everyone had already gone," Andi said.

Cooper said, "I stayed behind. Just working on a new song."

"It's lovely."

"Thanks. I'm writing it for my brother's wedding."

"That's nice." *Really nice. Who are you, and where's the obnoxious guy?*

Cooper set his guitar back in the case.

"So, are you headed out on a job?"

"Yes," she nodded. "I was unsuccessful this morning, so I'm hoping to snatch the car after the skip gets off of work."

"I still can't believe you repo cars. I mean, I know you do. I've actually seen you in action," he laughed. "Would you mind if I rode along? I'd love to see it from your side of the dashboard."

"I don't think that would be a good idea," she said, hesitating. "It's boring most of the time."

"Oh, I don't know. The car chase with Russell's Mercedes was pretty interesting."

"Yes, well." Andi looked away.

Cooper just knew she was going to tell him no. *Again.* This wasn't working. He needed a new approach.

"Oh, I get it," he nodded, "You're afraid." He crossed his arms and gave her his best smart-ass grin. "Don't feel bad. I have that effect on women."

She gaped at him for a moment and then lifted her chin, "I'm *not* afraid." She straightened her shoulders. "Especially of you." She narrowed her eyes and folded her arms across her chest.

"Great, then let's go," he smiled, grabbed his jacket and headed for the door.

Wait. What just happened? Andi chased after him out the door.

Cooper walked over to her car, and she ran over to the driver's seat and got in. He opened the passenger door and stared in shock. The passenger floor and seat were full of stuff.

"Hold on, let me move a few things out of the way," Andi told him while she moved a large metal shovel to the back seat.

Holy Shit, Cooper stared at the inside of her car. "Why do you have all this in your car? Want me to move anything into the garage for you?" he asked helpfully.

"No. Everything in here is important for my job," Andi replied.

Why the hell did she need a shovel? Cooper frowned as Andi tossed several items in the back seat.

Jesus. She must be one of those hoarders. He saw a show once about them on television. Except her house wasn't cluttered. But her car. *Wow.*

She finally finished tossing things in the back seat, so he could sit down in the passenger seat. He got in and buckled up.

Andi pulled out of the driveway and headed down the street.

He looked over at her and grinned, "So what's the plan, Repo Girl?"

"Well, I've got to pick up a sandstone Toyota Camry belonging to Thomas Milner. Unfortunately, he had to work today which is why I came home early this afternoon."

"Why didn't you steal, I mean get his car from the lot, like you took Russell's car?"

"Because Mr. Milner's car is secured in a fenced, guarded lot. He gets off in about 15 minutes, so my plan is to follow him and hopefully get an opportunity to grab his car."

She looked over at Cooper briefly, then returned her attention to the road. "Are you sure you're up for this, Rock Star? It's unpredictable work. That's one of the reasons I like it. No two repos are ever the same."

"Hey, I love a challenge," Cooper smiled and winked at her. "Bring your best game, Margarita. That's what I like about performing with the band. We play the same songs, but the feeling is unique with each audience. For instance, I've only ever had a tray of margaritas dropped at the end of a song one time."

They pulled into a bank parking lot. Andi reached into her purse and grabbed a pair of binoculars, slid her head through the strap and then held them to her eyes. She stared at the parking lot across the street.

"Damn! How old are those binoculars? They look like they weigh 30 pounds."

Andi grinned while still looking through the binoculars, "Who needs a gym with these? They were my grandmother's favorite binoculars."

"Did she keep an eye on Mrs. Barzetti and the other neighbors with those?"

Andi laughed. "No, she was an avid birdwatcher. She used to sit at the kitchen table and watch the birds at her feeder. She'd have heart failure if she knew what I was using them for now."

"So where's the car we need to pick up?" Cooper asked.

"See that sandstone Toyota Camry, third row from the street and seventh car from the right?" Andi checked her watch. "He should be out any minute."

As if on cue, the building doors opened, and about one-hundred employees poured out of the building and walked toward their cars. She spotted a man opening the door to the Camry. Andi started her car and unconsciously touched something shiny on her rearview mirror.

"What's that?" Cooper asked.

Andi looked at him in confusion, "What?"

"You touched your rearview mirror just now. What's that?" He pointed to the small metal object on the mirror.

Andi's face flushed briefly, and she said, "Oh, I didn't even realize I still did that. It's a St. Christopher medal. He's the Catholic Saint of safe travels. Gram used to always do that before she drove anywhere. I picked up the habit from her."

"So you were raised Catholic?"

"Most definitely," Andi said as she pulled out onto the road behind the Camry. "Spent 12 years in Catholic school and Sister Kathleen kept me in line." She glanced over at him with a wicked grin. "Mostly."

"Ah, now there's an opening for some interesting stories if I ever heard one." He returned her grin with one of his own.

"Looks like he's not heading home. If we're lucky, he'll stop somewhere for dinner, and we can scoop up his car and be home before dark."

At that moment, Cooper's stomach growled. Andi smiled. "Sorry, it's one of my least favorite parts of this job. No scheduled dinner breaks. Hopefully, we won't be very long. I've got some Cheese Curls in my purse if you're hungry. Help yourself."

Cooper grimaced.

A moment later she said, "That's odd." They watched the Camry pull into Diamond Auto Body Shop. Andi whipped her car into the adjacent gas station. Milner drove his car up to the garage door. Leaving the car running, he walked into the side office. A minute later, the large door opened, and Milner walked back to his car and drove in, the garage door closed behind him.

"Drat," Andi said.

Cooper looked over at her and smiled.

She pulled her binoculars and her wallet out of her purse. She reached into her wallet and handed him a ten dollar bill. "I'm going to keep watch. Would you mind getting me a water, and whatever you'd like for a snack? I'm just going to munch on these Cheese Curls."

She put the binoculars back up to her eyes, so she could get a close-up look at any movement at the body shop.

Cooper asked, "What if he leaves before I return?"

"There's not much of a selection to choose from in there. I'm guessing Milner is discussing the work he wants to be done on his Camry for another scheduled appointment." She glanced back at her watch and then looked back at the garage. "It's too late to drop off his car now and wait for it to be serviced."

"Let me ask the question another way. Will you leave me if he drives out before I return?"

Andi considered this and bit her lip. "Well, sure, but I'll come get you after I drop the Camry off at the Repo Lot."

"That's what I was afraid of. I'll be right back." He started to go and then turned back for a second, "Don't leave," and then he hurried into the store.

About five minutes later, he jogged back, opened the passenger door and sat inside, opening a plastic bag.

"What did I miss?" he asked while handing her a cold bottle of water and opening one for himself.

She had just popped a cheese curl into her mouth, so she smiled her thanks and opened the bottle of water and took two big gulps. Cooper thought it was incredibly sexy and then immediately bit the inside of his cheek to distract himself from such a ridiculous thought. With those kinds of crazy thoughts, it was no wonder the guys in the band were teasing him. What the hell was wrong with him?

"What's wrong?" Andi asked.

Shit. She'd just caught him staring at her lips, so he smiled at her, pointed to a spot at the corner of her mouth and said, "You've got some orange. Right there."

"Oh." She blushed and quickly reached into her purse, pulled out a fast food napkin, and wiped at her lips.

He held out his hand and said, "Here's your change."

She looked at him in confusion. "Change? You shouldn't have any change. What did you buy?"

"Two bottles of water and a bag of honey-roasted peanuts. Want some?" he asked as he offered the bag to her.

She snorted. "I thought you were hungry. They sell real food too. Pizza? Hot dogs?"

He made a disgusted face. "Yes, well I did see those, and that's why I got the peanuts."

"You should keep the change. Peanuts are hardly a meal."

The garage door opened, and the Camry drove out followed by a big black SUV. Looked like an Escalade.

Andi started her car, began to touch the St. Christopher medal, but her fingers were orange, so she quickly wiped them on her jeans and then pulled out behind both cars. Cooper grinned. The woman was a mess.

A minute later he asked, "What's the deal with that other car?" and then he popped a couple of peanuts into his mouth. He felt like he was watching a movie.

"I wish I knew. Doesn't make any sense." Andi thought for a minute. "Maybe Milner isn't a customer but a friend of an employee, and they're headed to dinner."

"We can hope they both go to dinner and then sit somewhere away from the window, so you can grab his car."

She looked over at him in surprise. "Why, Mr. Barnett, I believe you'd make a fine Repo Agent."

He grinned. "Well, I am being trained by the best."

They followed both cars for about 20 minutes until the cars turned into Mill Mountain Star and Park.

"This isn't good," Andi said.

The park was small and isolated, so Andi turned off her lights, drove up onto the grass, pulled behind a hedge, and killed the engine.

"Let's wait here. The park is small, and I don't want them to notice us. We'll be able to see anyone who comes in and out of the park from here too."

Cooper nodded and then said, "I don't think they're having dinner."

"Not unless it's a picnic." She scrunched her nose. "Or maybe a romantic tryst."

"Well, I know what I'd be doing at this park at dusk if I brought someone I found irresistible."

He gave her a dazzling smile, and his eyebrows rose in invitation. He'd meant it as a fun flirtation. He threw out these kinds of lines all the time, but as he looked over at this adorable Repo Girl, who was trying her best to ignore him by fiddling with those damn binoculars in the dark, he began imagining kissing her and holding her close to him. Wow, was it getting warm in here?

Andi knew his type. The man sitting next to her was a bona fide flirt. She was used to being the target of flirts and usually deflected their lines like bullets bounced off Superman's chest. The problem was Cooper was her kryptonite. When he directed that charm at her, she turned to goo. What was it about this guy? Life was so unfair. She was trying to ignore the man, so she looked out into the darkness with her binoculars. They weren't night vision goggles, for Pete's sake.

She pulled them over her head and placed them back into her purse before she looked any more inept. *Stop acting like an idiot*, she reprimanded herself. She turned to tell him she couldn't see anything, but he had somehow moved so close to her, leaning in, only a couple inches away, those chocolate brown eyes were looking right into hers, and in a voice that was barely a whisper, he said, "Andi, I" as headlights lit up the inside of her car.

Without thinking, she grabbed Cooper's face, a hand on each cheek and kissed him hard and fast. She was almost certain the car was hidden from view, but the headlights cut across them. There had been no time to think, only to act, and if the other car could see them, they'd think they were just lovers making out at the park.

Holy Mary Mother of God. The minute her lips touched Cooper's, she forgot to breathe, to think, pretty much forgot about everything but the soft feel of his lips on hers, and a feeling of falling as he wrapped his arms around her and deepened their kiss.

"Shit!" he exclaimed and pushed Andi back off of his lap.

It was like someone threw a bucket of cold water on her. What had she been doing on his lap? *Sweet Baby Jesus.* She had jumped the poor guy. She sat up quickly and moved back to her driver's seat, mortified, eyes closed, face burning in embarrassment.

"I'm so sorry. The headlights hit us. I panicked, and I kissed you. I'm sorry." She was so pathetic. *Pathetic goo.*

Cooper started to laugh which made Andi open her eyes and glare at him. That just made him shake his head and laugh harder. He sat up and picked up the half empty water bottle. With his laughter under control, he smiled at her and grabbed her hand and put it on his shirt over his flat hard stomach.

"The kiss was great. Better than great. It's just that in the middle of that *better than great* kiss, my water bottle spilled on me and drenched my shirt and pants, startling me." He gazed at her warm hand and then looked back up at her. "I think we should resume that kiss until the next car drives by. Just in case anyone sees us," he said in a soft tone.

He began to pull her over to his side of the car, but she shook her head and said, "No. Wait. The other car should have come out by now. They came in together. It doesn't make sense that they'd leave a car."

Cooper sighed. He wanted to explore the kiss further, but that wasn't about to happen. He could see her mind working to solve the puzzle.

She buckled in and started the car.

"Buckle up," she instructed and then said, "Maybe they decided to go to dinner after all and just took one car. Hopefully, they left the Camry."

She drove out of her hiding spot and over to the area where the other car was parked.

"Yes!" she exclaimed when she saw the Camry was the only car left in the parking lot. "Please be empty." She pulled next to the car. No obvious passenger.

"Okay." She reached into her purse and pulled out the key for the Camry. "Darn, I must have left the paperwork at home. Would you follow me in my car while I drive the Camry back to the repo lot? Then after we drop it off, I'll treat you to a real dinner."

Cooper pulled her in for an urgent, hot kiss, then in a low voice, said, "Deal, but I warn you, I'm starving."

Andi wasn't sure if he was talking about food. Breathless, she stared at him, handed him her keys, got out of the car quickly before she pulled him in for another one of those delicious kisses. She unlocked the door and opened it, but the interior lights didn't appear to be working. *Figures.* Probably one of the items Thomas was going to have repaired at the body shop. She started the engine. At least the dash lights worked. She turned on the headlights and backed out of the parking space. As she drove out of the park, she could see Cooper's headlights behind her.

In no time at all, she was back on the Blue Ridge Parkway. She drove carefully in the dark going the posted speed of 45 miles per hour. She glanced in her rearview mirror and saw Cooper following behind her in her Honda. She was on edge tonight, which was ridiculous, because this wasn't the first time she'd repoed cars at night in sketchy neighborhoods. It was reassuring not to be out here all alone. *This repo was going to work out after all.*

When she looked back at the road, she saw it—a large deer staring directly at her, and then, in a split second, he was smashed against her windshield. She had automatically hit the brakes hard, but it didn't really matter because the collision with the deer had brought the car to a stop. It all happened at once. The deer, the airbag, and then something heavy and wet pressed between her and the airbag.

Oh my God, the deer must have come through the windshield and was lying between her and the dashboard. *No.* That didn't make any sense because she was staring at the bloodied deer body on the other side of the shattered windshield. The inside of the car was dark, but there was definitely something heavy and wet pressed on her legs and against her chest.

She finally released the death-grip she had on the steering wheel and felt for the object pressing against her. It was a body. A human body. Warm, wet, skin pressed against her.

"Oh my God...Oh my God...Oh my God," she whispered these words in a hysterical chant over and over as she tried to move the very heavy body off of her. She tried to push it over to the front passenger seat since the dashboard had been pushed forward by at least a foot from the impact. She was trapped. Why couldn't she slide out from under the weight? Oh, yeah, the seat belt. With her right hand, she reached for the seat belt and felt something hard on the seat next to her. Metal? A gun? The "Oh my God...Oh my God," mantra became louder and more hysterical as she slid it away and finally found the release button for the seat belt. Her hand kept sliding off the button. It was slippery. *That's odd.* She didn't even want to consider why it was slippery!

She heard a banging sound at the driver's door, and then suddenly it flew open, and Cooper said, "Andi, are you alri...*Fuck*!"

She just shook her head no and repeated "Oh my God...Oh my God." Her eyes were wide and focused on the deer eye staring blankly at her. She wouldn't, no she couldn't look down at the body trapping her in the car.

Cooper had a mantra of his own which was packed with four-letter words as he leaned inside the car and tried to move the dead weight off of her. Finally, she successfully pressed the seat belt release button, and once she was free of the belt, she gave one last bench press push on the weight and escaped out of the car.

She ran across the street to put as much distance between her and the wreck and then immediately bent forward and tossed those Cheese Curls. She continued to heave until all the contents of her stomach had been emptied. Halfway through her stomach dump, she felt a hand on her forehead and another on her shoulder holding her up.

Cooper handed her a handkerchief that she used to wipe her face. She found a clean, dry spot of grass and sat down with her arms wrapped around her knees and just stared, not really seeing anything. She didn't remember much of what happened next. Cooper squeezed her shoulders and said something in a soothing voice and then there were lights and police and questions. She had begun to shake, not because it was chilly, it's just that her body began trembling, and she couldn't seem to stop.

A paramedic wrapped a blanket tightly around her shoulders, and she remembered him checking her for physical injuries and concussion symptoms. When the shaking finally stopped, her mind had sort of gone into a neutral gear to protect her from the situation that she was in no way capable of dealing with at the moment.

The police spent a lot of time asking questions that she apparently answered, but she didn't remember talking at all. They asked her things like, "What's your name? The car is registered to Thomas Milner. What were you doing driving this car? Do you have any identification? Are you in a relationship with Mr. Milner? Why is there blood all over your shirt?"

She heard Cooper say something like, "Seriously? Are we going through this again? This is such bullshit! She's covered in blood because a dead man was thrown on top of her from the back seat when she hit the deer like we've been telling you for the last hour! Can't you see that she's obviously in shock? Can't we just go home, get cleaned up, and meet you at the precinct first thing in the morning?"

It was at that point that Andi looked down at her blood covered clothes and went deeper into her safe place and didn't really remember any questions after that. She stayed in that blissful abyss until a female officer read them their rights, said that they were being charged with murder, and then they were handcuffed and tossed in the back seat of a patrol car. *Wait...did she say something about murder?*

*Huh...*She'd never actually seen the back of a police car much less ridden in one with her hands cuffed in front of her. She stared at the handcuffs in fascination. Seeing them burst her peaceful, gentle, protective bubble. *What the heck was she doing handcuffed in a police car?* Trying to make some sort of sense of this situation, she looked over at Cooper, who was busy muttering profanities under his breath. He suddenly stopped when he realized she was staring at him. His frown evaporated into a small smile of encouragement. No, she must have misread him because there was nothing remotely encouraging about this situation.

Then he said in a soft, soothing voice, "Hey, it's going to be alright."

Her facial expression must have shown how ridiculous she thought that statement was because he continued, "No really. I promise. We get one phone call, right? When you're arrested, you always get to make one phone call. Happens all the time on NCIS. I'll call my family attorney, and we'll be out of here in no time."

She continued to stare at him like he was insane.

"You know, one day, we'll even probably laugh about this. I mean, it is pretty funny when you think about it." He grinned as he held up his cuffed hands.

Her mouth dropped open in disbelief. The man was certifiable!

"Um, no. Not funny at all. I *killed* Bambi."

That seemed to be the easiest thing to deal with. Now that the initial numbness was gone, she was feeling angry. Yeah. The anger actually felt pretty darn good.

"Then, a dead guy flew up on my lap and trapped me with his dead weight. And I mean that literally. I *think* the police just *arrested me for murder* and with all his blood on my blouse and jeans, I'm sure they have an excellent case against me. If that wasn't bad enough, Jerry is going to fire me because I totaled the asset/Camry/car, whatever you want to call it, when I hit Bambi."

She took a breath, "Oh, but it's all going to be okay, right, because I won't need a job when they send me to the Correctional Center for Women. I'll be living the good life in the Big House with free meals. What was I freaking out about anyway? You're right, of course. I'll be laughing about this while lounging in my cell probably before I even go up for my first parole hearing in a good fifteen to twenty years."

Then she took a long breath and glared at Cooper, daring him to challenge her.

The officers up front chuckled. Cooper opened his mouth as if to say something and reconsidered. He closed his mouth and looked out his window.

They arrived at the police station without another word after Andi's angry outburst. The police took them to a small room with a single table, four chairs, and a mirror. No doubt it was a two-way mirror so that they could be observed like fish in a tank.

An attractive female officer came into the room, dressed in tan slacks, a professional, aqua-colored blouse with a strand of simple pearls draped around her neck. She wore a friendly smile and had long blond hair that fell loose around her shoulders.

"Well, y'all have had quite the night," she said in a soft, friendly deep southern accent. Andi guessed she was probably from Georgia or maybe Alabama. Cooper shot Andi a look she wasn't sure how to interpret.

"My name is Detective Richardson. Let's start by getting you out of these," she said as she removed their handcuffs with a key. "That's got to be uncomfortable." She removed Cooper's handcuffs first, and he gave her one of his flirty smiles but was unusually quiet. Then Andi's cuffs were removed, and Andi rubbed her sore wrists.

"I'll be working with Detective Kendricks to see if we can get this whole situation," she waved her hand in the air like their *situation* was a simple matter, "resolved as quickly as possible. Can I get y'all something to drink? Coffee or water?"

Cooper spoke up first and said, "Coffee would be great with just a little cream."

Andi desperately needed a warm cup of herbal tea from the Little Green Hive to calm her nerves, but she was sure they wouldn't have that here.

"Water please," Andi said, her voice came out a little scratchy. She was surprised she was able to speak at all.

Detective Richardson smiled and said, "Okay, then. Just try and relax, and I'll be back soon with your drinks." She walked out of the room, and they heard the door lock into place.

As soon as they were alone in the room again, Cooper leaned across the table toward Andi and whispered, "That was the Good Cop. Did you notice how she was friendly, made us feel comfortable by removing our handcuffs, and then asked us if we wanted a beverage like we were at a damn coffee shop instead of a police interrogation room? Yeah, she was definitely the Good Cop. As soon as we begin to relax," Cooper slammed his hand down suddenly onto the table making a loud sound, "Bam! They send in the Bad Cop who will, no doubt, rough us up to get us to talk."

He frowned as if perplexed by his next thought.

"Frankly, I'm kind of surprised they didn't separate us to get our stories individually. Then compare notes to see if they match up. I saw that same scenario on an episode of Castle."

"Shut up," Andi whispered. Her eyes were beginning to fill up. She refused to cry. She was afraid that once she started, she wouldn't be able to ever stop crying.

"What?" Cooper asked, confused by her reaction.

"Just please stop talking. You are making me crazy," she said as she slid the metal chair away from the table and stood up quickly. She began pacing the room and started talking quietly to herself. "Okay, take slow, deep, breaths. Don't panic. Maybe this isn't even real." She stopped pacing for a second and then said, "Maybe I'm having a terrible nightmare, although usually when I dream about Cooper, it's nothing like this." Andi looked over at Cooper and saw his eyes widen and mouth drop open. She shook her head and began pacing again. "But wait. I did eat those awful Cheese Curls. Mags is so right. No more processed food for me. Ever again."

Then she heard it; a bluesy melody coming from inside the room. Was that a harmonica? She turned towards the sound to see Cooper leaning back on two legs of the metal chair against the wall playing the harmonica like he was in prison playing blues. She put her hands on her hips and glared at him and then said, "Seriously?"

He stopped playing and looked up.

"What?" he asked innocently. Well, almost. There was a hint of a smile at the corner of his mouth.

"Music relaxes me." His smile spread into a full-blown grin.

"Are you intentionally trying to push me over the edge?" she asked. Her voice sounded an octave higher than usual.

"Hey." He put his hands up in surrender. "I was just trying to lighten the mood a bit. With that pacing and talking to yourself, I was afraid you were headed back to zombie-land. My intention was to relax us both with a little humor. It's been a tough night."

"A tough night?" she repeated, stunned for a second by the oversimplification of the horrific evening. Like "tough night" wasn't the understatement of the century. Then she looked down at her blouse, and a sob escaped her lips.

"I'm covered in stinky, sticky blood. From a dead man. I can't relax."

She began breathing more rapidly and paced in the small space like a caged animal.

"I can't *b-r-e-a-t-h-e*. I just see and smell the blood," she began to hastily unbutton her blouse.

"Andi, *what the hell are you doing?*" Cooper asked in a strangled voice.

He looked both alarmed and fascinated at the same time.

"I have to get the blood off of me. NOW!" she said hysterically.

Okay, she sounded a little Lady Macbeth, but the blood was freaking her out, and if she didn't get it away from her skin now, she didn't quite know what she'd do. The buttons were sticky, so she finally gave up and in a panic, just ripped her blouse open, yanked it off, and threw it on the floor. Then she pulled her camisole over her head because some of the blood had soaked into it too. She added it to the heap on the floor. That left just her lace bra covering the upper half of her body. She stood in place, still breathing hard, just staring at the clothes on the floor.

"*Damn,*" Cooper said in a slow, deep, sexy voice, and then quickly stood up, pulled off his jacket, and put it on her. As he zippered the jacket to cover up her bra, he whispered, "Well, this isn't exactly how I fantasized you would undress for me. Don't get me wrong, *you are totally sexy*, it's just that in my fantasy, your white blouse was soaked in margaritas instead of blood."

He zipped his jacket all the way up to her neck, stared at her lips for about 3 seconds as if considering kissing her, and then slowly and ever so gently touched her lips with his, like she was the most precious, fragile thing in the world. *WOW.* The kiss instantly changed to a hot, soul-consuming explosion. She didn't know if it was the adrenaline from their insane night or the fact that she'd been having hot dreams about the guy ever since she met him at Star City Bar & Grill, but the second his lips touched hers, she felt tingles travel down her entire body and then every inch of her skin felt on fire. It was the most amazing, exhilarating kiss she had ever experienced. She automatically reached her arms around his neck and pulled him closer, hanging on for her life.

The door to the interrogation room was shoved open and hit the wall with a loud bang startling both of them. Andi jumped back away from Cooper, alarmed as much by the interruption as by the intensity of that kiss. At the same time, Cooper pulled Andi close to his side, placing his arm protectively or possessively, she wasn't sure which, around her waist. He pressed his mouth next to her ear and breathed, "Bad Cop."

A man stepped into the interrogation room wearing a light blue shirt and striped tie. The knot on the tie was slightly askew like he'd been tugging at it for most of the day.

"My name is Detective Kendricks."

There was no smile, just a fierce look first at Andi, or rather at her chest as if he could see right through Cooper's leather jacket, and then directly into her eyes for what seemed like an eternity before his gaze dropped to her lips.

No way. She must be hallucinating. Andi briefly closed her eyes and opened them again. Nope, she wasn't imagining things. The man standing before her was tall, had broad shoulders, and resembled her favorite Avenger's character, *Thor.* Well, if Thor had short hair. She could feel her cheeks heat up. *Terrific.* Now was not the time to blush. It's just that she had a major fantasy about the Norse god, and here he was, staring at her mouth with such concentration. *Idiot.* He was staring at her because she'd been charged with murder. *Oh no.* She was sure he'd seen her lace bra and that kiss from behind the two-way mirror. Now, her face burned with embarrassment. Thor looked at Cooper, briefly assessing him, then at the floor where her ruined clothes were lying in a heap.

"Miss Sloan. You are not permitted to destroy any evidence from this case," he reprimanded.

He reached into his pocket and pulled out a latex glove and a plastic bag and quickly deposited her ruined clothes in the evidence bag and set it on the table.

"Why don't you both have a seat?" He motioned to the two chairs across from him. It was a polite order rather than a real question. Cooper pulled out a chair for her to sit in and then sat down next to her. The detective opened a manila folder and scanned through a couple of the pages.

"Can you tell me what you were doing driving the Toyota Camry, Miss Sloan?" Detective Kendricks asked Andi.

"Yes," she swallowed to make sure her voice was steady. "I'm a repo agent, and I work for The Repo Doctor. Jerry Harper is the owner. I was supposed to repossess the Camry, so I followed Thomas Milner after work. He stopped at the Diamond Auto Body shop, and then he drove his car to the Mill Mountain Star and Park." She paused. "Oh, and another car followed him from the body shop. It was a big SUV type, like an Escalade, maybe?"

"Do you have any proof of employment?" Kendrick's asked her.

"Um, no. I left the paperwork for the repo at home. You can call Jerry Harper, the owner. He'll vouch for me," Andi said.

Kendricks nodded and made a note in the folder.

"So, what happened at the park?"

Andi blushed, thinking about how she'd jumped Cooper when the car had gone by.

"When the big SUV left, we drove over to the Camry, and when we confirmed no one was there, I started up the Camry planning to drive it to the repo lot. Cooper followed me in my car," Andi said, and she glanced briefly at Cooper. He was watching her so closely, and when she looked at him, he gave her a slight encouraging smile. Andi swallowed and turned back to look at Kendricks.

"That's when I hit Bambi," she shook her head and said, "I mean the deer, and I got trapped under the body."

Andi looked down at her hands and shivered briefly.

Kendricks leaned forward, eyes narrowed. "Do you expect me to believe that you drove away with a dead body in the car and didn't notice it? He wasn't in the trunk, and it's not a big car."

Andi looked up, eyes wide.

"I would have never gotten in the car if I *had known* there was a dead body in there," Andi said.

"The body found at the scene is currently being autopsied by the medical examiner, but we suspect that his identity will be the same as the owner of the vehicle, Thomas Milner. Unfortunately, he has multiple gun wounds including his face, so it's taking a bit more time to ID him. We believe the murder weapon was the nine millimeter we found in the front of the Camry."

He looked at Andi with that same intense glare then said, "Your fingerprints were found on the gun, Miss Sloan. Can you explain that?"

She paled.

"I must have grabbed it when I was struggling to get out from under the body. I was pretty freaked out when I realized I was trapped under a dead man in the car. I was desperate to get out."

Andi was relieved that her voice was fairly steady.

The detective watched them both closely when he said, "The naked body found in the car had scratch marks all over it. We're going to need to get DNA samples from both of you as well as samples from under your fingernails to check for the victim's skin."

"No, no, no, no, no," Andi said in a voice that was barely a whisper as she shook her head to the left and then the right rapidly. *She must not have heard him correctly. He couldn't have said naked body.*

"Actually, yes. You will give us the samples Miss Sloan. We can do this the easy way or the hard way and frankly, it's been a long day. I'd prefer you go the easy way since I'm out of patience," the detective said in annoyed tone.

"No," Andi said exasperated still shaking her head.

She wasn't communicating clearly, but frankly, the panicked feeling was returning again, full-force. She obviously wasn't having any luck with the detective. Maybe Cooper could fix this. Cooper with the amazing kisses. She quickly turned to Cooper desperate to correct this misunderstanding. She was certain the detective couldn't have said *naked* body.

"Cooper? He wasn't *naked*, was he? I didn't look. I *couldn't* look. I was having a staring contest with Bambi. *Please* tell me he wasn't naked," she begged.

"He wasn't naked," Cooper said immediately and reached over and squeezed her hand.

Thank God for that. Why such a detail would make a difference in the scheme of things, she didn't understand. But this little fact was the thread that was holding her together. A dead guy's blood all over her was bad enough. *A naked, dead guy's blood...ew.*

"Actually, he was naked, Miss Sloan." Detective Kendrick corrected. "You can clearly see in these pictures."

He shoved the folder toward Andi and she looked down before she had a chance to think about what she was doing.

She heard Cooper say *"asshole"* under his breath as the room began to spin and she felt light-headed. She started to say, "Oh no...." when Cooper grabbed her by the back of the neck and lowered her head between her knees.

Then he said, "Easy there *Margarita*. Just breathe in through your nose, out through your mouth, nice and slow. Everything is going to be okay."

There was that soothing voice again. Cooper was gently rubbing her neck. After a few minutes of staring at the floor, the spinning had ceased and Andi noticed that if this was a restaurant, the health department would have written them up. The floor was filthy. She sat up slowly and gave Cooper a shaky smile.

"Thanks for that. I would have been really upset to faint on this filthy floor."

The Good Cop, Detective Richardson, returned with a cup of coffee and a bottled water. It took her long enough. Andi was definitely not leaving a tip. She shook her head at that insane thought as she drank her entire water bottle. God, Cooper's warped sense of humor was beginning to rub off on her.

The Bad Cop cleared his throat and resumed the interrogation. "So, where were we before all the theatrics? Oh yes. The victim's clothes were found scattered throughout the car. When was the last time you saw the victim? Was he dressed?" the detective asked.

Andi clenched her teeth. *Jerk!* Did he consider her almost fainting theatrics? Did he seriously believe she was capable of faking this emotional mess she'd been in since the wreck? Cooper was right when he'd called him an asshole. And he was most certainly the Bad Cop. Now he was looking for her to confess to murder or sex with the victim or both. Something snapped inside of her. She felt that anger again like she'd felt in the police car on the way over here. She would not allow this "Bad Cop" to push her around. She was innocent and had nothing to hide. She sat up straight and glared at the detective. *Fine.* She would gladly answer his insensitive and idiotic questions.

Cooper started to answer for her.

"Look, Andi obviously didn't...," but Andi put her hand on his arm.

"I've got this," she said to Cooper.

Andi squared her shoulders and tilted her chin up.

"Of course I can't explain it, *Detective Kendricks*. The man was obviously naked and dead when I got in the car, and his body was hidden somewhere in the backseat, or there is no way I would have ever gotten in the car. The last time I saw him was at the auto body shop, and he was definitely wearing clothes. I never got a good look at the body when it was crushing me in the car. It was dark inside the car, and once I realized what was pressing against me, I didn't want to see it. For my own sanity, I couldn't see it."

Detective Richardson spoke up for the first time since she'd entered the room with Andi's water.

"Miss Sloan, the last time you saw Mr. Milner for certain was at the Diamond Auto Body Shop. Can you describe the large car that followed the Camry? Any unique marks, license number, by chance?" she asked hopefully.

"No. I was only interested in the Camry, so that was my main focus," Andi answered.

"I don't suppose you got a look at the other car as it left the park? How many people were in the car?" she asked.

"I didn't see. I was hiding in my car behind the bushes and ducked when I saw headlights. I don't know for sure. I don't know when they killed Thomas. Could have been at the body shop? Could have been at the park? I was only trying to retrieve the Camry. I didn't want to confront Mr. Milner," Andi said.

Detective Richardson leaned forward, and in her slow southern drawl said, "Miss Sloan, I know this has been difficult for you to go through again after the night you've had." She smiled kindly at her. "In your investigation of Mr. Milner, did you ever see him at the Diamond Auto Body Shop before tonight?"

Andi shook her head. "No, I assumed he was going there to get work done on his car. Then, when he left the shop with the other car, I figured he must be friends with someone from the shop."

Kendricks made another note in the folder.

"I thought it was weird that they were going to the park at dusk," Andi said.

Kendricks stared at her for a minute with narrowed eyes and then turned his attention to Cooper.

"What is your relationship with Miss Sloan?" he asked.

Cooper looked at Andi with a look that made her face flush and then he looked Kendricks in the eye. "We're *friends*.

Our band is renting space in her garage for practice. My buddy Danny is dating her roommate."

Kendricks lifted an eyebrow and continued to look at Cooper.

"Mr. Barnett, I would say the kiss you shared with Miss Sloan when I walked in indicates you are more than friends. Did you know Thomas Milner?" Kendricks asked.

Cooper narrowed his eyes at Kendricks and shook his head.

"Why were you with Miss Sloan tonight?" Kendricks asked.

"I asked if I could ride along. I was curious about her repo job," Cooper said.

Kendricks looked at Cooper and then at Andi.

"The gun wounds on the body could be a professional hit or a crime of passion. The shooter obviously wanted Milner to suffer before he was killed."

Kendricks loosened the knot on his tie with his index finger.

"The thing I find most curious about this murder was that he was naked. Not typical of a professional hit which makes me think it was more likely a crime of passion," Kendricks said.

"Miss Sloan," he looked at her with those intense blue eyes, "were you involved in a romantic relationship with Thomas Milner?"

It took Andi a few seconds to make sense of the bizarre question. When the meaning of his question sunk in, her eyes widened and her mouth dropped open.

"No." She shook her head vehemently. "Absolutely not. Cooper was there with me tonight. He can confirm that everything I said is true."

Kendricks rubbed his chin again and tilted his head and glanced at Cooper.

"It's possible that this wasn't a repo job at all. Maybe you, Miss Sloan, had an affair with Milner. For some reason, it ended badly, and you bring your new *friend,* Mr. Barnett, with you to get rid of him. Or, maybe you're out with Milner at the park in his car, lose the clothes, and Barnett comes by and in a jealous rage, kills Milner. The problem with that scenario is that your prints, Miss Sloan, are the only ones on the murder weapon."

Andi stood up.

"You've got to believe me. I didn't know Thomas Milner as anything other than a skip on my repo case," Andi said. Her hands were in fists by her side and she was trembling with rage.

Kendricks looked up at her and said, "Have a seat, Miss Sloan. I'm just speculating. We'll conduct a thorough investigation. The first thing we'll do is verify that the Camry was scheduled for repossession."

The Bad Cop sighed, "Okay. I think that's all we're going to get tonight."

Andi sat up, "Does that mean we can go home now?" she asked.

"Not quite yet, Miss Sloan. You can't go anywhere, I'm afraid."

"What?" she asked in disbelief.

"You both have already been charged with murder at the crime scene. I'm afraid you aren't going anywhere. At least not until we can get you to court for a bail hearing. The earliest we can do that is tomorrow. Meanwhile, we have to collect your DNA samples, validate your place of employment, and finish the paperwork for your arrest."

"But I was just doing my job. I'm a victim as much as Thomas Milner," Andi said.

Kendricks lifted an eyebrow.

"Not quite. Thomas Milner is dead and you're alive," he said as he leaned back in his chair.

"Look at this from my perspective. The only thing I know for sure is that the body was in the car at the time of the accident and that the man was naked and shot multiple times. A shot in each knee, once in the right arm and then in the face. I suspect the victim is Thomas Millner. I suspect the weapon used to kill him is the same one we found in the Camry. You two are currently my only suspects in this case, and just because I don't know your motive, doesn't mean you don't have one. It could be a car theft gone bad, a relationship problem, jealousy, any number of motives. Bottom line is there's no way I'm letting you walk out of here. Actually, legally I couldn't even *if* I believed your story because you've already been charged with murder."

"Wait," Cooper said. "We'd like to talk to our attorney. Now."

"Sure, you can call him as soon as we finish booking you," Kendricks replied.

"No, no, no. We were making headway! Do you really think *I'm* capable of murdering someone?" she pressed her hand against her heart and looked directly into the eyes of the Bad Cop. *See me. See that I'm innocent,* she silently pleaded with the detective.

He stared at her lips and then into her eyes intensely for about ten seconds and then said, "Frankly, Miss Sloan, I have no idea what you're capable of."

She felt her face heat up again.

"It's no longer in my hands. You are in the legal system now, and we have to follow procedure."

***

The Bad Cop led them down the hall into a larger office with lots of desks, officers milling around, and what must have been the "booking" area. He left them with a quiet uniformed officer to do the menial work. The officer took their mugshots and collected their clothes, probably to check for more DNA and then let them wash up and change into orange prison-wear. At least Andi wasn't wearing anything that might have Thomas' blood on it. Cooper seemed completely fascinated by the entire process and even excited after he saw his mugshot.

"Excuse me, Officer? Is there any way I can get a copy of this? I'm a musician, and I'd really love to use it for an album cover," Cooper explained.

The officer just rolled his eyes and replied sarcastically, "Oh sure. I'll get right on that. Do you want it black and white or color?"

Cooper ignored the officer and grinned at Andi. "That's alright. I don't need that specific photo. I'm totally inspired. I wish I had my guitar and notepad and pen. The songs are just flowing through my head, and I need to record them before I lose them. I'm thinking a mugshot-type photo would be completely awesome for the cover, and the CD could be titled *Arrested*."

The officer took them through a locked, steel door, and they walked past about 5 cells, each containing a prisoner. The last cell was empty—*Thank God!*

"Well, we've arrived at your recording studio," the uniform said as he began unlocking the cell.

Oh great. A policeman with a sense of humor.

Cooper just grinned at the officer and said, "I bet the acoustics are great. Don't suppose you have a spare guitar down in *Evidence* that I can use while I'm here?"

The uniform actually cracked a smile and shook his head.

"No, but I'll see if I can get you some paper and a pencil," the officer replied.

Andi just shook her head. Cooper could charm anyone. Well, maybe not the Bad Cop, but probably just about anyone else.

What kind of crazy guy can joke about spending the night in jail? Must be his coping mechanism. Kind of like her blissful bubble of shock. She missed her bubble. Andi began following Cooper inside when the jailer said, "Oh, you're not staying here, Miss Sloan. Your cell is through that door."

"What?" she asked suddenly alarmed. Well, more alarmed than she'd been a moment before. She was reaching new levels of shock and terror tonight.

Cooper turned to her and cupped her face with his hands and stared directly into her eyes. "Look at me. It's going to be alright. *You* are going to be alright. I lost you for a little bit at the accident scene tonight. Scared the hell out of me to be quite honest. But you're back now and stronger than you realize. You handled the interrogation with the Bad Cop amazingly well. If you could handle that, then this single night in a quiet cell is going to be a piece of cake. Try to get some sleep and we'll be out of here by morning. Jerry will vouch, for you and my dad's attorney will represent us at the bail hearing."

Then he kissed her hard and urgently and she melted right on the cell floor.

The officer cleared his throat.

"And this is why you get your cell down the hall, Miss Sloan. This isn't the honeymoon suite. No conjugal visits tonight."

Andi took a step back from Cooper and stared at him a little breathless. *Wow.* The man's kisses curled her toes. Cooper was looking at her like she was a triple fudge sundae with sprinkles.

"Sweet dreams," he said in that deep, sexy voice and grinned.

Once she was safely standing outside the cell, she realized that the last thing she needed was to be locked in a small cell with Cooper Barnett. Cooper was right, too. She was going to be okay. Even though life in her bubble was great, she had to switch gears and focus on getting out of here and clearing her name. Obviously, the police already felt that this case was pretty much wrapped up now that they had arrested them.

Andi followed the officer through the locked door and down the hall. There was a woman in each cell they passed, and then they stopped in front of one that wasn't empty and he began to unlock the door.

No. No. No. Why couldn't she get a cell to herself? Really, life could be so unfair sometimes. She had to share one with a real criminal.

"Don't you have one that's empty?" she asked hopefully.

"Sorry ma'am, our rooms are all booked. Perhaps if you'd have called ahead, I could have had a room made up for you." He laughed at his own joke and said, "Man, I'm on fire tonight!"

Andi rolled her eyes and stepped inside the cell. The room was about the size of the small bathroom at her house. A bunk bed filled half the room and there was a person stretched out on the bottom bunk with her arms relaxed behind her head and, her legs crossed at the ankles. Her bleached blond hair was shaved close to her head except at the top where it stood straight up about 2 inches. There were three bands of blue coloring racing across the sides of her head and at the tips of hair on the top of her head. She had a couple tattoos visible on her arms where she'd rolled up her orange sleeves. Her ears, eyebrows, and lips were pierced and probably other places that Andi didn't care to know about.

The door slid closed and locked behind her. *God, what an awful sound.* She closed her eyes briefly and then heard a voice from the bunk ask, "So, what are you in for?"

Andi opened her eyes and looked down at the bed. The woman was still in the same position looking and sounding completely relaxed except for her eyes. They were assessing Andi and waiting for a response.

"Murder," Andi answered casually like she was used to answering that question all the time. "How about you?" Andi asked and prayed she wouldn't say me too.

She looked skeptical and then smiled and said, "Oh yeah, bet it was manslaughter." She nodded her head. "Car accident? D.U.I.?"

"No. Murder. Multiple gunshot wounds to the body, but the one to the head is what finally did him in." Again, Andi was going for casual but tough. She knew she had better build up a prison cred if she was going to survive the night.

"No shit."

She looked stunned and her mouth gaped open, and she sat up.

"Wait, I know," she snapped her fingers and smiled, "It was a hunting accident, wasn't it? You probably thought the dude was a deer and shot him. Bet the guy wasn't wearing orange either."

Oh, she killed the deer, alright, but she wasn't hunting. But her disbelief that Andi shot a man to death on purpose was very insulting.

"No," Andi put her hands on her hips and glared at her new roommate.

"We were in the city. The police caught me with the dead body and the murder weapon. My fingerprints were all over the gun."

Okay, so this was the strangest night of her life. A half hour ago she was trying to convince the police that she didn't kill anyone, and now she was mad because this punk girl didn't believe that she killed a guy.

"Hmm," she looked Andi up and down again then shook her head, "I'm just not feelin' it. Sorry. I'm a pretty good judge of character, usually, but I can't really buy into this story."

Andi let out a long frustrated breath, sat next to her on the bunk, put her elbows on her knees and rested her chin on her knuckles.

"Why couldn't *you* have been my homicide detective?"

She took a breath and then confessed. So much for her prison-cred. Somehow, this punker was easy to talk to, and it had been a long night. She was finally ready to dump.

"You're right. I didn't kill anybody. I've never even gotten a traffic ticket, much less murdered someone in cold blood. The only thing I've killed in my life that was larger than a house fly was the deer I hit with the car tonight."

She released another deep sigh and looked up at her.

"So what are you in for?"

The blond smiled at Andi reassuringly and said, "Oh, nothing as exciting as your charge of murder. Just assault, destruction of property, and resisting arrest."

"Wow. I don't know, that sounds like a pretty impressive rap sheet," Andi said.

"Yeah, well, you see, I was dating this guy. You know how I said I was a pretty good judge of character, *usually*? Well, the men I date are the exception. We met about a year ago. I was working at Under Your Skin Tattoo and Piercing Studio over on Williamson Road when this hot guy walks in wanting a couple piercings. His real name is William, you know, it was on his driver's license, but he goes by Axle because he works on cars. So, we went out a couple times, one thing leads to another, then he ends up moving into my place. I thought everything was great, and then I come home early from work, and he's in my house with another girl. Can you believe it?" she asked incredulously.

"So, you assaulted him?" Andi asked.

"Damn straight, but I didn't get arrested that time. I literally kicked his sorry ass to the curb and thought that was the end of it. Before I could have the locks changed, he used my key, came back to the house while I was at work, and took stuff that didn't even belong to him. I confronted him about it, but he said it was community property, and that I couldn't prove that it wasn't his. He said, 'Possession is nine-tenths the law.' He's such a total asshole. I can't believe it took me so long to realize it. Anyway, I guess I have anger management issues because tonight, I was on my way home when I spot his car parked in front of Charlie's Steak House, just three minutes from work. Did he ever take me there or anywhere other than McDonald's for dinner? Even then I paid. I was so stupid. So, I'm driving by, and I see his precious Mustang. I know it's his car because he has the vanity plates FX-IT. I don't know what came over me, but I whipped into the parking lot, parked right next to his car, and then began puncturing his tires. It felt so good, you know? So then I took my keys and scratched the entire length of the driver's side. I was a woman high on revenge at that point. Then, Axle comes out with the ho from before and starts screaming at me—like I'm the one with the problem. So I picked up a loose paving brick, stood at the front of his car, and lifted it with both hands over my head. Then he screams, 'You'd better put that goddamn brick down right now.' so I said 'Okay,' and threw it right through the front windshield. Axle lunges at me, and I kicked him in the balls and gave him a bloody nose before the cops finally pulled me off of him. I guess in the shuffle, I accidentally gave a cop a bloody nose too. So here I am."

She smiled a big smile.

"Let me just say, it was so worth it to see the bloody look on Axle's face when the police hauled me away. You'd think he would have been happy to see me sent to jail, but he was looking at his Mustang and wiping fat-ass tears off his cheek. That was sweet."

Wow. The woman definitely had rage issues. Andi would never make the mistake of getting on her bad side.

"So, did you call someone to bail you out?" Andi asked.

"Nope. I think they're hooking me up with a public defender because none of my friends have that kind of money to bail me out of anything. So I'm just chillin' and makin' new friends like you. Now, why don't you tell me how someone like *you* ended up *here?* We got all night girl. Hey, by the way, my name is Liz."

"Nice to meet you, Liz. I'm Andi."

Then she told her. Everything. From when she started working for *The Repo Doctor* until now. She even told her how she planned to find the real killer and clear her name. She left out her interrogation strip-tease and those hot kisses with Cooper. It was nice to finally be able to unload it all. After that, Andi was pretty much exhausted. She climbed up to the top bunk and collapsed on the vinyl covered mat. She didn't even want to think who else had been on it. It seemed like she had just closed her eyes when she heard the guard open the door and say, "Wake up Sleeping Beauty. You're headed to court for your Murder Bond Hearing."

Chapter Four

Andrea followed the guard out of the holding area back through the large area where they'd been 'booked' last night into a smaller office to the right. When she opened the door, she was instantly embraced by her support team: Ben and Maggy.

"Girl, no offense, but you look like hell," Ben said immediately

"You think? I'm so glad to see you, but what are you doing here?" Andi asked.

"Well, Daniel called me and told me about the accident, the arrests, and the *body*," Ben shivered and shook his head, "I had to hear from Daniel. Why didn't you text me directly? Apparently, Cooper called the guys to let them know what was going down."

"Sorry guys. It was a rough night, and I wasn't thinking clearly," she said.

"We're just happy you're okay. You'll come out of this great. You'll see." Maggy smiled at her and gave Andi another big hug.

"You guys are the best! Thanks for coming."

"You bet. You bring such excitement to our humdrum lives. You've had quite the wild night out," Maggy teased.

"Girl, you are front page news," Ben said and pointed to The Roanoke Times cover story. There was the mugshot Cooper wanted a copy of so badly along with a terrible picture of Andi. Why did Cooper's photo look sexy, and Andi looked like a crazy person with bad hair? The headline read, "Two Arrested in Brutal Slaying."

"Oh no. This is really bad," Andi dropped down in the chair.

"Well, you certainly look criminal in this current state. We found out you were scheduled for a bond hearing this morning at 10 am, so I brought emergency supplies," Ben said and held up a large duffel bag.

"And I brought you this," Maggy said and handed her a large paper cup filled with herbal tea from the Little Green Hive—Andi's favorite tea shop.

Andi inhaled the scent and took a sip, "Oh, you are an angel of mercy. Thank you."

Ben said, "I brought clothes, makeup, and hair products because this," he waved his hand towards her orange prison clothes, "is not a flattering look for you. We'll be transforming you from arrested violation to irresistibly innocent. And girl, we've totally got to go shopping once you're cleared. Your closet is very, very sad," Ben looked at her seriously.

She smiled and embraced both of her friends in a big hug.

"I really love you guys. Thanks," she said in a whisper.

An hour later Andrea Sloan's transformation was complete. She was wearing fresh, light makeup, a nice outdated conservative dress from the depths of her closet, and her hair was tangle-free and in a ponytail. The three of them went to a larger meeting/conference room where they joined up with Cooper, Daniel, Zach and an older guy Andi didn't recognize.

Cooper looked sexy this morning. He'd shaved for court and was wearing a suit and tie. Andi thought it was really a toss-up. The man looked amazing dressed up and in a t-shirt and jeans. That was so unfair.

He spotted her, grinned and looked at her in a way that made her face flush.

Just then, the door to the room flew open, and Jerry came bursting in, looked around until he spotted her, and said: "Thank God." He pulled Andi into a big hug, lifting her off the ground. When he placed her feet back on the floor, he kissed her on the forehead and then held her at arm's length to assess for damage. When he seemed satisfied that she was uninjured, he shook his head.

"*Jesus*, Andi. I've been running this business for five years, *five years*, and I've never had an agent find a dead body in one of my cars. Seriously?"

He shook his head and smiled tenderly at her.

"Only *you* would stumble into this kind of trouble. If anything happens to you, my grandmother will *kill* me."

"Sorry about the Camry, Jer."

Andi bit her lip and scrunched up her nose.

"I'm afraid I totaled it when I hit Bambi, and because of the dead body, the police have impounded it as evidence. Who knows when we'll be able to get it back?"

She braced for his reaction.

"Don't worry about the *damn car*. It's a loss. It happens. Our priority is to get you released, so you can get back to work. Our in-box will be overflowing if you're out of the office for more than two days."

He paused and looked her over again and grinned. Jerry pulled her ponytail like he used to when they were younger.

"What are you wearing? You look like you did back in high school."

Andi laughed.

"You can blame that on my personal stylist," she nodded her head towards Ben in the corner of the room who was talking with Daniel. "This is his *irresistibly innocent* look."

"Well, at least it's clean," he teased and tugged on her ponytail one more time. Then he got serious. "Hey, I heard your stray hired his hotshot attorney to represent you both. I need to talk to him. *Now*."

Cooper had been watching the interaction between Andi and her boss. He'd only met Jerry the one time when he'd chased Andi back to the repo office. That day, her boss didn't do more than grumble. His actions today were overly affectionate and very unprofessional. He was a little too *handsy* in Cooper's opinion. He didn't like it. So he focused his attention on Andi and *holy shit*, close up she looked like she was 16, maybe 17 years old. Cooper was frowning at them both as they approached.

Jerry's warm demeanor had vanished, and he was all business. He held out his hand to Cooper for a very firm handshake and introduced himself as Andi's employer and *close friend. What the hell was that supposed to mean?* Former boyfriend? Future boyfriend? Nope. Definitely didn't like the guy. Then it was Cooper's turn to introduce Andi and Jerry to his family attorney, Christopher Mills, who would be representing them at the bond hearing.

Mr. Mills' first question was for Andi, "I'm sorry, but I've got to ask. Are you old enough to drive?"

Andi smiled at him, and when his expression didn't change she said, "You're serious? Okay, this is ridiculous. Please just give me a second," she said, exasperated. She pulled the hair band out and shook her long dark hair loose around her face. "Apparently, Ben does the innocent look a little too well. *Jeez*," Andi mumbled to herself. "To answer your question, Mr. Mills, yes I've been driving for 9 years. I'm 25." She lifted her chin, defying anyone to challenge her claim.

Cooper grinned at her. He hadn't even had a minute to ask how her night in prison had gone. She was back to her usual sassy self so apparently, she was no worse for the wear.

With that initial concern addressed, their attorney described what they should expect at the bail hearing.

Mr. Mills looked at Cooper and then at Andi.

"You both have been arrested for first-degree murder, which is a felony. The police are going to transport you to the magistrate who will hear a summary of what happened last night and then set a date for your preliminary hearing. Because you're charged with murder, he may decide not to even allow bail. If that's the case, you'll have to stay in jail until your preliminary hearing."

"When will that be?" Andi asked.

"It can take a few weeks or it might even be a couple months," the attorney said.

"Oh no," Andi whispered.

Cooper swore.

"If we're lucky, the judge will set bail," Christopher Mills said.

He looked at Cooper, "Your father has authorized me to write a check for any amount to get you released." He looked at Andi and said, "If we're lucky and the magistrate sets bail, it's going to be high since you're charged with first-degree murder. Probably well over $500 grand. I would advise you to use a bail bondsman. They'll put up the money or promise to pay if you don't show up to court. You'll need to pay them a non-refundable 10% of the total bail amount."

Andi paled. She'd be hard-pressed to come up with $500 much less $50,000 to pay a bail bondsman. She was going to be spending a lot of time in a jail cell. How was she supposed to clear her name from there? She was feeling a little dizzy, so she dropped down into the closest chair.

Jerry crouched down next to her, put his hand on her shoulder and gently squeezed it.

He leaned close to her ear and whispered, "Listen, don't freak out about this, Squirt. I feel responsible for getting you into this mess. I know a guy. He owes me a really big favor, and I'm going to call it in. I'm sure he can cover your bail."

Andi turned to Jerry and whispered, "But I don't have that kind of money to pay him the 10%."

"Look, you can't spend *several weeks* in jail. Let's get you out of here, and then we'll worry about paying him back. We'll have several weeks to a couple months to figure it out. Plus, I'm sure he'll work out some sort of discount, so it won't be the full 10%"

Andi closed her eyes and blew out a long breath.

"Look, I don't see any other option. It's not like you can stay here," Jerry said and looked around and winced, "*indefinitely.*"

She opened her eyes and looked directly into his.

"Let's just get through this thing with the magistrate, and I'll talk to my guy and see what we can work out."

He stood up and ruffled the top of her hair.

She rolled her eyes, finger-combed her hair, and then stood up.

A uniformed officer stepped into the room and said, "I need Cooper Barnett and Andrea Sloan."

Cooper and Andi were transported back to the courthouse in the back of a police car. This time, without the handcuffs, and she wasn't covered in blood. They were still very much under arrest, and she felt just as desperate as she did last night. *God, was it only just last night?* Neither of them spoke. They were busy thinking about what was going to happen next.

When they arrived at the courthouse, Mr. Mills was already talking with Detective Kendricks and a man who must have been the Commonwealth's attorney. Ben, Maggy, Daniel, and Jerry were waiting for them in the hallway.

When it was their turn, they entered the courtroom with Mr. Mills, stood before the judge, and listened to the charges brought against them. Their charges sounded pretty bad. The judge listened intently and nodded his head.

Then the Commonwealth Attorney stunned them completely by saying, "The Commonwealth would like to recommend allowing bail for the accused. Neither has a previous criminal record. Andrea Sloan's employment with The Repo Doctor has been verified, so they were not involved in auto theft. Cooper Barnett's family is very active in the Roanoke community, and Andrea Sloan has spent her entire life here. While our office continues this investigation, we don't feel that Mr. Barnett or Miss Sloan pose a threat to the community, and our office does not consider them to be a flight risk."

The judge looked down at a file on his desk. "I normally do not permit bail for a murder of this gruesome nature; however, given the Commonwealth's statement, I will allow bail to be set at $700,000 dollars for each of the accused."

The judge gave them a cold, hard stare and pointed his finger at Andi and Cooper. "You'll need to report to the court, and stay out of trouble while you're released. Don't make me regret this decision."

Then he banged the gavel and said, "This court will reconvene for an arraignment hearing in three weeks."

They were dismissed and began to move out of the courtroom. Mr. Mills told them, "You'll be transported back to the jail. Cooper, I'll meet you there and take care of your bail." He turned to Andi and held out his hand, "Best of luck to you Miss Sloan."

"Thank you," Andi said and shook his hand, "for the representation and advice."

Andi and Cooper rode together in the back of the police car. *Again.*

Andi spoke first, "I'm sorry about this," she waved her hand in the air, "whole mess. I was so upset last night, I don't think I apologized for getting you arrested."

Cooper looked at her, eyebrows raised and snorted, "This isn't *your* fault. I tricked you into letting me ride along with you last night." He shook his head, "And it sure as hell wasn't *your* fault there was a dead body in that car."

She shrugged, "Well, I'm still sorry you got dragged into the mess that is my life. This is a whole new level of disaster, even for me."

His lips curved into a half smile.

Then he became serious and said, "Are you going to be able to make bail?"

She shrugged and bit her lip.

"Maybe. Jerry's working on it."

***

About three hours later, Andi was pulled out of her holding cell and taken to a discharge window where she was released on bail. The officer behind the counter returned her purse to her and handed her a clear plastic bag with all the items that had been in her purse. They must have collected her things from the Camry during the accident clean-up. Lord knew it was probably scattered all over the car after it went flying when she hit the deer."

As she walked out the door, she spotted Jerry pacing in the parking lot near his car.

He stopped when he saw her, smiled, and said, "Thank God you're finally out." He motioned to his car.

"Let's get out of here and go get your car from the impound lot. This place makes me itchy," he said and scratched the back of his neck.

Andi sat in the passenger seat of his blue 1969 Chevrolet Camaro, Jerry's pride and joy. She opened up the large plastic bag and began to dump the contents into her large purse.

Jerry glanced over as he was pulling out of the parking space.

"What is all that shit, anyway?" he asked.

"*Excuse me.* You've just caught a glimpse of one of the age-old mysteries. No man should ever truly know the contents of a woman's purse. Show a little respect," she grinned at him.

He smiled and shook his head. She was resilient, he had to give her that.

"I have no desire to *ever* know what's in your purse," he looked over at her and grimaced. "The thought actually scares me."

With her purse put back together, she turned to look at him.

"Thanks, Jer. You know, for getting me out of jail. I was okay for a night, but I think I might have gone a little crazy if I had to spend even another full day in there."

She took a breath and began the conversation she was dreading.

"So, give it to me straight. What's the name of 'your guy' and what kind of discount did he give me?" she asked then held her breath.

Jerry glanced over at her again, briefly. "I don't know his real name, but he goes by *The Broker*. He made arrangements with a local bail bondsman to post your bail. Listen carefully because this is important. You need to absolutely make sure you show up for court or things will get ugly, fast."

"Of course," Andi said.

Jerry looked over at her, his eyebrows raised.

"*Please*. I'm not going to miss my court date. Trust me," she said.

He seemed convinced, so he nodded.

"The normal rate for a bail bond is 10%. He's giving you a discount as a favor to me, so your rate is going to be 5%." He pulled into the parking area of the impound lot.

Andi's jaw dropped.

"But that's still a lot of money. I have to come up with $35,000! How the heck am I supposed to come up with that kind of cash in three weeks? It might as well be $70,000!"

"I've already thought about that. It's simple."

Jerry grinned at her. He really was a complete genius to come up with it.

"Just get a second mortgage on your house. I'm sure you've got even more than that in equity in your home," he said, then waited for her to beam with gratitude.

"Um, no!" she said and leaned her head back and stared the roof lining. "My grandparents took a second mortgage on their house to send me to Catholic School. My credit is terrible, and I've only had this job for two weeks. That's hardly steady income. Before I began working for you, I wasn't making enough as a waitress, and I got behind on my mortgage payments and was late for a couple of months. *No way*. They'd never approve me. *Never.*"

"*Damn,*" Jerry said and gripped the steering wheel tighter, "I was counting on you getting the cash out from your house."

"Well, I can't," she said and then sat up abruptly. "*Oh my god.* Now, not only am I charged with first-degree murder, I'm in debt to somebody named The Broker for 35 grand."

Andi looked over at Jerry, eyes wide, eyebrows raised, mouth gaping.

"I would have been better off in jail, Jer. Because if I can't figure out a way to get the money, I'll probably be the next body the police find."

She began to feel light headed.

Shit. Jerry grabbed a hold of her shoulders.

"*Listen to me.* We'll find a way to come up with the cash. Take the rest of the day off. Let's get your car, so you can go home, and try to relax and get some rest."

Jerry insisted on paying for her car to be released, assuring her he was going to expense it through the company. She got into the driver's seat and started the engine. Jerry stood near her driver's side door, looked down at her and said, "Things will look a lot better tomorrow," then he walked back to his car, started it up, and drove away.

Why did people always say that? In her experience, things usually looked a lot worse the next day. She shook her head and drove home.

***

Andi stepped inside her home and was greeted by a very excited Dodger. He welcomed her like she'd been gone for a week instead of just one night. It felt that way to her too. She'd just let him out in the fenced backyard to run around when the doorbell rang. With a sigh, she turned and walked back to the front door and looked through the peephole.

There they were, her pseudo grandmothers, waiting on the front porch. *So much for rest.* Not like she felt like resting anyway. She was too wired to relax. She opened the door and smiled as the three women began talking at the same time.

"Oh thank heavens you're alright," said Mrs. Harper.

"I told you she would be okay," Mrs. Barzetti said, "She's a tough girl."

"We were so worried about you," said Mrs. Davis.

Andi stood to the side and invited them into the kitchen. She put on a kettle of water for tea.

"We knew something was wrong when you didn't come back home last night," Mrs. Davis said.

"Then we saw your photo in the paper," Mrs. Barzetti said as she made the sign of the cross, "and I believe I aged ten years. I'm an old woman, dear. I can't afford that kind of time added on." She reached over and squeezed Andi's hand.

"I called Jerry first thing in the morning, and he said he was on his way to the police station to see you," Mrs. Harper said. "I told him I'd never forgive him if anything happened to you because of that job."

"Yes, he's the reason I'm not still in jail. He was able to help bail me out," Andi said.

Mrs. Harper leaned back in her chair and smiled as she took a sip of her hot tea.

"Well, isn't that the most *romantic* thing you've ever heard?" Mrs. Harper asked.

She turned to Gladys and Hazel for confirmation. Gladys sighed, and Hazel rolled her eyes and said, "Here she goes again."

"He's a good boy, my Jerry. I had always hoped the two of you would marry someday," she said and with sparkling eyes, looked over at Andi. "It's not too late, you know."

Mrs. Harper leaned forward and said, "He needs a woman in his life, and you'd be perfect."

Andi smiled and shook her head.

"I'm afraid that's not likely to happen. I do love Jerry, but like he was my brother rather than a potential husband."

Mrs. Harper always seemed to work that idea into the conversation whenever she talked to Andi about Jerry no matter how many times Andi tried to make it clear there was nothing romantic between them.

When they'd finished their tea and were convinced Andi was really alright, they said their goodbyes and left, so she could get some rest.

She couldn't rest. It was early afternoon, and she was feeling tremendous pressure.

The previous night still seemed unreal. She was the primary suspect in a brutal murder, and although she was released on bail and owed the man responsible for that bail a ridiculous amount of money, it was just like putting a Band-Aid on a hemorrhaging wound. Her fingerprints were on the murder weapon, and her DNA was all over Thomas Milner's body from when she tried to escape out from under him. Even though she had no motive for murder, there was enough evidence to put her away for life. That thought made her break out into a cold sweat.

She wasn't convinced that the police were motivated to look into this case and find the real killer. If she was going to stay out of jail, it would be because she figured out who killed Milner. What did she know about Thomas Milner, anyway? He was divorced and lived in a brick rental on Orange Avenue. She couldn't get into his house to look for clues. The last thing she needed was a breaking and entering charge. That would land her right back in jail. She knew he kept his car in a locked garage, which was why she had to follow him from work and not snatch it in the middle of the night. He worked for the phone company and drove a utility truck during the day. He was responsible for setting up phone/internet for residential and business customers.

If she was going to clear her name, she'd better begin now. She went into her bedroom to change out of her dress and into a pair of jeans and a black fitted sleeveless top. She slid on a pair of sandals, pulled her hair back in a loose hair band, let Dodger back inside, and locked up her house.

Her court hearing was in three weeks, and that wasn't a lot of time to investigate. Heck, she was good at finding people and things. She could do this. *Where to start?* She'd start at the last place she saw Thomas Milner alive—Diamond Auto Body Shop.

***

Andi parked in the same Gas 'N Go lot where she parked the night Milner was killed. *Had that only been last night?* There weren't many cars in the parking lot of the body shop, and she didn't see any activity outside the building. *Must be a slow day for business.* She got out of her car and carefully walked through the bushes that separated both businesses.

The body shop building was constructed with painted white concrete blocks, had two large garage bay doors in the front as well as a regular door that opened to the office. Along the side of the building were several large windows that were opened. Andi leaned against the side of the building, just next to the window.

She had considered taking her car in to get an estimate for some body work, so she could investigate from inside the building. Her car definitely could use a new paint job, so that part of the story would be believable. The problem was that she was very recognizable since she was on the front page of *The Roanoke Times* and the local TV channels as one of the prime murder suspects, so the employees would probably realize who she was too.

She took a quick look in one of the windows. There was a burgundy minivan up on one of the lifts, and a guy working on a fender near the front tire. Shelves lined the back wall of the garage and were filled with brown cardboard boxes, almost to the ceiling. *Okay. Nothing unusual there.* She was probably wasting her time here. This was the action of a desperate woman, for sure, but she was out of options. She wasn't sure what she was looking for, but this was the last place she saw her skip alive. She knew the answer to his murder was here.

She walked towards the back of the building and peered around the corner. The back lot was void of employees, thank

88

goodness. It just had a couple old oil drums, a large green dumpster for trash, and a pile of scrap metal. There were no windows on the back of the building, just a solid metal door that exited the garage bay area. She ran across the back of the building and cautiously peered around the corner to the side of the building that housed the office. There was a window on this side too, and it also was open. She approached it with care. She could hear the deep voice of a man. She gathered her nerve and took a quick look through the window. She saw him, his back to her, thank goodness, holding the phone between his ear and his shoulder, while he looked at a computer screen. He had a tattoo peeking out from his collar of a dagger with a snake wrapped around it. *Creepy.*

"Okay, we'll wipe the computers now and move the inventory tonight." There was a moment of silence, and then he said with a hint of frustration, "Look, we did exactly as you instructed. When he wouldn't tell us where to find the file, we *handled the problem*, away from the shop."

Silence for another 15 seconds.

"Well, there wouldn't be anything linking us to the body if it weren't for that damn *Repo Girl*."

Andi blanched and moved away from the window, pressing her back flat against the wall.

Holy Mary and Joseph. They did not just refer to her?!

"How do you want us to handle her?" he asked.

Another few seconds of silence and then she heard the man say, "Okay." He hung up.

What she wouldn't give to be able to hear the other side of the conversation!

She needed to leave. *Now.* Heaven only knew what they would do with her if they found her eavesdropping at the window. She moved soundlessly to the back of the building. It was still clear, thank goodness, so she ran across the back of the property, a decent distance away from the building.

Then she heard it—the unmistakable sound of a door opening.

She darted behind the green dumpster and crouched down low. The sound of heavy footsteps came closer, and she nearly had a heart attack when a loud thump sounded from inside the dumpster. She felt the green metal vibrate from whatever heavy thing was dropped inside.

She waited, afraid that her breathing and the pounding of her heartbeat could be heard by anyone within a 50-foot radius. She listened to the sound of retreating footsteps then finally heard the door close. She risked a quick look from behind the dumpster, and the lot was clear once again. She walked as quietly and quickly as she could, darted through the bushes between the two properties, got into her car, started the engine, and didn't relax until she was safely back on the interstate.

***

Five hours earlier, across town, Cooper entered the Barnett office building after being released on bail. Hell, he was already dressed in a suit from the bail hearing, might as well go in and deal with the fallout from last night's events. He could only imagine the office gossip. Plus, it wasn't like he'd get any sleep if he went home. He was too wired.

He shook his head in disbelief as he thought about all that had happened in the past 24 hours—watching Andi wreck the car, finding the bloody, naked body trapping her, getting arrested, cuffed, interrogated, and booked. *Andi.* He ran a hand through his hair. *The woman bewitched him.* Last night she'd displayed a kaleidoscope of traits: sexy, clever, *crazy*, shocked, freaked out, strong, resilient, and vulnerable. *Was she able to make bail? God, he hoped so.* He hated to think of her spending another minute in jail. He thought of how she looked when she had to leave him to go to her own cell last night and then that kiss. *Who was he kidding?* All those kisses they'd shared last night. What was it about this woman that made him feel so much?

He took the elevator to the 12th floor, and when he stepped off, he could feel all eyes on him. *Wouldn't it be hilarious if he spread his arms wide open, addressing everyone at once and just yelled—Did you see I'm charged with brutally slaying a man last night? Meet me in the break room for coffee and muffins if you want to hear how I shot the face off of Thomas Milner.* He grinned at the thought. As funny as that would be, it would probably come back to bite him in the ass during the trial.

Shit. Maybe coming to work today was not a good idea. He had to get his head on straight. He approached his administrative assistant's desk, right outside his office.

"Good morning, Kelly. Any messages?" he asked. She was a professional, efficient, forty-something woman, who was also a smart ass. They got along great.

She smiled at him sweetly and said, "Welcome back. The blue tie is nice, but I thought you might go with orange today."

Cooper rolled his eyes, held out his hand, and Kelly picked up a pile of messages.

"That's a lot," he said looking at the pile of white paper in her hand.

"Well, your clients have important questions now that you're a local *celebrity*. They want to know if you'll be able to continue to work on their portfolio from 'the big house'," she flipped to the next message and said, "This is one of my favorites, 'Was Milner one of your clients, and you killed him because he closed his account with you?'" She looked up over her reading glasses at him and smiled sweetly.

"Give me those," Cooper said and reached out and snatched the messages from her. *Jesus, what a mess!*

He turned to go into his office, and she said, "Wait, I'm supposed to tell you that you need to go directly to your father's office as soon as you arrive."

Cooper groaned and tucked the messages into his suit jacket pocket.

"Oh, and your mom will be there too." She smiled sympathetically.

Just great. Things continued to deteriorate after he'd entered his dad's office. His parents were obviously devastated, but not because he'd been at the scene of a brutal murder, or the fact that he'd been arrested and had spent a night in jail.

"You're a Barnett, by God, and your involvement in this murder is a poor reflection on our business and our family's reputation in the community," his father had said.

It was, apparently, bad for business to have one's son arrested as an accomplice in a homicide.

"What the hell were you doing repossessing a car? How did you manage to get involved with this girl, anyway?" his father asked.

"I'm sure he met her as a result of that rock music he plays," his mother said to his father. She looked directly at Cooper then and said, "Dear, if you would have practiced the cello more than that awful electric guitar, you would not be in this mess."

Leave it to his mother to blame everything wrong with his life because he gave up the cello.

She continued, "Nice girls go to orchestra concerts. Oh, what will the Junior League say when they read this?!" She pointed to the front page of the Roanoke Times that she'd been holding and dropped dramatically in a seat in front of his father's desk.

Mr. Barnett glanced down at his wife and then patted Cooper on the shoulder in a gesture meant to reassure him. "Christopher will get you out of this mess. That's why we pay him so generously. Once that's done, you'll need to drop this silly music hobby you've been playing at, son. It's high time you got serious about your position in the firm."

Cooper sighed. This was a recurring conversation they'd been having since he graduated college.

He looked up at his father. "Look, I give you my time during the workday. My free time is my own to do what I please and my music is exactly that. Mine. It's like asking me to give up my right arm. It's a part of who I am."

"Oh, don't be so dramatic, dear," said his mother.

Mr. Burnett continued, "We've let you keep your little hobby, but now it's affecting the firm. Reporters have been at the house and here at the office asking for a comment. They want to know why you were involved repossessing a car. Hell, I want to know that too. They asked if the man killed was a client of Burnett Investments. This event last night could cause us to lose credibility with our clients."

"What were you doing with that repo girl, anyway?" his mother interrupted.

Cooper sighed. He had no answer to that question. There was something about Andi that drew him to her, but he sure as hell couldn't explain it. Oh sure, he knew what he'd like to be doing with Ms. Andrea Sloan, but that was hardly an appropriate answer for his mother.

So instead, he said, "The band's renting her garage. We needed a place to practice."

His mother tilted her head, considering his excuse. "That still doesn't explain why you rode along with her." Then her jaw dropped. "Please, God in heaven, don't tell me you two are dating."

Sadly, no. "No, just friends. I was curious about her job, so I asked if I could ride along."

His father, an expert at closing the deal, said, "Well, it doesn't matter 'who struck John', or, in this case, Thomas Milner. The important thing is for you to follow our attorney's advice to the letter. I'm completely confident he'll get your charges dropped. If we're really lucky, you won't even have to go to court. It's not like *your* fingerprints were on the weapon. You'll be fine, son."

He gave Cooper a pat on the back as if that settled everything, looked down at his Cartier watch, "Time to get back to work."

Mr. Barnett leaned over and kissed his wife lightly on the cheek and held the door open. They were officially dismissed. Why did getting called into his father's office always make him feel like he'd been summoned to the principal's office?

As Cooper walked back to his office, a few of his colleagues gawked but said nothing. Thank god, no one had come up to him with questions about his new notoriety. Maybe they were afraid he really was homicidal. Just as well. He wanted to be left alone.

Once he was in his office, door closed, he was relieved to sit at his desk and completely immerse himself in the financial portfolios. Or at least he really tried to focus on the numbers, the accounts, and his clients, but after about thirty minutes, he finally gave in. Maybe if he could just clear his head, he could concentrate on the spreadsheets. He glanced at his watch. *Jesus*, he felt like some kind of addict. *Okay*. He'd give himself ten minutes. Reaching down to the bottom left drawer, he pulled out his music notepad, opened to a blank page and began filling in notes onto the empty staff.

He couldn't write the notes down fast enough. Before he finished, lyrics began to flow from him, so he wrote them down quickly on the page. It was the most incredible feeling. Almost as good as sex. He smiled and shook his head. He was an addict all right, a music junkie, and he was definitely on some kind of composition high. After he'd written music for over an hour, he leaned back in his chair, feeling euphoric.

His mother called him dramatic when he tried to explain, *again*, how music was an inherent part of him. His life, over the last few years, had become a composition of dull, repetitive notes and that had even begun to penetrate into his treasured performance with the band. He'd tried to change up the rhythm when he'd written the song, *Not Enough,* and worked up the nerve to perform it to a live audience, exposing a part of himself that he'd always kept tucked away. He laughed remembering the margaritas crashing to the floor at the end of the song. Symbolic. He had no idea then that that moment signaled the beginning of an entirely new song.

Oh, he'd changed his life's rhythm alright. He'd gone from a monotonous harmony to Mussorgsky's Night on a Bare Mountain, from pouring through spreadsheets to discovering dead bodies, from superficial, flirtatious flings to what exactly? An intense attraction to a bizarre, beautiful woman who repossessed cars for a living? There was certainly a chemistry between them, and his body wanted to explore where those fiery kisses might lead. And yet, it felt like more than just a strong physical attraction. It was stupid really, but he sensed this inexplicable connection to her ever since he'd sung that damn song. It was like she could see right through his masks. He had no name for this 'thing' between them, but it was new, terrifying, and exhilarating all at the same time.

His thoughts were interrupted by a knock on his office door. Cooper quickly tossed his notebook in the drawer as Russell Stewart came walking into his office, closed the door, and sat down in the chair across from his desk.

Holding up the front page of the Roanoke Times, he said, "So this is the same woman who stole my car from the parking lot? Didn't know you two were *friends.*"

Russell raised an eyebrow and sneered.

Cooper frowned. He really didn't want to speak to anyone right now, much less this asshole.

"She didn't *steal* your car. She repossessed it because you defaulted on your payments. It's her job."

"Well, I call it stealing when some crazy woman takes my car in the middle of the day while I'm simply trying to earn a living."

Russell leaned forward.

"I hope they lock her away for life."

Cooper narrowed his eyes. *Prick.*

"They're not going to lock her away because she's innocent."

He was getting irritated with people insisting she was going to be convicted. He was with her. She didn't kill anyone.

Cooper glared at him.

"Was there something you needed related to work?"

Russell stood up and walked to the door then turned to Cooper.

"No. Just wanted to welcome you back. You let me know if I can help you with any of your clients while you're working through this mess with your murder charges."

He grinned and stepped out of Cooper's office and whistled as he walked down the hallway.

Oh, Cooper was sure Russell would be happy to steal his clients right out from under his nose. He picked up his phone and called his shrink, Dr. Martin. He definitely needed to see her. What a hell of a day.

***

Andi didn't want to go home after leaving Diamond Auto Body Shop. She needed to keep busy and not sit around at home, worrying about her mounting list of problems. If she was out of leads for her investigation, the next best thing was to make some money. She had to come up with $35K in three weeks, after all. *When had her life spiraled so completely out of control?*

She drove over to the office, walked through the front door and waved hello to Jerry. He was busy on the phone and gave her a nod. Walking over to the in-box, she picked up two files. The in-box was always full. At least business was good, and there was an opportunity for her to earn some income. She took the files over to a desk with a computer and opened the first folder.

The skip's name was Nicholas (Nick) Ingram, and his last job was as a pizza delivery driver for Pyramid Pizza. He was two months behind on his payments for a Silver Ford Fiesta. Hmm. She was suddenly feeling hungry for pizza. Actually, she was *always* hungry for pizza.

She drove over to Pyramid Pizza to see who was working tonight. She ordered a small pizza and asked who was running delivery.

"I only ask because we had a bad experience with that kid, what is his name?" She pretended to not remember. "You know who I mean, he's about this tall," Andi held her arm up to her shoulder, picking some average height. People usually filled in the name for her.

"You mean Kenny?"

"Yeah, that was his name. Is he working tonight?"

"No. Nick is the only delivery guy working tonight."

Bingo

"Okay. Thanks."

Andi walked out to her car with her small pizza. She opened the box, took a bite and then texted Ben

Andi: `Where R U?`

Ben: `Home`

Andi: `Hungry for pizza? My treat☺`

Ben: `Always. XL Bacon, Jalapeno, and sausage`

Andi: `Yuk! You have an iron stomach. Don't give any of that to Dodger. Can you call it in? Order from Pyramid Pizza. I'll be there in about 5 minutes.`

When Andi arrived home, Ben's car was already parked in the driveway. *Perfect.* She pulled in behind him so the pizza guy, Nick Ingram, would have to park on the street in front of her house, making for an easy getaway.

She went inside. Dodger was the first to greet her with a big wet kiss on her face when she bent down to give him a gentle pat on the head. Then she filled Ben in on her master plan.

"Here's the plan. When Nick Ingram comes to the door to deliver the pizza, I need you to buy me some time. You know, keep him at the door long enough for me to hop in his car and drive off."

Ben beamed at her and clapped his hands in excitement.

"Yes! I have always wanted to be part of a sting operation!"

He pointed at her and said, "Look at you, girl. One night in the slammer and you're already running cons."

"This is all perfectly legit. Okay, I'm going to go hide in the shadows out by Mrs. Barzetti's rose bush near the curb."

"If it's so legal, why are you hiding in the neighbor's bush?"

She tilted her head and narrowed her eyes giving him her best threatening look.

He only laughed.

She turned to leave and then spun around.

"Oh, I almost forgot."

She reached into her front pocket and pulled out money and gave it to Ben.

"This is enough to cover your disgusting pizza plus a tip for the skip to get a taxi home. Are you sure you're okay with this?"

"I've got this, girl. If I weren't such a brilliant fashion designer, I'd be on Broadway. I'm a natural actor." Ben grinned at her.

"Uh huh. Let's see your academy award winning performance."

Ben counted the money.

"You should be called Repo Angel rather than Agent with all the money you're leaving for this kid," Ben said in a voice mimicking Mrs. Barzetti. He patted her on the cheek, laughing.

"Very funny" she smiled back at him. "Better stick with fashion."

She went down her front steps, crossed the street, and crouched behind Mrs. Barzetti's prized knock-out rose bush, closest to the curb. She checked her watch. Nick should be here by now. She held the key to the Ford Fiesta in her right hand, so she'd be ready to make her getaway and her purse hung from her left shoulder. *Jeez* her purse was heavy. She really needed to clean it out and see if she could get rid of anything to lighten the load. It weighed a ton.

Then she heard a sound that sent a chill down her spine.

Click-click

Click-click

Mrs. Barzetti said, "I've got you in the scope of my Remington 700 Bolt Action Rifle. Stand nice and easy with your hands up and slowly turn around. I'm an old woman, and I startle easy, so I'd hate to shoot you by accident."

"Mrs. Barzetti, it's me, Andrea Sloan. I didn't mean to startle you. I'm going to stand up now."

"Oh for heaven's sake," Mrs. Barzetti lowered the rifle. "What in tarnation are you doing hiding by my roses, young lady?"

Andi turned toward the loving neighbor that almost blew a hole through her.

"I'm working. Do you mind if I hide out here until the pizza guy comes?" Andi asked.

"Fine dear. Next time, be sure to let me know first," Mrs. Barzetti said as she turned back to go inside. "Young people," she mumbled and then closed the door.

A car sped down her street with a bright orange pyramid on the roof of the driver's side and pulled in front of her curb.

Andi ducked behind the rose bush. Nick Ingram must have been in a hurry because she was pretty sure he didn't even notice her.

Showtime. The driver left the engine running and hopped out of the car with a large flat pizza box. He jogged up the sidewalk to Andi's front porch and knocked on the door. As soon as she heard Ben open the door and begin talking, she ran to the street.

She slid into the driver's seat, removed Ingram's keys, put her new key into the ignition, and restarted the car. Ingram turned around when he heard his car ignition turn off and then start back up.

"What the hell?" Nick ran down the steps toward his car.

"STOP! My car's being stolen!" he screamed.

Ben hollered, "Nick, comeback. I didn't get to pay you yet!"

Andi threw out Nick's set of keys onto the front yard as she yelled, "Don't worry. It's all perfectly legal. I'm not stealing your car, just repossessing it!"

She made a right at the end of her street and headed to the Repo Lot. Then she looked down at the dashboard and saw the gas gauge was below empty.

"Oh, you've got to be kidding me," she groaned. She'd already spent her own money on the pizza for Ben, plus the tip, and now, she needed to buy gas for a car that was riding on fumes. She pulled into the first station she saw. She pumped $5 worth of gas into the tank, put on the cap and sat back in the driver's seat. Finally, she drove the car to back to the repo lot.

***

Cooper walked into Dr. Linda Martin's office and sat down on the edge of her sofa. She was already sitting in an armchair across from him, legs crossed, notepad and pen in her hand.

"Good afternoon Cooper," she said looking at him through her black framed designer glasses. A smile softened her face. "I assume you asked for this emergency session to talk about last night."

"You read the paper? Of course. Everyone read it." Cooper sighed. "Okay," he took a breath and placed his palms on his thighs. So you're probably going to think I'm crazy."

He laughed. "I bet all your patients say that." He shook his head. "My life is so damn complicated."

He exhaled and leaned back against the sofa.

"I met the most unusual woman a few nights ago. The guys and I were playing at a local bar and grill, and I finally got up the nerve to play the song I wrote. You know, the one I shared with you at our last session?"

She nodded. "Good for you."

"As I was performing the song, I noticed a waitress who just stared back at me, holding a heavy tray full of margaritas. She was completely transfixed on me like she understood what I was singing about, and she had lived through it too. I felt so connected to her in a way I can't explain. All I know is at that moment, she was seeing the real me, not the cocky guy. It was raw, real, and intense for both of us because as soon as the song was over, she dropped the tray of margaritas."

He smiled at the memory.

"Turns out she's a roommate of my buddy's boyfriend, so I got to meet her backstage. She's so different from any woman I've ever met."

"In what way?" Dr. Martin asked.

Cooper snorted. "Well, for starters, she wasn't impressed to meet the band and for some reason, she was particularly hostile toward me. But I saw the way she connected with my song as I performed it, and that made me kind of curious about her. I wanted to know her story. She didn't share my curiosity and didn't stick around for me to get to know her better. Margarita Girl definitely wasn't a fan which meant I'd probably never see her again, right? *Wrong.* The next day I spotted her in my office parking lot trying to steal my coworker's car. So I got in my car and chased her all the way across town."

Dr. Martin shook her head and opened her mouth to speak.

Cooper held up his hand to stop her. "Yeah, I know what you're going to say. I realize that was reckless, but as it turns out, my Margarita Girl is actually a Repo Agent. I ended up giving her a lift back to her car since she left it at my office. It gave us a chance to talk, which only made me more curious about her. When there was an opportunity to use her garage for band practice, I jumped at the chance. Then, last night, I talked her into letting me ride along on one of her repo pickups. You've read the newspaper article, so you know what happened next."

"Yes. That sounds like it was quite a night. How are you feeling now?" Dr. Martin asked.

"*Alive.* I feel like I'm finally waking up after sleeping through my life."

Cooper laughed at himself. He sure as hell sounded unbalanced, but then that's why he was in here after all.

"It's not unusual to feel that way after such an adrenaline-filled night. Finding a dead body is traumatic in itself. Being charged with murder just magnifies everything tenfold. All things considered, I think you are handling the situation remarkably well," Dr. Martin reassured him.

"Maybe too well. I should be worried about being arrested, the murder charges, my upcoming court date, the evidence against me, and the impact of my arrest on my family and my job, but I'm not. Not really. Instead, I feel invigorated, and all these feelings are flowing out of me in the form of lyrics and notes faster than I can write them down. I've already composed three songs, and I can visualize an entire CD."

"Why do you think you aren't worried about the impact of this arrest on your job?" she asked.

Cooper sighed and raised his hands in surrender.

"I don't know. Maybe because it's not what I want to do for a living," he said.

"Then why are you doing it?" she asked and looked at him over her glasses.

Cooper began shaking his right leg and then ran his hand through his hair.

"Because it's what my parents expect me to do. Ever since I was a kid, my father would talk about how my brother and I would take over the business he built for us. I've never felt I had a choice in the matter."

Dr. Martin made a note and then looked back up at him.

"So you stay at this job for your parents' approval?" she asked.

He shrugged.

"Do you have their approval?" she asked.

Cooper sat very still for a moment and shook his head and then said, "No. Not really. I work forty hours a week doing a job that is deadening. I'm really good at it, but it's not satisfying, you know? The only thing that keeps me relatively sane is composing and playing music with the guys in the evenings and on weekends. Now, after last night, my parents are insisting that I give that up too. It's like they don't get me at all. Music is not just a hobby to me. It is me."

"Do you feel like your parents will still love you if quit working at your father's company?" she asked.

Cooper stared at her like she had three heads. He'd never considered leaving a real option. But what if he did quit?

"I really don't know," he said honestly.

Dr. Martin looked at him and in a gentle voice said, "Conditional love isn't really loving at all. That's simply approval. Your parents' love shouldn't have to be earned."

Cooper frowned and looked away.

"What about this Repo Agent?" Dr. Martin glanced down at her notepad and then looked back at Cooper. "Andrea Sloan. How do you feel about her?" she asked.

He blew out a long breath and ran his hand through his hair and grinned. "Fascinated," he paused then became serious and added, "Terrified."

"That's an interesting combination. Why?" Dr. Martin asked.

"Together, we survived finding a naked, dead guy, an arrest, interrogation, booking, spending the night in jail, and a bail hearing. That sort of thing tends to make a bond stronger. She's kind of attractive, and there's definitely chemistry between us. She's unlike anyone I've ever met, and I have such strong feelings for her, which I find both fascinating and terrifying. Plus, ever since I met her, my life has turned upside down."

"So what's next?" she asked while tilting her head and raising her eyebrows.

Cooper leaned forward resting his elbows on his thighs and clasped his hands together.

"I think I need to ask her out on a date," Cooper said and then chuckled. "Something a little tamer that doesn't involve fingerprinting or spending the night in jail," he added, winked at Dr. Martin and said, "Although the handcuffs could be interesting."

Dr. Martin made another note on her pad.

He wondered what the hell she wrote on the notepad. She probably made notes that he was a smart-ass and whiny. He glanced over at the pad, but she kept it turned toward her, so there was no chance of reading anything. Or maybe she was bored and making a grocery list.

Then a thought occurred to him, and he sat upright and said, "That's it!"

She looked up at him.

"I'll invite her to my brother's wedding this weekend," he said grinning. *He was brilliant.*

Dr. Martin's jaw dropped open, and she looked at him like she thought quite the opposite. When she finally spoke, her face returned to her normal open, expression of patience.

"Weddings can be stressful under the best conditions. Maybe you should start with something a little more conventional, like dinner and a movie," she said.

Cooper shook his head.

"No. This is perfect. She thinks I'm this rich playboy, musician. Dinner and a movie is the type of move I'd make with the women I normally date."

He shook his head, feeling more certain of this decision.

"No. This isn't something someone interested just in a one-night stand would do. It'll show her I'm serious, and my parents will see I'm serious too."

Yes, this was a great idea. He couldn't wait to see Andi.

***

Andi sat in the driver's seat of her car at the Gas 'N Go and peered through her binoculars next door at the Diamond Auto Body Shop. The inventory was being moved tonight, according to what she overheard this morning. She prayed she hadn't already missed it. Blowing a sigh, she let the binoculars hang down around her neck as she reached for the share size bag of plain M&Ms she purchased in the Gas 'N Go about twenty minutes earlier.

She saw a parts truck pull up to the garage bay, heard the horn, and then the bay door raised and the truck slipped in, the door shutting behind it. *Figures.* What she needed was x-ray vision. Or a drone. She was so frustrated. Everything was hidden behind those doors. She ate a few more M&Ms and moved the binoculars back to her eyes.

Just then, there was a tap on her driver's window, and as she jumped, the binoculars dropped to her chest, and a couple M&M's spilled from her bag.

She turned to see *Thor* leaning his muscular arm against the top of her door, staring down at her. Heaven help her, she really must stop thinking of him as Thor, but he'd just scared the bejeezus out of her. Detective Kendricks looked mad. Or maybe that was his normal expression. She lowered her window.

With her best good Catholic girl smile, she said, "Good evening detective."

"Miss Sloan. What are you doing here?" he asked in a quiet, stern voice that would have made Sister Kathleen proud. Wow, he had the most beautiful, sky-blue eyes.

Andi swallowed and held up her bag of M&Ms. "I stopped for some chocolate on my way home from work. Would you like some?"

"No thanks," he said in a brisk tone. "What were you just doing with those?" He pointed to the binoculars hanging around her neck.

Andi looked down at her Gram's binoculars and said the first thing that popped into her head.

"Birdwatching."

Well, it wasn't great, but it was better than admitting to spying on murderers. She looked back up at him and gave him her most winning smile.

The corner of his lips turned up with a hint of a smile, those ice blue eyes softening for a fraction of a second, and then his serious cop face was back in place.

"Miss Sloan." He sighed.

Andi could feel a lecture coming, so she interrupted him. "Please, call me Andi." She smiled and dropped three M&Ms into her mouth. "Are you sure you don't want any?"

He stared at her mouth for the briefest moment and shook his head no. He returned his gaze to her eyes. "Andi, according to your statement, this is the last place you saw Thomas Milner alive, and yet I find you here, the day you're released from jail, interfering with my investigation."

"Your investigation? You're looking into Diamond Auto Body Shop?" She placed her hand on her chest, over her binoculars. "Thank God. I was afraid that since my prints were on the murder weapon, there wouldn't be much more of an investigation."

He clenched his jaw and spoke slowly. "Of course there's an investigation. My partner," he pointed to an unmarked black Chevy Tahoe with dark tinted windows, "and I are following up on all aspects of this homicide."

She glanced at the car, back at the body shop, turned back to him, and lowered her voice. "When I came by this morning to do some investigating on my own, I overheard one of the mechanics on the phone with someone he referred to as "boss," and he said they were going to clear the computers and move the inventory tonight."

Andi looked meaningfully at Detective Kendricks and pointed to the shop.

"There's an auto parts truck in there right now probably moving evidence as we speak."

He shrugged. "Nothing incriminating about that. It's not unusual to find an auto parts truck in a body shop."

"I heard him tell the boss that they couldn't find the file, so they got *rid* of him." Andi raised her brows and chewed on her bottom lip.

Kendricks exhaled. "Look, you need to stop playing Nancy Drew and leave this to professionals. Again, they might have been referring to anything perfectly innocent, like firing an employee. Go home, Andi."

Andi just shook her head no and let out a breath of frustration. With her eyes wide, her brows raised, she leaned closer and said, "There's more. He said there wouldn't have been anything linking them to him if it weren't for that damn Repo Girl."

She leaned back in her seat and couldn't stop the slight shiver that went down her spine.

Detective Kendricks swore and rubbed the back of his neck. He crouched down, so he was eye to eye with her. She didn't move. He was so close to her face that she stopped breathing altogether. He looked so intense. Was he angry? Concerned? She wasn't quite sure.

His voice was deep, low, and very controlled when he said, "Andi, this isn't a game where you get to solve a puzzle or play detective. Thomas Milner is dead because he underestimated someone. That same person won't hesitate to put a bullet in your pretty head."

Andi swallowed hard. *Wait, did he just call me pretty? Focus Andi.*

Kendricks continued, "The way I see it, you've got two choices. The first is you can stay here, and I'll arrest you for interfering with my investigation where you can spend your time safely in jail until your court hearing in a couple weeks. Or, the second choice is for you to go home and not come within 5 miles of this place. Do you understand?"

Andi nodded, her eyes huge. "Yes. I'd definitely prefer option number two. I think I'll go home now."

She gave him a giant fake smile, the kind she used when she was a waitress serving an obnoxious customer.

Kendricks reached into his shirt pocket and pulled out a business card and handed it to her. "Call me if you think of anything else that might be important to the case, and *I will investigate it.* Are we clear?"

She just nodded again.

"Good," Kendricks' face relaxed, "now go home." He stood and tapped the roof of her car to send her off.

Andi promptly left, but she didn't go home. Instead, she drove straight to the Star City Bar & Grill. As she opened the door to the restaurant and took five steps toward the bar, she stopped in her tracks. Ben was there, working, but apparently, the Riot Act band members were also sitting at the bar. Before she could turn around to leave, Ben spotted her and called out her name.

Darn it. No way to sneak out now. She plastered another fake smile on her face and watched as the band turned toward her. *Great.* She should have headed home like Detective Kendricks ordered her to do, but she was kind of freaked out and not anxious to be alone.

She plopped down on a stool and dropped her forehead on the surface of the bar.

"Rough day? I know just what you need. Be back in a sec," Ben said and turned his back to her and began blending a drink.

Cooper asked, "So, how's life on the outside? Hope your day was better than mine."

"Definitely not," Andi mumbled.

"Oh, I don't know. Mine was pretty awful. What do you say the person who had the worst day buys the next round?"

Andi lifted her head and glared at him. "You're on."

Cooper grinned. "Okay, I'll go first. I got called into my dad's office for an 'intervention' from my parents."

Andi gaped at him. "Intervention?"

Cooper's lips lifted into a small smile. It was nice to see her look outraged on his behalf, then he shrugged because he expected no less from his parents.

"But you spent the night in JAIL!" People around them stopped talking and stared at her, and she realized she said that a little too loud. "Sorry."

"Well, they told me it was time that I dropped this music hobby," he grimaced, "because it was ruining their family and business reputation."

Andi stared at him with her mouth wide open in disbelief. He smiled and wanted to kiss her right here. He decided to leave off the detail where they blamed his music for involving him with people of questionable character – like her.

"I admit that does sound pretty terrible," Andi said. "Still," she cocked her head as if considering, "not as bad as my day."

Cooper continued, "Then, our buddy Russell Stewart cheerfully stopped by my office to offer to steal my clients while I worked through this murder thing."

With a flourish, Ben placed a beautiful yellow icy drink with a salted rim in front of Andi. "May I present you with my first ever Pineapple Lemonarita." He winked at her.

"Your first?" Andi asked with a little hesitation. "I'm your guinea pig?"

Ben grinned, "Of course. It's a signature drink I created just for you. I call it jailbird." He smiled wider. "First one's on the house, love," he leaned in close and said in a loud whisper, "because you look like hell."

"Gee, thanks," Andi smelled the drink and took a sip.

Cooper grinned, looked at Ben and said, "Andi will be buying the next round."

Andi snorted and took another sip. "Don't you believe it, Ben. He's definitely going to be the one to *pay*," she said as she slanted an evil look at Cooper.

Andi spun around on the stool, so she was facing Cooper. "If that's all you've got, then it's my turn."

Cooper grinned and said, "Take your best shot, Margarita," and then held up his beer bottle, "and thanks in advance for my next drink."

Andi narrowed her eyes and clenched her teeth, but refused to respond to his taunt.

Cooper just grinned—she was so damn sexy when she got all riled up.

"The best part of my day was the Pizza Delivery Repo cash I earned today. Of course, I had to deduct the cost of Ben's pizza, which I used to lure the unsuspecting pizza delivery car to my home, and the gas I had to put in the kid's tank to make it to the repo lot."

She took another sip of her drink.

Ben interjected, "And don't forget the nice tip you left him, so he'd have enough cash for cab fare back home. Although he was still really pissed you took the car."

Cooper looked at Andi in surprise and shook his head, "Well that was nice of you." He took a swallow of his beer from the long neck brown bottle and said, "Still, doesn't sound that bad."

Andi shrugged. "That was the *highlight* of my day. I made bail thanks to a favor a guy owes Jerry," Andi made quotation signs with both hands when she said 'a guy', "and I have to come up with the commission before we go to the hearing."

She tilted her head from side to side to release the tension that built up in her neck every time she thought about her bail situation.

"I was glad to hear you made bail. I worried about you all morning until Danny called to tell me you were finally out," Cooper took another swig of his beer.

"I'd say it's probably a tie for the worst day," he said.

"Ha!" Andi said and pointed at Cooper, "Not so fast. Since I'm still the prime suspect in the murder of Thomas Milner, I drove over to the body shop to do some investigation on my own this morning."

Cooper stopped smiling and set his beer down on the counter. It was his turn to stare in disbelief as he narrowed his eyes.

She continued in a matter of fact tone, "While standing outside a window of the shop office, I overheard a guy talking on the phone to someone he referred to as boss. They were supposed to 'wipe' the computer and said something about not being able to find the file. I'm guessing they meant a data file since they were talking about computers, but I can't be sure. Then, in so many words, the guy pretty much admitted to killing 'him,' but they said they didn't do it at the shop."

Andi's face paled as she came to a realization and then whispered, "Oh God. They must have killed Milner when we were at the park." She closed her eyes for a second, and then she opened her big green eyes and said very quietly, "They said no one would have been able to link the murder to them if it weren't for me."

Cooper swore and then asked, "They actually said your name?"

"No." Andi thought for a minute. "They said 'that damn Repo Girl,' but they might as well have said my name. I think all of Roanoke City knows me now and that I found and probably killed Thomas Milner."

"Please tell me you called the police," Cooper demanded.

"No," she said, exasperated. "I'm their prime suspect, remember?" She pointed to her chest, "I've got no proof. It would just be my word against theirs. And my fingerprints are the only ones on the gun."

Cooper stopped breathing.

Andi picked up her drink and took the last sip. She should have asked Ben to add a lot of alcohol, and she could have just taken a cab home.

"So I went back tonight," Andi said

"You've got to be fucking kidding me," Cooper said, putting his hands on her shoulders. He wanted to shake some sense into her or kiss her. God, this woman was going to be the death of him.

Instead, he said, "Promise me you will stay the hell away from there." It came out sounding like a demand, so he added a soft, "please."

"That's what Detective Kendricks told me when he caught me there tonight." She looked affronted. "He threatened to throw me back in jail for interfering with the investigation."

"Finally, bad cop and I agree on something."

Andi glared at him and then softened her expression. "At least he's looking into it. I was afraid they wouldn't look for the killer since they had me. Anyway, he told me to go home."

Cooper's lips twitched. "So you came here."

Andi was staring down at her empty glass. "It's on the way home. Sort of." She shook her head. "Not really. Not at all." She glanced up at him and with a wry smile said, "Truth is, I didn't want to be alone."

Cooper returned her grin, "Same. Plus, I was kind of hoping you'd be here too."

Ben swung by and cleared the empty glasses, wiped the bar, leaned his forearm and looked at them both and asked with a grin, "So, who's buying this round?"

Cooper said, "I've definitely got this one. Andi won hands down for having the worst day"

Ben winked at her.

"That was a sucker bet. Andi always wins that contest."

"So, what will it be?" Ben asked Andi.

"I'll have another jailbird. Better make this one a virgin because I'm driving."

Cooper said, "I'll just have a Coke. Thanks, Ben," then he handed Ben his credit card and turned back to Andi.

"Since we never made it to dinner last night, I'd like to take you out this weekend. You know, on a real date, not one of your repo pickups or another romantic evening like last night at the police station. I'd like to explore this thing between us," he said with a grin.

Andi looked down at her hands, took a deep breath, and then looked back up at Cooper and said, "No. I don't think that's a good idea. This thing between us isn't *real*. It's just a psychological result of us being thrown into an extraordinary situation."

She reminded herself that he was a player, and despite the attraction she felt for him, or maybe because of it, she needed to draw a line in the sand and put him neatly into the friends' zone where she'd stay safe.

So predictable he thought. She'd already made it perfectly clear she didn't want anything to do with him the first time they met. He must be sadistic because he couldn't seem to stay away from her. How was it he had known her for such a short time, and yet he felt he really knew her? He wasn't used to being turned down, but he knew for sure that flirting and charm weren't going to work with her.

"That's exactly why we need to try out a normal date," he said.

She shook her head.

"No, I'm not interested," she said not meeting his eyes, "but thanks."

"Oh, I get it," he nodded and then said, "it's because of those kisses we shared last night. Are you afraid to go out with me because you're already half in love with me, *Margarita*?"

He gave her a sympathetic look and patted her on the knee and couldn't help letting his hand linger.

"Don't feel bad, you aren't the first woman to lose her heart to me."

Andi glared at his hand on her knee, and when he didn't remove it, she pushed it off and narrowed her eyes at him.

"*Oh please*. I'm not afraid of you, *Rock Star*, and I'm certainly not in love with you. You are really quite full of yourself. Unbelievable," she said shaking her head.

"Then there's no problem. You'll go out with me," he said and shrugged.

"There wouldn't be room at the table for me and you and your gigantic ego," she frowned back at him.

"Oh, it's much worse than I thought," he said doing his best to keep a serious face.

He shook his head and said, "You're actually *terrified* to go out with me."

She snorted. "Are you drunk? Do I look terrified?"

"I'm completely sober." He pointed to himself and smiled. "You're just chicken."

Ben came back with their drinks and handed Cooper his credit card.

"Who's chicken?" he asked.

Cooper spoke up, "Andi's afraid to go out on a date with me this weekend."

"What, are we in ninth grade?" she said and rolled her eyes and mumbled, "And I'm not chicken."

She took a sip of her drink.

Ben grinned at her and nodded at Cooper when she wasn't looking.

"She'll go out with you this weekend. Where are you taking her? Better be someplace nice," Ben said.

Andi gaped at Ben. *Where was the loyalty?*

"My brother's getting married, so the rehearsal dinner's Saturday night, and the wedding is on Sunday. Both events are at the country club," Cooper said.

Andi nearly choked on her drink. She turned to look at Cooper.

"You want to take me to your brother's wedding. On our *first* date? With your entire *family*?" she asked.

"Well, technically it's not our first date. We've gone out a couple times already." Cooper held up his left hand and began counting on his fingers.

"First, I bought you lunch the other day after you stole Russel's car. Second, you treated me to peanuts and bottled water during our stakeout. And treated me to a night I'll never forget, at the police station. So this would be our third date. I'd say our relationship has gotten serious pretty fast."

Cooper gave her one of his charming smiles. The kind that made her stomach do a little tumble.

He raised an eyebrow and said, "Handcuffs were involved." In the next moment, he shook his head and said casually, "So, yes, my family will be there. Oh, and both events are formal."

He took a sip of his Coke.

Ben and Andi spoke to Cooper at the same time.

Ben said, "Yes, she'll definitely go."

Andi said, "No way, not happening."

Andi glared at Ben as she said, "Even if I agreed to go," she looked at Cooper and said, "because I'm not chicken," she looked back at Ben, "I have nothing formal to wear unless you count my high school prom dress, and I can't wear that for both events."

Ben shuddered, "No, I'm afraid I tossed that hideous Bubble Yum Pink dress in the trash this morning when I went through your closet looking for clothes for your bail hearing. But don't worry love, I've got the perfect gowns for you."

Ben turned to Cooper, "She'll be there."

Then Ben turned to Andi, crossed his arms, smiled and said, "You owe me. I'm calling in the marker from the *Valley View Mall* incident."

Andi opened her mouth ready to object and then sighed and said, "Fine. I'll go."

She pointed at Ben and said, "But now we're even."

He grinned and said, "Deal."

Ben held out his hand to Andi, and they exchanged some sort of bizarrely complicated handshake.

Cooper said, "What's the Valley View Mall incident?"

Andi narrowed her eyes and pushed her pointer finger on Ben's chest.

"What happened in Macy's stays in Macy's. It will never be spoken of again or the deal is off."

Then she turned to Cooper with her hands on her hips and said, "Sorry. Ben's sworn to secrecy."

Ben grinned at him and shrugged, "Hoes before Bros."

Cooper looked at Andi and Ben in complete fascination. He wasn't exactly sure what just happened except that Andi agreed to go with him to the wedding this weekend. *Thank God.* Usually sure of himself, he was afraid she was going to turn him down. Now he was the one indebted to Ben.

***

Half an hour later, after enjoying her free virgin jailbreak—*thank you Cooper Barnett*—and having goofed off with Ben and the band guys—*who knew they were so much fun*— Andi was feeling much lighter. She said goodnight to everyone and refused Cooper's attempt to walk her out to her car. Chivalrous as his offer was, she was really afraid that he might try to kiss her goodnight and more importantly, that she wouldn't be able to resist him. A woman could only take so many of those molten kisses before losing herself completely. No, the safe plan was to keep her head by maintaining her distance around the man.

She was just about to unlock her car door when a black sedan pulled into the space next to her. A large bald man stepped out of the passenger front door. He was about her height, but he was as broad as a defensive lineman. He grabbed a hold of her arms, pulled both her hands behind her back, and the next thing she knew, her hands were restrained behind her in some kind of plastic. *Zip-ties?*

"Andrea Sloan. The Broker has requested a face-to-face meeting with you."

Holy Trinity, she didn't think it was possible, but her day just got a whole heck of a lot worse.

She tried to turn her head to get a good look at the man, but he effortlessly shoved her to the back door of the sedan and then opened it. *Oh no.* Nothing good ever happened to victims once they got into the car. Seized by panic, Andi glanced around the parking lot filled with cars. Apparently, everyone else was still inside having a great time, so no one was outside to hear her scream. So she did the first thing she could think of and kicked him as hard as she could in his shin.

"SHIT!" he yelled and then forced her into the car, pushing her head down and closed the door.

"HEY!" Andi hollered as she fell onto the seat. It took all her effort not to fall on the floor of the car. She heard the loud click that indicated the doors were locked. It was too dark inside the car to see anything, so she turned her back to the door and frantically searched, using her tied hands, for some sort of handle to open the door. She felt nothing but a smooth surface. *Great.* Well, if she couldn't get out through the back door, maybe she could get out the front. She pushed toward the front seat planning to launch herself over the seat and— *Ouch*—banged her head against some sort of glass barrier that separated the front and back seats. *Trapped.* She took three quick shallow breaths. She needed to calm down. Having a panic attack wasn't going to get her out of this mess.

"Please relax Miss Sloan."

Judas Priest! There was a man in the back seat next to her. It was so dark inside the car—*tinted windows?* The car began accelerating and made a sharp turn. Andi quickly sat back in her seat and leaned against the car door to be as far away as possible from the man on the other side of the car.

"I mean you no harm. I would suggest you sit back in your seat. My driver tends to drive a bit fast, and I would hate for you to get injured while we chat."

She took a slow deep breath and wet her lips.

"Are you *The Broker?*" she asked.

Now that her eyes were adjusting to the dark, she could just barely make out the profile of the man sitting in the back seat with her. His outline was hardly visible—not helpful in identifying him, which was no doubt his intention.

"Yes. I make it a point to have a face-to-face conversation with my clients. I find this eliminates any misunderstanding of the terms of our arrangement."

Andi snorted. *Yeah right—hardly face-to-face if it's too dark to see anything. More like let's scare the bejesus out of the client.*

"I would have been happy to meet you at your office. There was no need to *abduct me* at night in a parking lot and *handcuff me,*" she said with more bravado then she felt. *Grams had always said sometimes you've got to fake it 'til you make it. Seemed she was doing that a lot lately.* "My friends are expecting me back inside. They'll come looking for me," Andi lied.

She heard him chuckle.

"You *are* spunky. I figured you were somebody quite special for our mutual friend to call in the favor I owed him. When we parted ways a few years back, he made it quite clear that he would never do business with me again."

He paused, then said, "So I've done a little research on you, Miss Sloan. It appears you have poor credit, so it's unlikely you'll be able to get a loan to pay me back. You certainly don't make enough money working at your job to come up with that kind of cash. Do you have any assets of value that I'm unaware of?"

"No," Andi said and swallowed. Unfortunately, he'd spelled out her problem. Well, the guy was direct—she'd give him that much.

"So how exactly are you planning to get the $35,000 to pay me back before your court date, Andi? You don't mind if I call you Andi, do you?"

"Not at all. Since we're on a first name basis, what shall I call you?"

He chuckled again, "You may call me The Broker."

"The only thing I've got is my grandparents' house. I still have a mortgage on it. There's more than fifty thousand in equity in the house."

And it was worth a heck of a lot more than that to Andi. She suddenly felt sick to her stomach. She'd be losing the only home she'd ever known to this creep.

He sighed, "The last thing I need is an old house in a questionable neighborhood with a mortgage. No, I'm afraid I'm not at all interested in your house, Andi."

Thank goodness. She should be offended by his dismissal of her childhood home if she weren't so darn relieved that he didn't want it.

"Perhaps we can work out another form of payment," he said.

"I won't do anything illegal—not even to pay off the debt I owe you," Andi said fiercely.

"I'm not asking you to do anything illegal. I'm only interested in the results—the means you use to obtain them are completely up to you. The man you are charged with killing took something that belongs to me. I want you to retrieve this, and return it to me before anyone else gets hold of it. You do this for me, and I'll consider it repayment for the $35,000 you owe me."

Okay—she could do this—she was good at finding people. Heck, she was on a mission to find the killer anyway. She'd probably stumble across this missing item in her search.

"So, what am I looking for?"

"He took a digital file that belongs to me. You'll know when you find it. Confidentiality is critical. You must not tell anyone about our meeting or our arrangement. It's important that I get that file before anyone else finds it—the murderer, the police, *anyone*. Failure is not an option, and your life depends on it. Are we clear?"

"Do *you* know who killed Thomas Milner?" Andi asked.

"No and I don't care—I just want my file back. You don't have much time until your court date, Miss Sloan. Don't worry about finding the killer. You need to focus all your efforts on finding my file. If you fail, you won't be going to jail. You won't be going anywhere. Do you understand?"

Jesus, Mary, and Joseph.

"Yes."

The Broker tapped on the glass, and a few minutes later, they pulled next to Andi's car.

"Remember, this new payment arrangement is confidential. If you speak to anyone about it, our arrangement will be *terminated*. Understand?"

"Yes," she said. *How many times was this jerk going to threaten her life? Jeez, her nerves could only take so much in one night.*

Her door opened, and she scrambled to get out of the car. Baldy was there again, yanking her out by her arms, then freeing her hands before slipping into the front seat of The Broker's car. She watched as the car vanished down the street. When she could no longer see the taillights, she began to tremble. She unlocked her car, sat inside, and had a little trouble getting the key into the ignition because of her unsteady hands. She laughed—a sort of wild sound coming from her. Oh my goodness—her life was crazy. She shook her head, let out a shaky breath, and drove home.

***

Across town, a black Lexus pulled out onto Campbell Avenue. The driver was tired and frustrated and selected a phone number from the contact list of the smartphone. It was getting harder and harder to find competent help. The call was answered on the second ring.

"The Repo Girl somehow heard your end of our conversation from this morning, and she told the police about it. You were already under surveillance since the debacle with Milner, and now you can expect a warrant by tomorrow. Make sure the place is clean. Am I clear? I'm pulling your building completely off the list until further notice. And one more thing. I need you to assign someone discreet to follow the Repo Girl. See if she's playing dumb or if she knows anything about our operations. Do not make contact with her. Don't be seen."

The Boss hung up without waiting for a reply and merged onto I-581. This mess was an inconvenience, but still manageable, as long as there were no more mistakes.

Chapter Five

The next few days flew by for Andi. There were no more surprise visits from The Broker, and work had been uneventful and easy, which frankly was a relief after the naked, dead guy job. This morning, she had looked over the file for her latest acquisition and checked online for background information. The skip had a cell phone number as his primary business line and lots of social media pictures with him hanging with people, drinking. Either he was one of those people who generally took a bad picture, or he was high much of the time. That was horrifying considering he drove an ice cream truck for a living.

She drove by his house and spotted his truck. Unfortunately, it was parked in his backyard, behind a 4-foot wooden fence. *Darn.* Considering most people didn't eat ice cream for breakfast—she was an exception to the rule—she decided to stay and wait for him to leave. She parked across the street in front of a neighbor's house and waited. Waiting was one of the downsides to her job. Well, that and finding dead bodies.

About an hour later, Andi was munching on Cheese Curls and texting with Maggy when James Foley finally came out of the house and unlocked and opened the gate. She watched him start up the colorful truck and pull out onto the street. Starting her car, she followed his truck, careful to stay back far enough so that he wouldn't notice her tiny Honda. She tracked him to a baseball field and watched him park and set up on the opposite side of the field. At least this was more of a food truck and not one of those ice cream trucks that were in constant motion, driving around neighborhoods, luring kids out with music. That was a little too creepy.

He began serving ice cream to little league players, fans, and a bunch of other folks that happened to come by just to buy ice cream from him. *Odd.* Must be good ice cream. Better sample some of the goods—a definite job perk.

She got out of her car and walked behind the backstop, cheering for a little guy who hit the ball and was running to first base. Near the bench of the team that was up at bat, she picked up a neglected baseball cap from the bench, placed it on her head, and walked over to the ice cream truck. In recon missions like this, it was important to blend.

When it was her turn, she stepped up to the window. Jimmy Foley was wearing jeans and a green t-shirt that read, *I only party on days that end in Y.* He leaned closer to the window, and she could see his eyes were red. *Great. Probably high.* She automatically glanced down at his arms, and she saw the tell-tale marks that indicated he shot up regularly. He looked her over in a way that made her skin crawl.

"What can I do for you, *babe?*" he asked.

"Just the fudge bar, *pal,*" she said firmly and gave him a stern look as she held out the exact change for the ice cream.

He shrugged, took the money, then slid open a glass door and pulled out her ice cream. He handed it to her and grabbed onto her wrist when she went to take it.

"You just come on back to see me if you need anything else, *darlin',*" he said.

Andi twisted her wrist out of his grip and turned away. *Ew. Oh, I'll be back alright, you cretin. To take your truck.*

She opened up the ice cream and took a bite. It wasn't even very good—freezer burn—so she tossed it in the trash and then took a seat on the bleachers where she could keep an eye on the truck. She noticed the truck still got plenty of customers, some of them coming just for the crappy ice cream. *Weird.* Maybe the other flavors were fresher.

Finally, the break she was looking for presented itself. Foley closed the window on the side of the truck and put up a "Be Right Back" sign. He stepped away from the vehicle and—*YES*—headed to the brick public restrooms near the road. Andi quickly ran over to the truck, key in hand, and peeked in the driver's side. She slipped into the truck and turned on the engine. Uh oh. Loud ice cream music began to play. *Time to put this baby in gear and head to the Repo Lot.*

She pressed on the gas, and the truck began moving forward slowly then suddenly, the engine finally received the fuel and she began racing forward, heading toward third base. She swerved so as not to take out the cute little third baseman and shortstop. She looked in the rearview mirror in horror to see that Foley was trying to grab onto the truck's bumper. She pressed down on the gas harder and headed toward left field with a very angry ice cream truck driver yelling and chasing the truck. The truck had outpaced the driver, but with the back door wide open, ice cream sandwiches, fudge bars, and Choco Tacos were bouncing out of the bins. *Huh, the doors must have slid open with that last wide turn.*

This was going to be a home run if she could manage not to run over any baseball players while she headed out to the main road. Foley reached for the back door as she drove over the bumpy grass in the left field. Just as he began to grab hold of the door to climb in, she turned the wheel a hard left before she ran over any outfielders. The skip couldn't hold on and went flying off the back of the truck. She glanced in the review mirror after safely pulling onto the road. The game had been forgotten as all the players made a run for the ice cream that fell out of the truck. Andi kept driving until she safely pulled into the Repo Lot.

She parked in the secured lot and stepped into the back of the truck to assess the damage. What a mess! There were wrapped ice cream pops all over the floor and counter. Luckily, most of the ice cream was still in the wrapper because it was a melted, gooey mess. She began picking them up and putting them in a trash bag.

That was when she noticed it. Several ice cream boxes had fallen onto the floor from the open cabinets under the counter, and they had assorted flavors of an entirely different kind. *What the heck?* She found prescription drugs like Codeine, Fentanyl, Hydrocodone, Oxycodone, and Morphine scattered on the floor along with small bags of white powder! With dread, she opened a cabinet door and saw cardboard boxes labeled with ice cream names but not refrigerated. She opened a box of Choco Tacos to find it was filled with bags that she could only guess contained cocaine.

Oh my god! This could not possibly be happening to her. She grabbed the box of Choco Tacos and ran into the office. Jerry was at his desk on the phone busy listening and writing something down. She set the open box down in front of him and stood back, hands on her hips.

He looked down into the box and said, "Mother Fu...Hey Bill, something just came up. Let me call you back in a bit," and hung up. Jerry looked up at her.

"Where in the *hell* did you get this?"

"They were in the ice cream truck I just repoed! I went to the back to clean up the ice cream bars that went flying while I was driving away, and I found drugs, Jer—lots and lots of drugs."

"*Holy Shit.* Andi, do you know what the street value in this box must be?" He looked back into the box incredulously. "I could retire just on these," he read the side of the box, "Choco Tacos."

"And there's a bunch more out in the truck. I know our policy is to return whatever items were in the vehicle back to the owner, but I'm guessing we'd better call the police," Andi said, biting her lip.

"Or take one hell of a vacation," he looked back down into the box and then back up into Andi's shocked expression.

"*Or pay off The Broker.* Jesus Andi, this solves your problem, right here."

Jerry stared back into the box.

Andi stared at him, mouth wide open. That would take care of her financial issue with The Broker, whoever the heck he really was, but it was still illegal. If she traded the drugs for what she owed, she really would be guilty of a crime. Not murder, but still. She bit her lip.

"I can't, Jerry," she said and dropped down into the chair across from him. "I'll find another way. I can't, no *won't,* use drug money to pay The Broker."

Jerry stared at the box a few more minutes and shook his head.

"It's a damn shame," he said and then picked up the phone to call the police.

"Not to mention, I hate to deal with the police."

He closed his eyes for a brief moment and took a deep breath. *Relax,* he thought to himself. It's not like he was doing anything illegal. *Now.* That was all in his past. He had a legitimate repo business. It's just he hadn't had to deal with the police with drugs since he was a teenager and had been involved with the wrong crowd. He opened his eyes and made the call.

In less than five minutes, two patrol cars and an unmarked police car pulled into the Repo Doctor parking lot with sirens blaring and flashing lights.

Jerry walked up to the front window.

"Jesus, with all this commotion, people are going to think you discovered another dead body. I still haven't decided if that was good or bad for business. We've definitely got a lot of free advertising out of it, that's for sure."

Three uniforms and a suit rushed into the office. The suit introduced himself as Detective Sanchez, and he was obviously in charge. Jerry and Andi walked everyone back to the secured lot and into the truck. One officer took photos of the inside and outside of the ice cream truck while two other officers took inventory of the drugs and then secured them. While the officers continued working in the truck, Detective Sanchez asked to speak with Jerry and Andi back inside their office.

Detective Martin Sanchez was in his early thirties and clean shaven. He wore a suit and tie and had coal black wavy hair that fell just to the top of his collar. By all outward appearances, he was just another detective in a suit, but there was something about him that set Andi on alert. When he looked at her, she felt a ripple of apprehension slide down her spine. She thought it might be his dark, hard eyes that showed no expression, or maybe it was his lips that were pressed together to form a thin straight line. The man oozed danger.

Jerry motioned for the detective and Andi to sit across from him at his desk.

Sanchez addressed Jerry first. "I'm going to need all the records you have on James Foley."

"Sure," Jerry said and hopped up quickly to get the files.

In fact, Andi had never seen him move so quickly. *Nice, Jer. Thanks for leaving me with the scary cop.* She rolled her eyes.

"Miss Sloan." Andi turned to face Detective Sanchez. "When and where did you last see James Foley?"

Andi swallowed. "Last time I saw him, he was at the River's Edge Sports Complex, in left field on the second baseball field."

She checked her watch.

"About 40 minutes ago when he finally let go of the truck bumper."

She grinned at the memory. Thank goodness he lost his grip before he could climb on the truck. That was a little too close. She'd had *no idea* he was a drug dealer.

Detective Sanchez had been taking notes and looked up at Andi, eyes narrowed, assessing her.

"Is there something you find *amusing*, Miss Sloan?" he asked.

The grin fell from her lips and her eyes widened. "No, sir."

He made a quick call from his cellphone to send a patrol car to the location to apprehend the driver.

"When did you discover the narcotics?" he asked with impatience.

The tone he used was more like an accusation. It made her feel like she'd been the one selling them in the truck. She refused to be cowed by Detective Sanchez, even if he looked like a cold-blooded killer. Andi sat up straighter in her chair, raised her chin, and stared down her nose at the detective. Sitting down, she was about 3 inches taller than he, and she wasn't above using her height to her advantage.

"Not until I got back to the Repo Lot. I brought in one of the boxes to show Jerry, and then we called the police immediately." *Well, maybe not immediately, but as soon as Jerry stopped fantasizing about how he'd spend the money he'd earn from selling the drugs.*

"Was this the first time you saw James Foley?" he asked, pointing that laser-stare at her.

"Yes. I drove by his house this morning. The ice cream truck was secured in his backyard so, I came back a little later and staked out his place and just waited. When he finally left, I followed him in my car to the ballpark, waited until he left the truck to go to the bathroom, then drove the truck back here." *More or less.*

"Is this all the drugs? Did anything fall out of the truck, Miss Sloan?" he asked.

Oh no. She hadn't considered that.

"I," she paused shaking her head, "I don't know. I know ice cream fell out of the back because the little league players were running behind me picking them up. It stopped the game. At the time, I had no idea there was anything other than ice cream in the truck."

She could just picture the little guys picking up ice cream sandwiches and bottles of OxyContin. She grimaced.

Jerry returned with a couple of file folders.

"This is all we've got," Jerry said as he handed the files to Sanchez.

Sanchez nodded. "Okay then. I think I've got everything I need," he said and tucked his notebook into the pocket of his front suit jacket and slid the files under his arm.

He handed them each a card.

"Here's my direct number in case you have any questions or problems. We should be able to pick up Mr. Foley today. Even if we're delayed in his arrest, I don't believe you're in any real danger."

They both nodded.

He narrowed his eyes at Andi and asked, "Do you mind if I ask you a question about the Thomas Milner homicide?"

Andi realized at once that he wasn't asking for permission. It was more like a warning, so she continued to make eye contact with the terrifying man, her head held high and nodded her consent with a confidence she didn't feel.

"I read the police report, of course, but I'm curious about your research into Mr. Milner before you followed him the night he was murdered. Did you have any indication that he might have been involved in any illegal activity involving narcotics?"

"No. His social media presence gave the impression he was kind of nerdy and a little boring. Divorced, close with one or two co-workers and a buddy from high school. Otherwise, he kept to himself. I talked with his neighbors and they considered him quiet."

He stared at her long and hard.

Was he waiting for her to confess something?

"That's all I've got. Nothing else." Andi shrugged like she hadn't a care in the world when really she felt prickly all over like a swarm of bees were crawling all over her skin, waiting to sting.

He looked at her with impassive eyes for another five seconds and then turned and walked back to the truck to oversee the inventory process.

Jerry and Andi stared at the door and then looked at each other.

Andi finally took a breath. "Sure glad that's over."

Jerry shook his head and said, "Wouldn't want to get on his bad side."

***

Saturday night arrived and Andi found herself sitting in the passenger seat of Cooper's car wearing the most beautiful dress. It was pretty enough that she almost forgave Ben for wrangling her into this date, no make that two dates, with Cooper. *Almost.* He had modified a vintage peacock blue, full-length gown into two pieces so that it fit her tall frame perfectly. The off-the-shoulder bodice was cropped and sprinkled with delicate stones that gave the illusion that the material was covered with a thousand diamond chips when the light hit them. The bottom was cropped just below her ribs, so a few inches of her flat stomach showed before the plain full satin skirt flowed to the floor. She wore her hair up in a French twist and her gram's faux diamond necklace sparkled around her neck. Matching earrings dangled delicately by her face. She felt like a million bucks. This gown filled her with confidence to face an evening with the millionaires of Roanoke—she hoped.

Cooper had been speechless, for a change, when she opened the door to let him in the house. When he finally regained his composure, he told her she looked stunning. It was no surprise that he looked elegantly handsome, wearing a black dinner jacket with matching trousers, a white shirt, and a bow tie. The man looked delicious wearing a t-shirt and jeans, so put him in a tuxedo and what did she expect? It was one of the things she found most annoying about him.

She fidgeted with her matching blue clutch. Ben had created it with leftover fabric from her dress. The man was truly a fashion wizard. She blew out a breath. God, she was so nervous it was getting irritating. This was one of at least one hundred reasons she didn't date. Lord have mercy, it was going to be a long night. She needed to focus on something. Better get some intel on Cooper's family so, things would go smoothly this evening.

"So, tell me about your brother, the groom," she said, breaking the silence.

Cooper glanced over at her and smiled. Hearing her cheeky tone in the darkness of his car relaxed him. He was familiar with this sassy Andi, not the gorgeous goddess that answered the door. The woman continued to surprise him.

"Phillip is my only sibling. He is four years older and is the perfect son my parents wish I would be. He actually loves his job at Barnett Investments. Phil is marrying his high school sweetheart, Brittany Rainier, who is the daughter of my father's business partner and an active member of my mother's clubs. Annoying perfection aside, Phil's actually a pretty great brother. We've always been close. And Brittany, well, you'll see when you meet her. She's absolutely perfect for him. I'm really happy for them both."

"Okay, how about your parents? What do I need to know?" she asked.

Cooper laughed and shook his head. Her inquisitive nature was probably why she was so damn good at her job.

"Well, we're here now, so I guess you'll get to find out for yourself," Cooper said, then stepped out of the car and came around to open her car door.

Great. She hated going into a situation blind. She'd done her own internet search on his parents, but all she found were articles about Barnett Investments and some photos of Mrs. Barnett at galas for her favorite charities. She needed more personal information, especially if she was going to better understand Cooper.

She'd heard about the country club but had never been there. It was a three-story white brick mansion with large white columns, huge windows, and a few balconies. The outside lights spotlighted the building in the darkness and it reminded Andi of one of the old southern plantations in the deep south. Once inside, there were lots of people in gowns and tuxedos already milling around. Cooper introduced Andi to so many people she knew she wouldn't remember all their names. Then they approached a man who she knew must be Phillip because he bore a resemblance to Cooper with much shorter hair. He shook her hand and gave her a warm smile as Cooper introduced them.

"It's a pleasure to meet you, Andi. Coop's told me a lot about you."

Andi elbowed Cooper in the ribs while smiling at Phillip.

"Ow," Cooper grunted.

"I wish your brother would have shared more information about your family with me," she said sweetly and then glared at Cooper, "instead, I'm walking in here completely blind."

Phillip chuckled and looked at Cooper with a nod, "*Finally*, you're dating a woman who speaks her mind."

Phillip turned back to Andi and grinned. "I'm glad you're keeping him in line. Lord only knows I could use the help." He winked at her. "It's a full-time job."

Ignoring his brother's comment, Cooper held his hands up in defense and stared back at Andi.

"Hey, I haven't had much time to talk about basic stuff like family with you distracting me with a dead body, murder charge, and an arrest. That's why I brought you here tonight, so you could meet everyone."

"Whatever story you want to tell yourself, pal" she rolled her eyes and spoke directly to Phillip and pointed her thumb toward Cooper, "Was he always this full of it as a child or did this condition develop in his adulthood?"

Cooper raised his eyebrows and said, "*Hello??* I'm standing right here."

Phillip laughed, shaking his head and said, "Oh my god, where have you been all my life? That's it—I'm adopting you as my little sister."

Then Phillip grabbed her hand and said, "Come with me," as he pulled her across the room, "you've got to meet my Brittany."

Looking around the crowded room, Phillip spotted his fiancé and walked right up to her, tugging Andi behind him. Two beautiful women with blond hair were in the middle of a conversation when Phillip and Andi stopped in front of them. One woman had long wavy blond hair and the other had a chic, short hairstyle. They looked like they might be related. Sisters or maybe cousins?

Both women stopped talking and starred at Phillip.

"Phil, what's wrong?" the short-haired blond asked, placing her hand on his arm.

He leaned in and gave her a brief kiss and smiled and said, "I'm sorry to interrupt. I just wanted you to meet Coop's girlfriend before we started rehearsing for tomorrow's ceremony."

Girlfriend? Date would have been fine. Acquaintance would have been better.

Andi opened her mouth to correct him when Phillip spoke, "Andi, let me introduce you to my beautiful fiancé Brittany Rainier, soon to be Brittany Barnett," Phillip smiled at Brittany and kissed her again then continued, "and her lovely sister Jessica. Ladies, this is Andrea Sloan, but she prefers to go by Andi, right?"

Phillip looked at her for confirmation.

Andi smiled and said, "Yes, please call me Andi. Congratulations Brittany."

Cooper caught up with them at that moment, stood next to Andi and placed an arm over her shoulder casually as he said, "Hey Brit, Jess, you both look lovely tonight."

The long-haired blond, Jessica, looked at Cooper as she said, "Thanks. We were just getting to know your *girlfriend*. I didn't know you were seeing anyone."

"We're not da," Andi began to say, but Cooper cut her off with a quick kiss on the lips.

He pulled away and gave her a long look.

What in the world was going on? Again, if he had only briefed her on these people, she might have a clue. He was so lucky she didn't punch him in the gut, right now. Instead, Andi only narrowed her eyes at him.

"Yes, well our relationship is fairly new. Andi's best friends with Danny's boyfriend. We met at one of our gigs and went out a couple times, got arrested." Cooper smiled devilishly. "It's been a wild ride."

Jessica's mouth dropped open and her eyebrows rose.

"Wait, you're the Repo Girl? From the paper?" Jessica asked and tilted her head.

She stepped closer and examined her face, "Oh my god. It is *you*."

Cooper grinned and looked at Andi, his smile growing even wider as he watched Andi frown.

"Yeah, her picture in the paper really doesn't do her justice," Cooper said and gave her a kiss on her temple, "Although, I still thought she looked pretty hot."

He felt her elbow jab him in the ribs, but he was prepared for it this time, so he just chuckled.

At that moment, Mrs. Barnett approached their group.

"It's time to practice the line-up for the procession. You'll all need to head up front now."

Phillip smiled as he took Brittany's hand, brought it to his lips for a kiss and then they walked toward the front of the room.

Jessica addressed Mrs. Barnett, "Madeline, have you met Cooper's *girlfriend* yet?"

Mrs. Barnett's eyebrows drew together, and she tilted her head as she turned and smiled at Andi.

"This is Andrea Sloan, the *Repo Girl* from the newspaper," Jessica said before turning to join her sister up front.

Madeline Barnett's smile turned an expression of horror for a moment before a mask with a bright, fake smile blanketed her face. *What the heck had Cooper gotten her into? No wonder he hadn't briefed her on his parents.* Obviously, Cooper talked to Phillip about her, not his mother, and his mother was not pleased. *No siree.* Also, what was the deal with the bride's sister anyway? The woman had emitted a passive aggressive vibe toward Andi. Was Jessica one of Cooper's former girlfriends?

Mrs. Barnett addressed Cooper, "Dear, you're the best man. You need to get up there with Phillip. Don't worry about Andrea. She and I can spend this time getting to know each other better," she said with a smile.

Shit. Cooper had seen the look on his mother's face. No way did he want to leave Andi alone to deal with her, but he couldn't stay and shield Andi from his mother. He had to be up there with Phillip. Damn, he hadn't really thought through this rehearsal dinner date. Then, he looked over at Andi and relaxed, marginally. Her chin was lifted in that superior way she had – as if she was looking down her nose at her subjects. *She wouldn't be steamrolled by his mother. Probably. Oh shit.*

He leaned in and gave her another quick kiss on the lips. He couldn't help it. It felt right. When he pulled back he could see she was surprised and then irritated. *Damn, she was adorable.*

He smiled at her and said, "This shouldn't take too long. I'll be back before you know it."

Then he leaned in to kiss his mother on the cheek and whispered "Be nice to her, mother. I *really* like her."

Madeline smiled and patted him on the back in their hug and said, "Of course, darling."

Andi smiled at Mrs. Barnett. *Oh, this was going to be uncomfortable. Terrific.*

Then she said, "You must be so excited about the wedding. Phillip and Brittany make such a lovely couple."

She really meant that too. The looks and touches that Phillip and Brittany had exchanged just in the short time Andi had spent with them were filled with genuine love and affection.

At the mention of her oldest son, Mrs. Barnett turned to look at Phillip and smiled—a real smile.

"Yes. Phillip and Brittany have been best friends forever. My husband and Brittany's father have been business partners for decades, so all four kids pretty much grew up together."

She looked directly into Andi's eyes and said, "I had no idea Cooper was dating anyone."

Before Andi could explain that she was not his girlfriend, Mrs. Barnett said, "You probably know that he and Jessica have had an on-off relationship for *years*."

No, but that certainly explained a lot.

Mrs. Barnett turned back to look toward the ceremony area of the room, and they both watched as the bridesmaids practiced walking down the aisle. The groomsmen were up front at the altar, and Andi watched as Cooper caught her eye and blew her a kiss. She rolled her eyes and shook her head. Cooper laughed, and she couldn't stop the half smile that slid onto her lips. Philip whispered something to Cooper, and then he playfully smacked Phillip on the back of his head.

Mrs. Barnett noticed the exchange and turned to Andi and placed a hand on her arm.

"Oh sweetheart, I love both my boys. I should warn you that Cooper has always been the restless one. Whenever he and Jessica break up, he's quick to jump into another relationship. It usually only lasts a couple days before he moves on to the next girl. I blame his erratic behavior on his rock music."

Mrs. Barnett looked back to the wedding party. Jessica was standing next to her sister.

She said, "I imagine Cooper and Jessica will be walking down the aisle together in the not too distant future."

She turned to look at Andi and said, "They are the next 'it' couple. You might have seen them written up in the society section a few months back."

Mrs. Barnett smiled and said, "*When* they do get married, they'll have the reception here at the club of course, with all the *right* people. My husband and I were married here too. It's a family tradition."

Mrs. Barnett sighed and looked at her watch.

"Oh, excuse me, dear, I've got to check with the caterer to make sure they're ready for dinner."

Mrs. Barnett gave her another huge fake smile and then turned and walked out of the room.

Wow. Message received. Could she be any more direct? According to his mother, Andi was only one of Cooper's many rebounds. Oh, and the implication that she wasn't one of the 'right' people. *Ooh*, she was so mad, she could punch someone. She took a deep breath.

So why the heck was she feeling irritated at the thought of someone else with Cooper. That was completely ridiculous. She folded her arms across her chest. They hadn't even known each other that long, and they'd been dancing around this intense attraction that had only magnified since their arrest. And wasn't that the point of this date, getting to know each other in a normal environment. But there was nothing normal for Andi about conversing with high society at a Country Club.

Andi watched as Cooper escorted Jessica back down the aisle, both of them laughing. Even though they were paired up as best man and maid of honor, she could see them as groom and bride, and she suddenly felt queasy, with Mrs. Barnett's comments playing on her insecurities.

She bit her lip and contemplated how a relationship with Cooper could never work—this, she looked around at the fancy room with wealthy people, was a foreign world to her, and she would never belong. He was raised in society and fit in so easily, but she was much more comfortable in her part of an old neighborhood in Roanoke. *God, what was she thinking? Why did she ever agree to come? This was a mistake.* She needed to get out. *Now.*

She turned abruptly and nearly collided with an incredibly good-looking man standing in front of her.

"Whoa!" he said as he handed her a glass of the champagne and flashed her a devastating smile.

"You look like a woman in need of a drink," he said, then leaned in closer and in a low, conspiratorial voice added, "My sincere apologies for not having something stronger to offer you. Had I been truly brave, I would have rescued you sooner, but alas, I'm but a mere mortal and no match for the intimidating Mrs. Barnett."

He stood back and with a devastating smile designed to make a woman swoon, he raised his glass, "To beautiful women and the men foolish enough to leave them unattended," he clinked their flutes together in a toast. "I'm Pierce Hargrove, a friend of the family, and you must be the beautiful and mysterious woman that Cooper has kept tucked safely away. Smart man."

He smiled at her and took a sip from his glass.

She raised her glass in a toast and drained the contents of her glass at once.

The bubbles tickled Andi's mouth and throat, and she could feel them float to the top of her head. *Okay, maybe that wasn't her best idea.* She looked back at the man in front of her, squared her shoulders – daring him to comment.

He looked at her empty glass, then back at her, and the corner of his mouth quirked up.

"Thank you," she said. "I was thirsty," she added as an explanation for downing her drink like it was a shot glass of tequila rather than an elegant flute of champagne.

He was gorgeous, charming and a nice distraction from her confusing thoughts about Cooper.

"How is it we have never met?" he asked smoothly, "I thought I knew every stunning woman in Roanoke."

She smiled and replied, "We've probably never run into each other because you are financially responsible and make your car payments on time."

Her lips curved into a gentle smile at his confused expression.

"Allow me to introduce myself properly," she held out her hand for a shake, and he took it, bowed slightly, and kissed her fingers.

She laughed thinking he was adorable. He kind of reminded her of Dodger.

"My name is Andi Sloan, Repo Agent Extraordinaire, at your service."

Pierce smiled and shook his head in disbelief. "Now you're just playing with me."

"No, true story."

She raised her right hand like she was under oath. *She'd better get used to that.*

"I only bend the truth when I'm in pursuit of a vehicle, and your name is certainly not on my skip list."

His eyes lit up. "No way. Are you the woman that Cooper was arrested with last week?"

"The very one," she said.

"You really are a repo agent? I bet you have a million interesting stories."

"Well, I'm a newbie. I've only been officially repossessing cars for less than a month. But it's been an interesting month, for sure."

They talked and laughed over Andi's more humorous situations.

When Cooper was finally free, he spotted Andi in the crowd laughing it up with Pierce Hargrove. *Jesus, nothing but sharks at the club.* And here he'd been worried about leaving her alone with his mother. He came up beside Andi, put an arm around her waist and pulled her close to his side, in a territorial way, making it clear that Andi belonged to him. Okay, it was a little neanderthal, but damn, he couldn't help the feeling that washed over him when he saw another man cozy up to *his woman.* He was feeling oddly territorial over Andi Sloan, another first for him. Cooper smiled, pressed a gentle kiss to her temple, *mine,* and said, "Pierce, thanks for entertaining Andi while I was detained with my best man responsibilities."

Sensing the best part of his evening was about to end, Pierce smiled at Cooper, sighed and said, "The pleasure was all mine, truly."

He addressed Andi when he said, "I came to rescue you, Andi, but you were the one who ended up rescuing me. I can't remember the last time I laughed this much with such a beautiful woman. You are a delight. Please save me a dance tomorrow." and with that parting note, Pierce bowed slightly, then turned to join another group of men in tuxedos.

Cooper glared at the back of Pierce as he departed and muttered, "Jackass."

Andi just laughed and poked him in the side.

"What?" he asked innocently, but couldn't help grinning back at her when he looked into her smiling eyes.

After that, Cooper kept Andi close by his side, and they had a fun time teasing one another.

She managed to enjoy dinner and miraculously kept her dress free of food, *thank God*. Ben would have killed her if she ruined his latest creation with one of the fancy sauces they served at the five-course meal. Several women genuinely admired her gown, and she proudly told them it was created just for her by hot new Roanoke designer, Benjamin Palmer.

"He's a genius. I'm sure he'd be happy to work up a unique something just for you if you're interested."

She gave out several of his business cards to the interested women.

The evening ended pleasantly enough, but as Cooper drove them back to her house, Andi remained quietly lost in thought.

Cooper had sensed a shift in Andi as soon as they got into the car. She was too damn quiet. Something was wrong. What had changed? Did she fall head over heels for Hargrove in his absence? Not likely but still, something had happened.

He finally broke the silence, "I'm a complete idiot." He waited a minute for her to contradict this statement. *Nothing. Not good.*

"When I invited you to the weekend wedding events, it never even occurred to me that I would be leaving your side so much for my best man responsibilities. I'm really sorry."

He stole a quick glance in her direction and said, "Forgive me?"

She was staring out the passenger window still lost in her thoughts, "Oh, you're fine. Everyone was very friendly," *with the exception of your ex-girlfriend and your mother,* she omitted.

He tightened his grip on the steering wheel. "Yes, I noticed Hargrove was especially attentive."

Andi snorted, "Yes, Pierce is quite something, isn't he? Lays it on a bit heavy, but he seems like a decent guy."

That didn't sound like a proclamation of her undying love for the man, but still, he couldn't help adding, "Well, he's got quite the reputation as a player at the club."

She shrugged, dismissing it. Pierce wasn't the one troubling her this evening.

"Your mother and I had an interesting conversation," she said.

Shit. Of course. My mother. One of the reasons he'd started going to therapy.

"She mentioned that you and the maid of honor have a long history together."

He sighed as he pulled the car into her driveway behind her Honda. He turned off the engine and faced her, resting his left arm on the steering wheel.

Well there it was, Cooper thought. They hadn't talked about past relationships. Frankly, he didn't want to imagine Andi with any man other than him, but it looked like they were going to talk about it now.

Hell. Was it getting warm in here?

He undid his bow tie and unbuttoned his top collar, so he could breathe. That was marginally better. He looked into her eyes and explained.

"Yes. She's Brittany's younger sister, and we all grew up together. You know, friends. Then Phil and Brit started dating and things worked out well for them, obviously since they're getting married tomorrow. So, we gave it try. It was okay, as in, it wasn't a disaster or anything. We were friends, after all, ran in the same circles. It was easy. We got along well, but there was no spark. No sizzle. So we broke it off, mutually. I think because it was easy, we fell into the relationship thing a few more times until we officially called things off for good a couple months ago. That was the most serious relationship I've been in. Until now. This thing between us," he pointed at her and then back at himself, "definitely *not* easy."

He smiled at her nervously and swallowed. "But you make me feel…," he searched for a word. *Amazing, terrified, jealous, unstoppable* then shrugged and said, "Everything."

Jesus, Mary, and Joseph. His heartfelt words were even more dangerous than his searing kisses. It felt like the floor had just dropped out under her feet, and she was free falling with him, eyes locked together until he spoke the next words that brought her crashing to the ground.

"Your turn. Past relationships." Cooper said, and braced himself for the answer he was dreading.

It took a few seconds for the meaning of those words to register. *Right. My turn.* She felt nervous, but he'd been straight-forward about his past, so she could do the same. *Maybe.* He was still silently waiting for her answer, his face set in a hard, serious expression. He was never serious. Even when they were handcuffed in the back of the police car. *Okay. Here it goes.*

She took a breath and said with a self-deprecating chuckle, "Okay, well, this will be brief. I don't do relationships."

Cooper stared at her, expectantly. *Bullshit.* He knew by the way she swatted away men like pesky flies that she was abstaining from relationships currently. "*Past* relationships," he clarified.

"Right. Okay, so I went out on a horrific date with Billy Stanslowski to prom. My senior year."

He continued to wait her out. A full minute passed.

"And I've had a long distance, one-sided, love affair with Chris Hemsworth, you know, Thor, from The Avengers. For *years.*"

She smiled at him with a spirited grin.

Cooper suppressed a smile and quickly looked away from that delectable mouth that he so wanted to ravish. Before he gave in to the urge, he moved his gaze back to her eyes.

He was tough. She thought she'd get a laugh out of him, but he just there patiently waiting for her to come clean. *God this was so hard. Just get the humiliation out on the table. Then it will be over.* She just couldn't look at him while she confessed.

"I met him before my grandparents passed when I was still going to the community college. He was in my calculus class, and he was gorgeous, an outrageous flirt, you know the type," she looked pointedly at him. "And for some reason, he directed all that hot energy at me. So, I was kind of swept away by it all. Thought I was madly in love with the guy, thinking of a long and happy future with him. We were together for almost the entire semester. I tutored him in calculus. Who knew differentials could be so much fun? What I failed to recognize was that apparently he took more classes than calculus, and there were other 'tutors' besides me."

She had been such a fool. After that heartbreak, she'd vowed never to let that happen again. *Ever.* What had she been thinking, falling for a guy like that? And what was she doing right now? Letting history repeating itself?

As if reading her mind, he said, "He was an asshole, Andi. He obviously didn't deserve you.*"

There was so much pain and sadness in her expression. *Shit. Not good. And now for the million dollar question…please let the answer be NO.*

"Do you still love him?" he asked.

"No," she answered without hesitation, and she looked like she had just eaten something very unpleasant.

Thank God. He took a breath and just as seriously, he asked, "Do you want me to kick his ass?"

Because he would if she really wanted him to. How weird was that? Another first.

She seemed to consider his offer.

"Maybe. Which ass are you offering to kick? Stanslowski, Thor, or Mr. Calculus?" and then she grinned.

Cooper remained serious despite her effort to lighten the mood. Their roles were certainly reversed tonight.

"You're worried I might be just like the loser that cheated on you."

Andi didn't say anything, which spoke a loud *yes* to Cooper. He reached out and took her hand, and she looked at their joined hands and then looked up into his face.

"I'm not like him, Andi, because I'm not an ass, usually, and obviously I'm not taking Calculus," he gave her another one of his smiles but then turned serious, "But most importantly, and here is the key difference, *you* are the only woman who interests me. No one else but *you*."

Oh my goodness, the man turned her insides to goo.

He gently cupped both sides of her beautiful face with his hands, glanced at her mouth, and then looked back into her eyes. *Damn, she looked so vulnerable.* He leaned forward and kissed her gently at first until she leaned into him and moved her hands up around his neck, deepening the kiss at which point he lost track of all thought.

Bam, Bam, Bam—They were startled by the loud banging sound against the car.

Jesus Christ.

They both pulled away from each other. A bright light was shining through Cooper's window, so he turned toward it, shielding his eyes with his left hand, ready to throttle whoever had interrupted them.

"Andrea Sloan, what would your grandmother say if she saw you making out in a car in her driveway?"

Mrs. Barzetti.

Cooper turned toward Andi and grinned. He wasn't about to pummel Mrs. Barzetti. He started laughing. Hell, he hadn't been caught making out in a car since he was sixteen.

Andi couldn't see anything except white light, but she could sure hear Mrs. Barzetti. And Cooper's laughter.

She held her hand up to her face to try to block the light, which no doubt was Mrs. Barzetti's new flashlight she bought from an infomercial on television.

"This is not funny," she whispered to Cooper.

"I know. I'm sorry," he laughed again, "Okay. I'm good. I got this," he told Andi.

They both got out of his car.

"Good evening Mrs. Barzetti. I was just going to walk Andi to the door," he said politely.

She pointed her finger up at him and in a stern voice said, "I'll make sure she gets in safely. I believe you've already gotten your kiss goodnight. You get in that fancy car of yours and head home."

Cooper looked over the roof of his car at Andi and grinned, "Good night, Andi. I'll see you tomorrow."

Then he turned to Mrs. Barzetti, "Good night ma'am," and picked up the hand that didn't have the flashlight and kissed it before getting into his car.

She smiled and said, "Oh, you're a rascal."

Cooper began to pull out of the driveway, and Mrs. Barzetti looked over at Andi, already walking up her porch steps.

"You'll need to watch out for this one. He's smooth."

Then she placed a hand over her heart.

"Reminds me of my Henry, God rest his soul," she said as she watched Cooper drive down the street.

***

The driver opened the car door of the Lexus, got in and started the engine. Once the car was safely out of the police parking lot and headed for the interstate, the driver sighed and made the call.

"Any news on the girl?"

"We've been following her the last few days, Boss. She ended up repossessing one of our distributors at a little league game, so we just watched like you instructed."

"Tell me something I don't know." The stories of the Repo Girl and the ice cream truck driver were circulating around the police station faster than cars racing around the

Martinsville Speedway. There were even clips on the internet from parents at the baseball fields.

Idiots.

"The repo was legitimate, so it probably was a fucking unlucky coincidence, but just to be sure, I want you to search her house. We're looking for anything that can be stored electronically like a flash drive, her computer, her phone if you can get it. Just search when no one is home. I don't want any more dead bodies. At least not yet."

***

The next day, Andi got ready to go to the wedding. Last night's gown had been vintage, classic, with a touch of elegance. For today's date, the masterful Benjamin Palmer had designed a beautiful sleeveless deep v emerald green chiffon maxi dress that was voluminous, modern, and sophisticated. This gorgeous number featured feminine layered ruffles, a center ruched bodice with waistband, and a sexy open back cut. It was perfect for dancing when paired with single sole heels for a drop dead gorgeous ensemble. She might have lived in a somewhat questionable neighborhood, worked an unconventional, dangerous job, but wearing this dress made her feel completely comfortable mingling with this group of millionaires. Thank you, Ben! Her very own personal fairy god-brother.

After she parked her Honda, she walked confidently onto the lawn of the Country Club, invitation in hand. Cooper was busy with his best man duties and nowhere in sight, so she was escorted by a groomsman to a seat on the groom's side. About three minutes later, the dashing Pierce Hargrove slid into the seat next to her.

"You look dazzling today, Miss Sloan," he said with a grin.

He studied her eyes and said, "Hmm. Do you have contacts to match each dress? I know for a fact your eyes were a beautiful blue last night, but today, they are most definitely an intense green color."

Her hazel eye color had that effect, but she just smiled at him and in a conspiratorial whisper said, "All part of the disguise, Mr. Hargrove. Perhaps I'm pretending to be a guest today while secretly crashing this wedding in pursuit of a skip. Maybe I'm planning to drive off in one of the luxurious cars parked over there. You know, this wouldn't be my first wedding repo."

He smiled at her, completely charmed.

"You can drive my car, the cherry red Jaguar F-Type, Miss Sloan, only if you promise to take me with you. Or I could default on my car payments if that's what it takes to have you pursue *me*."

She laughed. Just then, a string quartet began to play, and she watched as four men walked to the front of the gazebo.

Cooper stood next to the groom and scanned the faces of the guests until he spotted her. *God, she was beautiful when she smiled at him like that.* She wore her hair down today, and he knew he was probably grinning like a fool. Couldn't be helped. She rolled her eyes and shook her head no while she continued to smile at him. *Wait. Why was she shaking her head no?* He really couldn't help it. That's when he noticed Hargrove, sitting next to her, undoubtedly flirting with her. *Again.* But Andi was looking and smiling at him, not the jackass, so that was a slight consolation.

Andi thought the ceremony was beautiful and magical, watching the way Phillip and Brittany looked at each other, recited personalized vows they had written to each other, exchanged rings, and kissed sweetly after they were pronounced husband and wife. *Lovely* was the only word Andi could think to describe it. And okay, *envious.* What would it be like to love and be loved and most importantly trust in someone enough to make that kind of forever promise? *Terrifying.* So, she'd come up with three words. She watched the bridal party file out in pairs and tried to calm the jealous beast growling inside of her as she watched Jessica arm-in-arm with Cooper walking down the aisle. Yes, they had been *lovers*, on and off for *years*, but Cooper assured her that their comfortable, lackluster relationship had been over months ago. Could the man actually read her mind? At that moment, he turned to look at her with an irresistible smile that made her want to melt right there on the spot.

The bridal party stayed behind with the photographer while the guests were directed to the large ballroom inside the Country Club. There was a sea of round, white, flowing tables set with beautiful china and the most elegant fresh flower arrangements in the center of each one. The room was filled with at least a couple million fairy lights. Pierce stayed with her and escorted her into the huge room while they navigated to finally find her table. Jeez, there must have been 500 wedding guests.

"Looks like it's my misfortune to be assigned to a table on the other side of the room from you. I really do hate to leave you here with strangers."

His disappointment reminded Andi of the look Dodger gave her when she left for work. She was tempted to pat his head and tell him he was a good boy. He was a ridiculous flirt, but underneath all the silly lines, he was a really sweet guy, so she gave him a reassuring smile instead.

"Pierce, thanks so much for escorting me to my table. I'll be fine. Plus, they won't be strangers for long."

He smiled back at her and shook his head.

"No, I don't believe there are strangers in your world, Andrea Sloan. Don't forget to save me that dance."

And with that, he turned and walked toward the front of the room.

Since she was an unexpected guest, Andi was seated at a table with the other stragglers. Or perhaps this was all Mrs. Barnett's doing, who knew for sure. There were no bad tables at this shindig, but they were sitting in the very back corner of the room, the farthest from the bridal table, where Cooper would be dining. Next to the maid of honor, no doubt. And wasn't it the bride's duty to make sure her bridesmaids looked hideous in expensive gowns she made them buy? Brittany failed at that terribly, which kind of made Andi like her even more. Jessica looked gorgeous in the Tiffany blue colored gown that fit her like an elegant glove showing off her "assets." *The shrew.* Even though she was too far away to capture any sizzling looks Cooper might have thrown her way, she also wouldn't have to endure watching the friendly camaraderie between Jessica and Cooper. *Get over it. He said last night that there wasn't anything special between them. Jeez.* She hadn't been jealous of a guy since Billy Stanslowski in 12th grade.

When it was time for speeches, Cooper made a funny, personal, and elegant toast about Phillip and Brittany and the wonderful love they shared. Then Jessica made a toast about how great it was to be in love with your best friend. Was she only talking about Phillip and Brittany or was she also referring to her feelings for Cooper?

Luckily, Andi didn't have to spend a lot of time thinking about Cooper. Well, not too much anyway. The other guests at her table were eclectic and fun and it was difficult to eat because of all the laughing. These weren't polite chuckles, but gut-busting uproars where she laughed so hard that she cried. Thank goodness she had on waterproof mascara. She prayed she wouldn't spill anything on the masterpiece of a gown Ben created for her.

This is so stupid. That's all Cooper could really think while he sat next to Jessica Rainier at the bridal table, listening to her talk about a fundraiser committee she was heading for the children's hospital. He was trying to be a polite listener, but he was so distracted. What had he been thinking when he came up with this brilliant plan to take Andi on a real date at his *brother's wedding?* Why didn't his therapist talk him out of this lunacy? He could have just made reservations at a nice restaurant where they would be sitting right now at a romantic, candle-lit table for two in a dark corner while he got to enjoy her all to himself.

Instead, he brought her to an event where there were way too many single guys, soon to be drunk, and he wasn't even able to stand next to her with a stick and beat them back.

He'd finally spotted her in that green exotic dress in this ridiculous crowd of people, way, way in the back. She was so far away, he needed those damn binoculars she always carried in her car in order to see her beautiful face. Well, on the bright side, Hargrove wasn't at the table with her. *This was so unfair.* He sighed as he stared over at her table again and mindlessly moved his food around the plate with his fork. She even got to sit at the fun table. He could hear their laughter all the way up front. Of course, no matter where she sat, it would be the fun table. He exhaled deeply. Phillip leaned over and nudged his elbow, "So are you going to enjoy this fabulous food or are you just going to stare at her and pout?"

"I am not pouting," he grumbled.

Phillip laughed as he looked at Cooper's expression.

"*Oh my God,*" Phillip said. He pointed his fork toward him, "You look just like you did when you were five, and I wouldn't let you play with my video games."

Cooper smiled at that thought and patted his brother on the back, "Don't mind me. This day is all about you and Brit. Now you're an old married man. Seriously, I really am happy for you both."

"Thanks. You know, I don't believe I've ever seen you act this way over a woman."

"Not surprising since I've never met anyone like her."

"Interesting. What are you going to do about it?"

Cooper frowned, "Damned if I know."

***

Andi was having a grand time during the meal with her fun table companions. It was time for the bride and groom's first dance, so everyone gathered around to watch, and then the bridal party paired up and joined them on the dance floor. Andi frowned as she watched Cooper dance with Jessica. They were talking, laughing, and Jessica just leaned in to whisper into Cooper's ear. Sure, he said they were friends, but she couldn't help wondering if maybe there was something more. Someone tapped her on the shoulder.

"May I have this dance?"

Pierce. Andi turned to face him, smiled, and held out her hand. The guy had impeccable timing, she'd give him that.

"Coming to my rescue again?" she asked with a smile.

"I was hoping you would rescue me." He dipped her and she laughed, "*Again.*"

As they moved gracefully around the dance floor, her eyes kept wandering to find Cooper and Jessica.

Finally, Pierce looked into her gorgeous green eyes and asked, "I don't stand a chance, do I?"

Then he spun her around and pulled her in even closer.

Oh, he was a sly one. But as grateful as she was to have his attention when she'd been seized by jealousy, she wouldn't lead him on.

"No. I'm sorry, Pierce. I'm not looking to get involved with anyone right now," she said.

He gave her a half smile and said, "Right."

Pierce sighed, held onto her close as they swayed to the music and said, "I wish I would have met you first, Andi Sloan, Repo Agent Extraordinaire."

He looked over her shoulder and leaned in and whispered, "If you decide to ditch that idiot, please look me up. I think I could fall for someone like you."

"Hargrove," Cooper said with a low growl.

Pierce grinned at Cooper over Andi's shoulder.

"Barnett," he said with a big smile on his face.

"I was just keeping Andi company while you were dancing with your *ex*," he said with an eyebrow raised and then turned his attention back to Andi.

"Thank you for the lovely dance. I hope to see you again. *Soon*," he grinned at her, kissed her cheek, and then turned and left.

Cooper narrowed his eyes mentally launching a rocket at the back of Hargrove's head.

"Bastard," he muttered.

Andi grinned at him, happy to be back in his company. "Somebody's grumpy." She patted him on his flat stomach and said, "You need chocolate. I saw a chocolate buffet over by that humungous cake. Let's go check it out." She grabbed his hand and pulled him across the room.

"I'm not grumpy," he growled.

They reached the long buffet table filled with every chocolate concoction she could imagine. Andi stood frozen for a moment in awe.

"I think I've died and gone to heaven," she said as she reached for a chocolate truffle.

"Brittany's got a thing for chocolate."

"Brittany is magnificent. She's my new best friend," Andi said and then popped the truffle in her mouth and sighed. "Oh look, they've even got a chocolate fountain! I love those!!"

She reached over and picked up a deep red strawberry on a stick and dipped it into the dark creamy liquid chocolate that flowed from the fountain, held it over a small plate and took a bite. Andi closed her eyes and savored the sweet juice of the strawberry as it blended with the even sweeter taste of the dark chocolate.

"Mmm," she moaned.

When she opened her eyes, she saw Cooper staring at her with the strangest expression on his face.

"What? Is there chocolate on my lips?" she asked, taking a napkin from the table and wiping her mouth.

Cooper just took a step closer, grabbed hold of her waist, glanced at her mouth, and then looked into her eyes.

Oh no. He was going to kiss her. Right here in front of the chocolate fountain.

An older gentleman with thick white hair put his arm around Cooper's shoulder and said, "Don't you just love chocolate fountains?"

Cooper turned toward the voice, slid an arm around Andi's waist, and smiled at the man standing next to him.

"Pops," he said, "This is Andi Sloan, the amazing woman I was telling you about. Andi, I'm pleased to introduce you to my grandfather, the first Cooper Barnett."

"Oh, Mr. Barnett, it's very nice to meet you. Cooper's spoken fondly of you," she said and shook his hand.

"Oh please, call me Pops. That's what everyone in the family calls me. So Cooper tells me you're a hard worker and very good at your job," he said.

She smiled and poked Cooper in the ribs with her finger.

"Ouch," he said and laughed.

"Thanks, but I think your grandson *exaggerates*. I've still got a lot to learn," she said.

Pops smiled at her and nodded as he spoke to Cooper.

"She's humble too. I like that."

He turned to Andi, arched an eyebrow and said, "I read the article about the ice cream truck that you repoed—the one that led to one of the largest drug busts this year. That's pretty impressive work, young lady."

She smiled, modestly, "I was lucky."

"There's always an element of luck involved in any business deal."

He tilted his head and studied her, "But it only helps you so much. The rest of your success is based on pure determination, which is something I suspect you have a lot of."

"Well, my determination didn't help me much when I got the two of us arrested last week," she said.

Cooper shook his head, "Trust me, Andi, you had a hell of a lot of determination to stand up to Kendricks during the interrogation. You should have seen her, Pops. She was incredible."

Pops looked from Cooper to Andi and he grinned. *Ah, to be young and in love.*

"I bet. Andi, your determination may decide whether you get convicted or not," Pops said, serious again, "Well, that and a good attorney. Do you have someone representing you?"

"A public defender. I can't afford to pay someone," she said.

"Nonsense. You'll have the best criminal defense attorney in Roanoke. I'll talk to your father, Cooper, and we'll make sure Mills represents you both."

"Oh no, that's much too generous. I couldn't possibly pay you back," Andi said.

"In addition to determination, you need to learn when to ask for and accept help. Plus, you misunderstand. It's not an offer or even a request, and you absolutely will not pay me back. This is non-negotiable. You will have Mills represent you. It's purely an investment on my part. *In you*," he said.

"But," she said.

Pops held up a hand.

"There's nothing left to discuss, young lady."

Well, now she knew where Cooper got that persistence.

Pops rubbed his hands together and approached the table.

"Now that that's settled, let me try out this chocolate fountain," he said and picked a giant marshmallow on a stick.

***

The rest of the reception was filled with laughter, dancing, and finally a slice of that gigantic cake. Andi had never tasted such a delicious cake in her life. Then Phil and Brit left to head for their honeymoon in Bora Bora after a spectacular fireworks show. She and Cooper said goodnight to everyone, including Mrs. Barnett, who seemed quite unhappy to see Cooper taking Andi home rather than the lovely Jessica. Jessica didn't appear to be any happier than Mrs. Barnett. Andi just smiled sweetly at both of them, head raised slightly in a regal way when what she really wanted to do was put her thumbs in her ears and stick her tongue out at both women.

She and Cooper walked hand in hand out to her car. This was nice – being with Cooper was just so *nice*. She breathed in the night air and looked up. The sky was lit with tiny stars despite the country club parking lot's bright lights. *Hmm, not as much fun for a good night kiss under this wattage.* Then they finally reached her car. That's when she saw it.

"Oh, you've got to be kidding me," she said as she let go of Cooper's hand and bent down to get a closer look at her front tire.

It was completely flat. She walked around her car to check the other tires. Thankfully, they were fine.

"What am I going to do?" she asked, hands in the air in surrender. "I can't change my tire in Ben's dress. He'll *kill* me if I get anything on it."

"I'll change it for you," Cooper offered.

Andi rolled her eyes.

"*Please,*" she waved her hand at him, "you look like a model from the cover of one of those bridal magazines. I'm not letting you ruin your tux over my stupid tire."

Cooper grinned. She was adorable when she was all riled up like this. He was sure she didn't even realize she'd complimented him. He couldn't help it. He grabbed her by the waist and pulled her flush up against his body and then leaned in for a fast, hard kiss, wrapping his arms around her, his hands flat on her bare back holding her close to him. *Jesus.* He'd been wanting to do this all damn day. *FINALLY.* It was ridiculous how much he craved her.

A wolf whistle pierced the air and then the familiar voice of one of the groomsmen, Garrison, hollered out "*Yeah Cooper.*"

Damn. He forgot they were in the middle of the parking lot for everyone to see. He stepped back, turned toward the sound and there they were—up on the hill headed to the parking lot, three groomsmen and their dates. He waved and then turned to look at Andi. He was relieved to see that she was as affected by the kiss between them. Her lips were parted, her face was flush, and her eyes were unfocused. *He needed to kiss her again. He would kiss her again. Just not right here under these bright lights and with an audience.*

"Let me drive you home. I'll give you a lift here tomorrow, and we can fix your tire," he said.

She gave him that look—the one he was coming to know so well—that meant she was about to argue with him.

Before she said anything, he said, "Look, I'd be driving you home anyway if I hadn't had to ask you to meet me because I had to be here so early with Phillip for the wedding. Let's not stand out here and argue about it. Come on. Let me just drive you home."

He gave her his most charming smile.

"*Please.*"

He was too cute for his own good. She sighed and rolled her eyes and said, "Fine." and then in a softer tone she said, "Thank you."

***

Cooper tightened his grip on the steering wheel as he pulled onto Andi's street. Earlier this evening, he had worried that bringing her to the wedding had been a mistake, but she didn't seem to be interested at all by that prick Hargrove. Cooper still wanted to beat the shit out of him for kissing her. It was only a brief kiss on her cheek, but still. This jealous, possessive feeling was foreign to him. Andrea Sloan was unlike any woman he'd ever met. *He hoped she invited him in tonight.*

Andi glanced over at Cooper as they pulled into her driveway. How was it that this man broke through all her defenses? She had been so sure her strange attraction to him was caused by all the adrenaline from her job and being arrested, but tonight there were no dead bodies or car crashes, and she still felt like goo when he was around.

Why him? Pierce, who could have been Mr. December on some calendar of hot men, said and did all the right things and was genuine, romantic, and caring, but he only made her feel mild affection. With Cooper, she felt like she was standing in the glorious, rough surf at the ocean, and it took all her energy when she was with him to keep her feet solidly on the ground and not get swept out to sea. And even that effort only worked some of the time. And the rest? Well, she was way in over her head. The man made her crazy. One minute she wanted to punch him and the next she wanted to kiss him. The urge to kiss him won more times than not. Like now. *Jeez.* She was going to invite him in.

Cooper cut off the engine and turned to her with a half grin.

They both spoke at the same time.

Cooper said, "Do you think Mrs. Barzetti will call the police if I kiss you now?"

Andi said, "Do you want to come in?"

They laughed and answered at the same time.

Andi said, "No."

Cooper said, "Yes."

They laughed again and got out of the car and walked up to her porch.

"Is Ben working tonight? I don't see his car" Cooper asked. *Okay, he knew it was a lame question, and Andi would undoubtedly see right through it, but damn he needed to know.*

"No. He and Dodger are sleeping over Daniel's place. He said he hoped I'd get *lucky* tonight, so he was *removing all possible obstacles* because I needed all the help I could get. He's insufferable. I don't know why I put up with him," she said.

"Ben is great. I love Ben," Cooper said with a grin.

Andi turned the key, unlocked her door, stepped in and flipped the light switch.

"*Oh. My. God,*" Andi whispered.

Cooper stepped around her. *Fuck.* Her house was a mess. Seat cushions were on the floor and slashed open, tables knocked over, lamps shattered on the floor, and *Jesus*, even her big screen television looked like someone put their foot through the center of it. She stepped forward into the house and on pure instinct, he grabbed her and pulled her quickly back down the steps until they stood next to his car. *Thank god she wasn't at home when this happened.* With that thought, his stomach suddenly felt like he'd swallowed a gallon of acid.

Looking at her, he saw big tears rolling down her face. He pulled her into his body and wrapped his arms around her, holding on tight. That's when a sob escaped her lips. He squeezed her tight for another second and then pulled her back arms-length, holding onto her shoulders, so he could look into her eyes. She was trembling.

"Listen. I need you to stay out here with me in case someone is still inside. I'm going to call the police. Okay?"

Andi nodded once, and he pulled out his cellphone and called 911 then he immediately pulled her back into his arms, so he could hold onto her, for his sake as much as hers.

"Hello. My name is Cooper Barnett, and I'm calling to report a break-in," Cooper said and he gave her address.

"No," Andi cried out, pulled out of his embrace, stormed up the steps of the porch and into the house.

"Fuck! Andi wait!" Cooper yelled and ran up the porch stairs after her. She'd already entered the house. He heard the voice of the 911 operator on the other end when he stepped into the living room and said, "Just send the police. I don't know if they're still in the house, and my girlfriend just ran inside."

Then he pushed the end button and threw his phone into his jacket pocket and ran to the kitchen looking for Andi. He found her—*thank god*—standing in the middle of her kitchen which, as impossible as it was to believe, looked worse than the living room. Every cabinet drawer was open, its contents dumped on the floor, a leg to the kitchen table was broken off, so with only three legs left, the table had fallen on its side. Cooper picked up the broken table leg and held it like a baseball bat. Hell, if anyone was still in the house, he'd at least have a weapon. He watched as Andi bent down on the floor and picked up a broken ceramic handle and held it to her chest. She wiped at her face again. *Shit.*

In a quiet, fragile voice, Andi said, "This was a teapot I made for Grams when I was twelve."

She sniffed.

"She took me to the pottery shop downtown for Mother's Day," she looked up at Cooper, "which was a hard holiday for me to get through, so we'd always try to do something fun together on that day."

She looked at the handle again.

"It's *stupid,* you know? They're only *things,*" she wiped angrily at her tears again, swallowed and said, "*Thank god* Ben and Dodger weren't here."

"I know, Andi," Cooper said and pulled her into an embrace. "Hey, do me a favor? Let's wait outside for the police, okay? I don't think anyone's still here, but I also don't want to mess up the crime scene any more than we already have."

He held up the table leg.

"Okay," she said quietly, with the teapot handle clutched tight against her chest and walked with Cooper back out to the front porch. That's when they saw Mrs. Barzetti marching across the street, armed with her Remington 700 Bolt Action Rifle.

"*Holy Shit!* Is Mrs. Barzetti packing?" Cooper asked Andi in a low voice.

"Oh Andrea, dear, I heard about the burglary on my police scanner. I called the girls. Gladys and Ethel are bringing hot cocoa and some cups. They'll be here in five minutes." She cocked the rifle and began walking up the porch steps. "Meanwhile, you two wait out here while I go inside and make sure no one is still in the house."

Before Andi had a chance to stop her, a police car— lights flashing and sirens blaring— swerved into the driveway. A uniformed officer stepped out of the police car with his gun raised and aimed at Mrs. Barzetti.

"Place your weapon on the ground and slowly put your hands in the air where I can see them."

Andi spoke up immediately. "Officer, it's okay! This is just my next door neighbor, Mrs. Barzetti. She came over to check on me."

Mrs. Barzetti slowly lowered her weapon to the ground and turned around to face the young officer. She looked at her watch. "I clocked you at a response time of eight minutes. That's not too bad, but I think you can do better. I was just about to go inside to see if the perp is still inside. Want to follow me while I investigate?"

The uniformed officer stared at Mrs. Barzetti, his eyebrows raised, his mouth hung open, but he said nothing. He shook his head and quickly moved up the steps of the porch. "No, ma'am. I'm going to need you to wait out here while I check out the house."

"But I'm part of the neighborhood watch. Plus, I'm armed. You might need backup."

The officer grinned, glanced down at the rifle, and looked back at the spry older woman. "I'm sure you know how to handle that ma'am. With all due respect, please allow me to do my job. You should stay outside with your neighbors and keep them safe." He started to go inside the house and briefly turned back to Mrs. Barzetti. "Please do not touch the rifle until I get back." He headed inside, checked all the rooms, and came back out to the porch, reporting that no one was inside and every room pretty much looked like the living room and kitchen.

By that time, Mrs. Davis and Mrs. Harper had served the hot cocoa and began to put the living room back together – enough so that Andi and Cooper could at least have a place to sit. That's when Detective Kendricks and Richardson walked through the front door and conversed with the officer.

Andi held a mug of hot cocoa in both her hands. She felt so cold, and although her hands had stopped trembling, she still felt shaky inside. Cooper sat next to her with his arm wrapped protectively around her shoulders.

Detective Richardson and Kendricks sat on chairs across from them.

Richardson spoke first, "It looks like the intruders broke in through the kitchen door. We spoke with your neighbors, and no one noticed anyone suspicious. Was your front door locked when you arrived home?"

Andi nodded.

"Yes, I had to use my key to get inside," she said and took another sip of cocoa.

Detective Kendricks, with the intense blue eyes, looked at her and asked, "Have you noticed anything of value missing?"

Andi took a deep steadying breath. She felt Cooper squeeze her shoulder.

"They broke *everything* of value to me," her voice cracked, so she took another deep breath and said, "The only things I have of any monetary value they've destroyed, like my flat screen," she pointed to the mess by the living room wall.

Detective Richardson asked, "How about other electronics, like a computer?"

"I just have my phone, which I always keep with me, and the laptop that I use for work was in my car."

Andi gripped the mug tighter.

"Where's your car now? It's not in the driveway," Detective Kendricks fixed her with his ice blue gaze.

"At the country club. My car had a flat tire, and since it was late, Cooper gave me a ride home," Andi said.

Detective Kendricks nodded and then narrowed his eyes as he looked over at Cooper.

What the hell was that look for? Cooper really didn't trust bad cop and apparently, the feeling was mutual.

Kendricks turned back to Andi, "Was the tire slashed? Did it look like vandalism?"

"What? No. Just one tire was flat," she said, "Do you think someone did it on purpose?"

Kendricks glanced at Cooper for a moment and then said, "Not necessarily. I'm just collecting information right now and frankly, trying to figure out a motive since the theft of valuables doesn't appear to be one of them."

"What about anything you might have brought home from work?" Detective Richardson asked.

Andi frowned.

"The paper files from my skips and laptop are the only things I would have, and they were in my car."

Detective Richardson leaned in and in her kind, southern drawl said, "I'm thinking more along the lines of items from a car you may have repoed. Like, personal items the owner might have left in the car at the time you took it. Where would you keep something like that?"

Kendricks gave Richardson a strange look and then turned that intense gaze back to Andi.

Andi just shook her head.

"Anything that's left in the vehicle that we repo is returned to the owner. We're only responsible for the vehicle that's returned to the lender. Like the other week, I repoed a car at a wedding, and the newlywed's luggage was left in the trunk. We returned it. The only exception would be the drugs I found in the ice cream truck this week. We called the police to collect that."

Kendricks said, "Based on the way the drawers were opened and dumped out, I'm guessing that your intruders were looking for something. Of course, whoever broke in did a lot of damage to your property, which could also mean it was someone you've made really mad. Do you know of anyone that falls into either of those categories?"

"I could think of a few skips that are pretty angry that I took their cars, but enough to do this?" she motioned around the room.

She thought a moment.

"Definitely the creepy ice cream drug dealer, but I'm pretty sure he's in custody, right?" she asked. *She hoped so.*

Kendricks nodded and jotted down a note on his pad.

"I'll follow-up to make sure he didn't make bail," Kendricks said.

"Maybe Dodger's owner?" she looked at Cooper, who was staring at her, frowning.

"Who's Dodger?" Richardson asked.

"He's the pit bull I rescued from the skip with the red Dodge Charger. His name is Clyde Finch. Big, mean guy who left his abused dog in his car on a hot day with just the window barely cracked. So I took the car *and* the dog."

Kendricks shook his head as he wrote the name down on his notepad and under his breath said, "Of course you took the dog."

Andi's eyes widened, and she looked at Detective Richardson. "I guess I did bring someone's personal property home. But I don't think he wants his dog back. He could have come back to the office to demand we return it to him, and Jerry, my boss, has never heard from him."

"We'll check him out and see where he was tonight," Kendricks made another note, "Anyone else?"

Andi briefly thought about The Broker, but he had no reason to trash her house. He wanted her to find a mysterious file. She definitely wouldn't be sharing that with the detectives.

"That's it unless you think it could be related to Milner's murder somehow?" Andi asked.

Detective Kendricks looked up at her from his notes and glared at her.

Andi stilled, like a deer that knew it had been spotted.

She reminded herself that she was the *victim* of a crime, not the criminal. She lifted her chin slightly and began to breathe again, willing herself to relax under his intimidating stare.

He raised an eyebrow.

"Is there any *reason* you think it's related to Thomas Milner's murder? Because I thought I made it clear that you were not to get anywhere near my investigation," Kendricks said, his voice was like hard, cold steel.

The man was completely intimidating. She swallowed hard and then narrowed her eyes at him, pretending she was a tough, not easily cowed, woman—the complete opposite of how she actually felt at the moment.

"No specific reason and I haven't done any investigating on my own. I only bring it up because I thought it was weird that this break-in happened soon after the dead body dropped in my lap."

Kendricks relaxed, exhaled and rubbed the back of his neck. *Okay.* At least she wasn't investigating on her own—*that was something.* Although even with his most intimidating glare, she didn't flinch. *Shit, he even admired that about her.* So, she wasn't meddling in his investigation, but damn, she was a magnet for trouble. Tales of her huge drug bust with the ice cream truck had been all over the news. She had a dangerous job and obviously could have made someone mad enough to vandalize the place. *But something just didn't feel right about this.* It looked more like someone had searched her place. Recklessly, but still. *What was he missing?*

He nodded at Richardson and then looked back at Andi while he tucked his notepad in his pocket.

"I think that's about all we can do for tonight. We'll check into the two possible suspects. The officer secured your back door temporarily, but you'll need to get that door fixed tomorrow." Kendricks said.

He scowled at Cooper—*he definitely didn't like the boyfriend*—and then looked at Andi.

"Do you have a *girlfriend* you can stay with tonight?" he asked.

What the hell? Cooper was already on edge, the adrenaline from this evening making him want to hit something with his table leg weapon, so he leaned forward, pointed his thumb to his own chest and said, "*No. Andi will be staying with me.*"

He hadn't meant for it to come out like a growl, but *Jesus*, the woman next to him made him act like a freaking caveman. Of course, he immediately realized that it sounded like an order which would earn a *big* negative from Andi, so he turned to her and pleaded his case.

"Look, Andi, it just makes the most sense. I'm already here, you can grab whatever you need, and I'll drive you to my condo. It's right here in the city, I've got a second bedroom you can sleep in," Cooper looked at Kendricks, "*my building has security*," he turned back to Andi, "so you'll be *safe*," he said and then exhaled.

She didn't respond, just looked down into her empty hot cocoa mug.

"*Please.* Let me do this," he said.

She looked at him, and he touched the side of her face and gently caressed her cheek with his thumb, "*I need to do this, okay?*"

She nodded, too exhausted to think much less argue about anything.

Thank god because her refusal was not an option he could accept.

After the police left, her grandmotherly neighbors finally left, but only after promising to come help clean up tomorrow morning. Andi called Ben to let him know what had happened, and once she'd assured him she was okay she hung up. She just wanted to curl up in a ball, in a room that wasn't ransacked, and cry herself to sleep. But the tears didn't wait. Once she stepped into her bedroom, they began to drip from her eyes like a leaky faucet. Her closet had been emptied, and all her clothes and shoes had been scattered all over the floor. Just like the kitchen, drawers had been dumped, her underwear flung all over the room.

A shiver slid down her spine. The patrol officer called this a non-violent crime because there was no force or injury to a person, but Andi definitely felt injured and violated. Strangers had touched and broken her stuff. *All of it.* She hugged herself, blew out a long breath, and quickly grabbed some of the basics she'd need for tonight. For now, she just wanted to get out of here. Things would be better tomorrow.

***

Cooper pulled into his secured parking garage. This was not how he imagined bringing Andi back to his place—and he had fantasized about it *a lot.* Instead, they quietly took the elevator to his floor, he unlocked the door and showed her the guest bedroom and bathroom she could use to change out of her formal gown. He put on some water for tea and went to his bedroom to change out of his tuxedo into a pair of sleep pants.

Cooper grinned when she walked into the kitchen. She'd washed off her makeup, pulled her hair up in a ponytail, and wore a pair of pink shorts with donuts printed all over them and a tank top that read "I Donut Even Care." She looked adorable, *sexy as hell*, and all he wanted was to scoop her up and carry her back to his bedroom to explore every inch of her body. *He was a total ass to even be thinking about sex when she'd just been through hell.*

He shook his head and handed her the cup of tea.

"Sorry, it's just regular black tea. Unfortunately, I don't have that special blend you drink to help you relax."

"Thanks," she said and tried not to stare at his abs— *Oh. My. God.—the guy was ripped.* Sure, she knew he was solid. She'd felt the firmness of him when they'd embraced and danced, and he looked great in the fitted t-shirts, but *hello*. She shook her head to clear her stray thoughts. She looked up into his eyes. *Focus.*

"So, do you want to drink the tea in the living room or, no, you're probably ready for bed, of course. You must be exhausted," he said and ran a hand through his hair.

She took a sip and hid a smile. He was being so sweet, gentle and *nervous*—treating her like her broken teapot. She felt broken.

"Would you mind if we just sat up for a bit?" she asked.

They sat on his leather sofa that faced a huge window with the Roanoke downtown skyline outlined by the lights of the buildings. It was a beautiful view, and they were both quiet while he drank a beer, and she sipped on her tea, knees pulled up to her chest, her bare feet on the edge of the sofa, her painted pink toenails occasionally wiggling. She could feel the heat from Cooper's body next to her, he'd draped an arm casually across the back of the sofa, and she allowed herself to lean into his warmth, feeling safe for the first time since she'd walked into her vandalized home.

When she finished the tea, they both got up and walked to the kitchen, she rinsed out her cup and set it in the sink. Cooper walked her to the guest bedroom, gave her an awkward hug and kissed her gently on her forehead.

"My bedroom is just down the hall. Come get me if you need *anything*, okay?

"Thanks for everything, Cooper," she reached out and squeezed his hand before she turned, walked into the spare bedroom, and closed the door.

Andi felt exhausted, but every time she closed her eyes, she saw her ransacked house. When she would finally start to relax enough to fall asleep, she'd see two faceless thugs wandering around her house smashing her things and laughing. She wasn't going to be able to sleep. She wiped the tears away and sat up.

Cooper had been lying wide awake for the last hour, images of their day together at the wedding, the incredibly hot kiss in the parking lot, and then the shock of walking into her home and the terror he felt when she went running back into the house. He was so damn exhausted, but he just couldn't relax enough to sleep.

He heard a knock on his bedroom door.

"Um, Cooper, are you awake?" Andi asked in the softest voice, opened his bedroom door and stepped into his room.

Huh. Cooper figured he must have fallen asleep, and this was the beginning of an erotic dream. Andi had been starring in them ever since that first night they'd met. He smiled. *Finally.*

Andi thought that he looked awake, but he was just staring at her with an odd smile on his face. *Okay, just say it. Get it over with.*

"I can't sleep. Would you mind just holding me? You know, like you did in the living room?" she asked.

She could feel her face burn with embarrassment, but she was desperate.

Sweet Baby Jesus. This was definitely not one of his hot dreams.

"Sure," he said in his best *we're just platonic friend's* voice.

It was a miracle that his voice didn't crack. He pulled the covers back and patted the space next to him. Thank god he'd kept his sleep pants on.

She swallowed and said, "Thanks."

Andi slid under the covers next to Cooper. He rolled onto his side and pulled her close to him, her face resting against his chest, his arms wrapped protectively around her.

"Are you comfortable?" he asked.

"Yes, thank you," she whispered, her warm breath tickled his chest.

Andi was so grateful that he understood exactly what she needed tonight. She listened to his steady breath and the slow, easy rhythm of his heartbeat and felt safe once again.

She drifted to sleep almost immediately although Cooper stayed awake another hour, tortured by the heavenly scent of her hair, her soft curves, and gentle breathing. He finally began to relax, and then he heard it. She was snoring. He smiled and drifted off to sleep.

Chapter Six

Andi smiled into a pillow that smelled just like Cooper. She snuggled deeper into the pillow wrapping her arms around it to hug it close. *Cooper's bed was so much bigger than hers. Cooper's BED?* She sat up, immediately wide awake, and noticed, with tremendous relief, that she was alone in the bed. Everything from last night came rushing back to her. Discovering the break-in at her house, finding her things handled and broken by strangers, being interviewed by the police, coming back to Cooper's house to spend the night, and asking to sleep with him in his *bed*. She covered her face with the pillow and fell back on the bed, letting out a long groan.

He stood in the doorway of his bedroom, showered, shaved, and dressed in a charcoal gray suit for the office, although he wasn't sure he was going yet. First, he had to make sure Andi was okay.

He'd been standing there long enough to see her panic when she woke up in his bed. The morning after could be tricky, although he'd never had one quite like this, sleeping with a woman without having sex. But everything about Andi seemed way more complicated. Her moan was so damn sexy even though he was sure that wasn't her intention.

"Good morning, *Sunshine,*" Cooper said, a smile hidden behind the coffee cup as he took a sip.

At his greeting, she jumped completely out of bed, standing to the side of the mattress while holding his pillow tightly in front of her tank top as a protective shield. Her hair was a mass of wild curls, sticking up in odd places, and her cheeks were flushed with embarrassment.

Andi had a pretty good idea what she looked like. Mornings had never been kind to her between her wavy hair and being a restless sleeper. Nothing like being startled by an incredibly good-looking man, while in his bed, after asking to sleep with him. She was pathetic. And she'd bet her next repo check that he was smiling behind that stupid coffee cup.

She raised her chin, looked at him with a cool, "bite me" glare and with a smug smile, said, "Good morning, *Wallstreet.*"

Damn. She was a beautiful, hot mess, in ridiculous pink doughnut shorts, and he'd like nothing more than to set his coffee cup down, walk over, pick her up and toss her back on his bed to kiss away that sassy expression. Best to stick with his original plan. Keep things light and then evaluate the situation over breakfast. In the kitchen. Far away from the bed.

"I made you breakfast," he said in a rush.

Her lips softened into a genuine smile.

"Really?" she asked, surprised.

"Yes. I didn't know what you liked, so I made pancakes, waffles, French toast, eggs, sausage, and bacon."

He'd woken up at 4 am, wide awake and aware of every warm part of her skin that was touching him. A guy could only take so much torture, so he'd gotten up, taken a very cold shower, shaved, and dressed for work. He was ready by 4:30 am, so he put on his apron and began cooking breakfast.

She frowned and looked down at the pillow she was crushing against her chest.

Cooper's smile faded. He set his coffee cup down on his dresser and took a step into his bedroom but was still a safe six feet away from her.

"I can make you a bowl of oatmeal if you'd prefer."

She looked up into his eyes and shook her head.

"No. It all sounds amazing."

She looked back at the pillow and picked at a loose thread.

In a soft voice that was only slightly louder than a whisper, she said, "No one, besides Grams, has ever made me breakfast. Thank you."

Her eyes were extra shiny when she looked at him again and with a slight tremble in her voice, said, "And thank you for last night."

Shit. Was she about to cry? She looked so damn defenseless, standing there, thanking him for what? Holding her all night? Keeping her wrapped in his arms where he knew she was safe from whoever broke into her house? Hell, he should be thanking her. So what if he only got a couple hours sleep last night. How could he sleep with her soft, curvy body pressed up against him and the scent of vanilla from her hair? *Shit. Keep it light.*

With his best cocky grin, he said, "Well, you knew it was only a matter of time before I slept with you, *Margarita*."

A laugh bubbled up from her, and she lifted that sassy chin again, and with a snort said, "In your dreams, *Rock Star*," and then she threw the pillow at his head and ran past him, laughing, as he chased her into the kitchen.

Andi stopped when she reached the kitchen counter.

"Oh my goodness," she said as she looked at the food spread all over the counter, "Who else is coming?"

Cooper chuckled and reached into his cabinet then handed her a plate and took one for himself.

"I guess I got a little carried away," he said, "I was up early and just started cooking, wasn't sure what you liked, so I cooked all the breakfast food I had. *What do you like?*"

Andi grinned and said, "All of it," and took a little bit of everything until her plate was full and then sat at the kitchen table and dug in. *She was ravenous.*

Cooper just shook his head, grinned and said, "How do you manage to eat like that and look," he waved his hand at her, "like this. Most of the women I know would never dream of eating anything more than a plain non-fat Greek yogurt for breakfast."

Andi gave a half-shrug and smiled, "I'm not like most of the women you know," and then she scrunched her nose and said, "and I don't like yogurt anyway. Oh, unless it's frozen with hot fudge sauce, then it's okay."

She took a bite of her waffle covered in maple syrup.

"Mmm," she said and finished chewing, wiped her mouth with a napkin then said, "This is delicious. Thanks so much. After breakfast, I'll just grab a cab back to the country club and change my tire then head home. What time do you have to be at the office?" she asked.

"I already took care of your tire. Well, *I* didn't take care of it personally, I called a service that repaired your tire. They found a nail in it, so at least you didn't need a new tire. I thought I could drop you off at your car and then head to work. Or I can just as easily cancel my appointments and take the day off to help you at your house. I know it's going to be hard to go back there and deal with that mess."

"You shouldn't have done that. Fix my tire," she breathed out a sigh – well, it was done now – no sense arguing about it.

"How much did it cost?" and where was she going to get the money to pay him back? Lord, she didn't need any new debt.

Cooper frowned. He'd dated women who expected him to pay for everything and then would get bitchy if he didn't shower them with gifts. Andi wouldn't let him do anything for her.

"Let's not argue about it, okay?" he ran his hand through his hair, "It's just something I wanted to do for you—like a gift. It's rude if you offer to pay for a gift."

She looked at him and said "Thanks," and then her lips curved into a wide smile because it really was a thoughtful thing for him to do. She just wasn't used to anyone doing things for her.

Her face turned serious, and she pointed her finger at him and said, "But no way will you take off from work today.

You've already done so much for me. I'll be fine. Plus, I'll have lots of help from Ben and my neighbors."

They cleaned the kitchen, teasing each other, and then she quickly got dressed, and Cooper dropped her off at her car. She got out of his car, and he lowered his window.

"Are you sure I can't play hooky today and help you?" he asked one more time with a charming smile, "*please?*"

"Nice try, *Wallstreet*," she said, "Go make millions of dollars for your clients."

She smiled at him, got in her car, started it up and blew him a kiss as she pulled away.

Cooper leaned his head against the headrest and blew out a breath. *Damn. He was in way over his head.*

***

Andi called Maggy and Jerry to let them know about the break-in at her home. She told Jerry she was taking off today to try to put her house back together. When she pulled into her driveway, she was relieved to see Ben was already home with Dodger. She opened the door and was greeted with a sloppy kiss from Dodger and hugs from Ben and the Golden Girls who had insisted on coming over to help with the clean-up. She was so lucky to have such a wonderful support system.

It was easier to have a positive attitude about the clean-up while she was relaxing inside Cooper's clean, organized kitchen, enjoying the warm breakfast he'd prepared for them. She smiled thinking about the way he'd teased her into laughing throughout their brief morning together. Now, six hours after cleaning, washing, sweeping, throwing out broken dishes, glasses, picture frames, and furniture, she was not just mad. *She was furious.*

The five of them had taken a break and were eating homemade chicken salad sandwiches, potato salad, and drinking Cokes.

"Whoever did this to you, dear, didn't take anything valuable," said Ethel and then took a sip out of her can of cola.

"They smashed anything they could have sold for drug money, like that flat screen TV you had in the living room. Why would someone do that?" asked Hazel.

"Looks like a hate crime. Did you make anyone mad lately?" asked Gladys.

Andi took a bite of her potato salad and thought about that for a minute. She swallowed and then said, "That's what the police asked. I repo cars for a living. I try to take them without being seen, but there were a couple angry skips."

"Like the pizza delivery guy," Ben offered.

"Hmm, I was thinking of someone more like Dodger's owner," Andi said.

"Or the ice cream truck drug dealer," said Hazel, "I read about that one in the paper. You're becoming quite a famous young lady."

"He's in jail," Andi said, "but I still think this is related to Thomas Milner."

"Oh, you mean the dead, naked man?" Gladys said, her eyes lit up. She loved a good murder.

"Yes. My photo and name were on the front page, so everyone who read the paper knew the details of the homicide and that I followed Thomas from the time he got off of work until I found the body." Andi took a sip of her soda. "I think whoever killed Thomas must think I know something or have something."

"What do you have, dear?" Ethel asked.

"Nothing. I found the body. The police impounded the car."

Ethel leaned in with a loud whisper, "But *they* don't know that."

"You need to find out what *they* are looking for, Andrea," said Gladys.

"How is she supposed to find what they're looking for if she doesn't even know, Gladys? You watch too much NCIS," Ethel said.

"No, she's right. I'm really good at finding cars and skips. I'll just treat this the same way. I'll be right back."

Andi jumped up and ran out to her car. She opened the back door and pulled out her laptop and brought it back into the kitchen. She opened it and turned it on.

"Okay," she clapped her hands together and rubbed them while she waited for her system to turn on.

"Normally, when I begin looking for an asset or car, I find the skip, the person who is behind on his car payments, and then it's easy to find the car. I scan through social media like Facebook, Twitter, Instagram, and Snapchat. It's amazing what people put out there to share with the world." She shook her head in disbelief.

"Oh, this is so exciting!" Gladys said

"But your skip is dead," Ben pointed out.

Andi scrunched her nose and shook off a chill that ran down her spine. She didn't like to think too much about the dead, naked Mr. Milner. *It still gave her the heebie-jeebies.*

"True, but I've already done a bunch of research on him." Andi pulled up a file she'd saved on Thomas. She scanned her notes. Nothing interesting stood out to her.

"Sounds like a *dead*-end," Gladys said and laughed at her own joke.

"I'll just have to find any co-workers, friends, his ex-wife and talk to them," Andi said.

"I'm sure you can get the ex-wife to dish," Ethel said, "They all love to complain. Remember Deloris after her divorce? The woman would not shut up about Barney."

Andi did a quick Google search on Thomas Milner. She saw a couple articles on the murder investigation and "Bingo."

"What did you find?" Hazel asked.

"His memorial service is tonight! All the people who were closest to him will be there. It's the perfect place to go and see if I can find out what he was involved in. You don't get shot like that if you're a boy scout. I'm sure he was into something illegal. I just need to find out what it was."

"Nope. It'll never work," Hazel said, shaking her head.

"Why not?" Andi asked.

"Because, like you said, everyone already thinks that you're the one who killed him," Gladys said.

Andi's face fell. They were absolutely right.

"We could go for you. You write up the questions, and we'll interrogate his loved ones," Gladys offered.

Andi smiled. She could just imagine how that would go over. Her neighbors were loving, generous, outrageous, and kind, but they had never been subtle.

"Thank you, but I couldn't ask you to do that. It's too dangerous. I don't want the murderer to know you are involved in any way."

"She's right. We can't risk our *Strike Queens* on this mission." Ben smiled tenderly at his golden girls, and then his eyes widened, and he looked at Andi. "What if I could change your appearance, Andi, so that you would be the one asking just the right questions and no one would recognize you?"

Ben smiled winningly at Andi, and she returned his grin.

"I'd say it looks like I'm going to a memorial service tonight."

***

Two hours later, she was standing in the lobby of the Tranquility Funeral Home and Crematory, wearing a black knit plunging v neck dress with small rhinestones along the neckline that drew attention to her exposed cleavage and a hemline that stopped mid-thigh, black leather boots with three inch heels, a short blond wig with spiked bangs, and dramatic makeup that transformed her face completely. Her own Grams wouldn't have even recognized her, and thank goodness she wasn't alive to see her dressed in this get-up at a funeral, no less. Andi made the sign of the cross, just at the thought.

Ben wanted to go with her this evening, but luckily he had to work. Although she appreciated his help, she didn't want to put him in harm's way. She was smart enough to recognize that this reconnaissance mission was risky. Suppose the person behind Thomas' death was at the memorial service too? She'd go in, make some subtle inquiries, and be out before anyone could get too suspicious. *Simple.* She was going by the alias Tiffany Flannagan. Her backstory was that she'd gone out with Tommy on a couple dates through an online dating site before he was killed.

The room was fairly crowded—she counted at least 25 of Thomas Milner's mourners in the room. *Hmm.* The first person she needed to speak with was the ex-wife. She looked around the room and recognized the woman immediately from her Facebook profile page. The ex-Mrs. Milner was a brunette, about 5'8", with dark eyeliner, and bright red lipstick. She was closest to what must be an urn and an 8x10 photo of Thomas Milner. He was smiling in the picture, oblivious that four bullets from a nine mm would penetrate his body. Andi took a deep breath, cleared her mind of the image of Thomas' dead body, and thought about a litter of fluffy golden retriever puppies as she approached her first target. With a warm smile, Andi offered her condolences and introduced herself

"Mrs. Milner? Hi, my name is Tiffany Flannagan. I just wanted to tell you I'm so sorry for your loss."

She looked up at Andi, "I'm sorry, have we met?" She stared up at Andi's face then her gaze dropped down to her boots and thoroughly inventoried her entire outfit. "How did you know Tommy?"

"No. We've never met. I met your ex-husband online. We'd only gone out a couple times before he was murdered," she said.

His ex-wife chuckled, "That *Repo Girl,* the one that killed Tommy, did you a favor, sweetheart."

Andi blanched at this, but her make-up was so heavy she felt sure that Mrs. Milner didn't notice. *Think of fuzzy puppies.*

"My ex-husband was a lazy son-of-a-bitch, always looking for the next sure thing." She leaned into Andi and touched her arm. "He drank too much and spent way too much money on lottery tickets and gadgets. He always had to have the latest technology, best equipment, no matter how much it cost. The man could never manage his money. Thank God, I got the house before he lost that too. Having the best attorney in town paid off."

"What kind of gadgets did he buy?" Andi asked.

"All kinds. If it was new and hot on the market, he'd buy it. Surveillance equipment, night vision glasses, spy gear, like those little flash drives that look like innocent things like watches, pens, stuff like that."

"Since Tommy spent more than he had, do you think he might have borrowed money from someone less reputable? Maybe when he couldn't pay, they killed him?"

She laughed. "Are you asking me if I think he borrowed from a loan shark? No way." She shook her head with certainty. "They already have his killer." She leaned in close again and whispered, "I, personally, think it was some sordid love affair. He probably tried to have sex with her in lieu of making his back car payments. You know, they found him naked at the crime scene." She nodded her head. "That makes the most sense. I know I often dreamt of shooting the bastard when we were still married," she said smiling at the thought.

Andi felt bile rise in the back of her throat. His ex-wife would give a pretty convincing testimony if the prosecution called her to the witness stand. She seemed so certain that Andi killed him and even worse, had sex with him. *Yuk.* She said goodbye before she tried to convince her that he wasn't murdered by his repo agent. That wouldn't be helpful at all. *Focus.* After talking with the ex, she realized how important it was that she find the real murderer. She didn't want to spend her next 20 years in prison. Andi scanned the room for her next target and spotted him by the vase of white calla lilies. She touched her hair to make sure the wig was still in place. It should be. Ben must have used one hundred bobby pins to secure it to her scalp.

She introduced herself to Keith Marshall, friend and co-worker of Thomas. She'd also found him on social media. He happened to work for the same phone company as Thomas.

They'd been 'friends' on Facebook for six years, so she was hoping he'd be a good source of information. Andi noted that Keith was a little heavier in person than his profile picture.

She walked confidently up to Keith, introduced herself as Tiffany and lied, saying that Tommy had spoken fondly of him.

"I only had a couple dates with Tommy, but I really felt a connection, you know? Like it was love at first sight." Andi brought out a tissue and carefully dabbed the corner of her left eye as if she were wiping a tear. "I was devastated that he was killed. Do you mind if I ask you a little about him? I think it will help give me closure." Andi gave him a small smile.

Keith stood a little taller feeling the responsibility of this new request. A little final something he could do for his buddy. "Of course, Tiffany. I'd be happy to answer any of your questions."

Andi placed her hand over her heart and smiled. "You have no idea how much this means to me," she stated honestly. "What did Tommy do for the phone company?"

"He installed Wi-Fi and internet service for residential and businesses. He was really good at his job." He chuckled. "He used to tell me about the crazy shit people kept on their computers."

"What do you mean?"

"Oh, Tommy was a complete geek freak with computers."

He reached into his pocket and pulled out a silver pen and opened it to reveal it was a flash drive.

"He was always showing me these cool gadgets he bought, like this one. He had an extra, so he gave it to me. Sometimes he'd take them to his job sites and copy information to check out later back at home. Then he'd come into work and tell me about the shit on their computers, porn sites, gambling, you name it. It kind of made me wonder if maybe he saw something he wasn't supposed to see." Keith glanced around the room to make sure no one was listening and then in a low voice said, "Now that I think about it, he told me a couple days before he died that he'd finally found his cash cow and he'd be coming into some long overdue money. I never made the connection until now that maybe he was selling the information he'd copied off someone's system."

The lines between his brows creased, and he breathed a profanity.

Andi leaned in and whispered, "You think he was *blackmailing* someone?"

He nodded, but then realized he was talking ill of his buddy, so he shook his head. "No. I'm sure I'm wrong. Forget that I even said anything."

He gave her a friendly smile and reached out and gave her hand a gentle squeeze.

"He was one of a kind. I'm glad you two got to meet, even if your time together was cut short. I'm going to miss him."

Andi plastered a smile on her face for Keith. *Blackmail—certainly would be motive for murder.* Well, it was obvious she wouldn't be getting any more dirt from Keith since he didn't want to implicate his co-worker any more than he already had. She returned his hand squeeze and said goodbye. She needed to find Tommy's best friend and see what he knew about his little side business. She looked around the room for Douglas Woods.

***

Detectives Kendricks and Richardson stepped into Thomas Milner's room at the funeral home. They had no leads and Kendricks was feeling frustrated. He tugged at his tie with his index finger, just to loosen it a bit, so he could breathe. If they could break open a lead or two to this homicide, he'd sleep a lot easier. Attending this memorial service was a long shot, but considering they had nothing, it was worth the time to investigate.

A couple days ago, they'd finally gotten the warrant to search Diamond Auto Body Shop, and they'd found nothing out of the ordinary. He'd thought about what Andi had said she'd overheard that day he caught her snooping around and wondered if they'd been moving evidence right under their noses while he was sending Andi home.

He scanned the room. *What the hell?* Kendricks spotted Detective Sanchez chatting it up with Milner's ex. Their paths had crossed before since narcotics often resulted in homicide, but there had been absolutely no hint of drugs in the Milner case. He didn't like anything about the detective—his attitude, methods, hell, he simply didn't trust him. Kendricks rubbed the back of his neck and swore under his breath.

At the sound, Richardson turned to look at him and followed his gaze, touched his arm and in her slow Georgian accent said, "Let me go find out what he's doing here. I'll be more subtle than you. You can mingle."

She flashed him a sweet smile and sashayed over in her designer pastel suit to pay her respects to the ex-wife and find out why Sanchez was really here. They had already interviewed some of the people here the day after Milner's body had been identified and hadn't uncovered anything suspicious or any motives for murder. Kendricks was scanning the attendants at the service when he spotted a very tall woman he didn't recognize and wondered how she knew the victim. She towered over most everyone else, standing 6'3" in those high heels. There was something familiar about her, but he couldn't quite put his finger on it. She had short blond hair and was talking to Douglas Woods, the vic's best friend.

Kendricks walked nearby until he was standing about four feet behind her, close enough he could eavesdrop on their conversation without being close enough for her to notice him in the somewhat crowded room. *Oh, Christ.* He knew that voice. Andrea Sloan, his lead suspect was at the god damn funeral—in disguise, no less—playing fucking Nancy Drew. He rubbed the knot of tension that had begun in his neck with his left hand as he listened to her conversation with Douglas Woods.

"Hi, you must be Doug. Tommy told me all about you. You guys grew up together right? My name is Tiffany Flannagan, by the way." She extended her hand for a handshake. "Tommy and I met on an online dating service. Unfortunately, we only got to go on a handful of dates before he was killed."

Doug shook her hand and held onto it for a minute longer than was comfortable. Well, that and the fact that he was staring at her chest. *Eyes are up here, Dougie.*

"That's weird. Tommy never told me about you." He looked her up and down. "Then again, I can see why he might have wanted to keep you a secret."

He gave her a sleazy smile while he was checking her out a second time.

Rather than cringe, she gave him a friendly smile, looked over his shoulder and *oh no, no, no!* She caught a glimpse of Detective Richardson and Detective Sanchez talking with Tommy's ex. Time to leave. Now. She looked at her watch.

"Wow. I didn't realize how late it is. I've got to go."

"Listen," he took her arm, "let's both head out of here. I know a place down the street. I'll buy you a drink, and we can get to know each other better."

Picking up your dead best friend's date at his funeral. Classy guy.

"Sorry, Tommy's death has been too traumatic for me. I'm going to take a break from dating for the next year." She took a good look at the loser in front of her, "Maybe longer."

Clueless, he held out his business card with his phone number. "Here, call me if you change your mind."

Yeah, that was never going to happen. Andi took his card in case she needed to contact him directly about *her* investigation, turned to make a quick exit and walked right into a wall of a man with angry ice blue eyes.

"Hello *Tiffany,*" Kendricks said.

She stepped back, steadied herself on her absurd boots, reached her hand up and touched her blond wig to make sure it was still in place and then managed a cheeky smile. "Hi, Detective. What a surprise to see you here tonight."

He grabbed her elbow and said, "I bet. Allow me to walk you out." He led her outside, took a moment to scan the cars until he found hers and shook his head, mumbling, "There it is," and then escorted her to the driver's door. He turned her around to face him and with sarcasm laced in his voice, said, "You know, I'm confused because I believe we've already had a conversation about your participation in *my investigation*."

Andi bit her lower lip. "How's our investigation going?"

His only response was a raised eyebrow.

"Okay, I know what you're going to say. It's just that I'm still the only suspect, right?"

More silence.

She nodded and lifted her chin in defiance since he'd just confirmed her suspicions. She would not be intimidated by the bad cop, even if he did look like Thor with short hair. Too much was at stake. She squared her shoulders and took charge of their one-sided conversation. "Exactly. Look at this from my point of view. You have no new leads, I've got thugs breaking into my house, destroying my stuff. Whoever killed Thomas must think that I have something they want. I'm just trying to find out what that is before I get killed or *worse*, go to jail for a murder I didn't commit."

He shook his head, swore, rubbed his neck and said. "Jail is better than *dead*, Andi."

He exhaled slowly, reining in his patience and then absently reached into his pocket and popped an antacid into his mouth. This woman drove him crazy.

"Look, I know you're frustrated and worried about the slow movement of this case, but you should also be scared. If you keep poking your nose into this investigation, you could end up as dead as Thomas Milner. Did you consider that Thomas' killer might be here tonight?"

Yes. As a matter of fact, she was counting on it.

Kendricks read her expression. He swore again.

"You seem like an intelligent woman, so I shouldn't have to tell you to stay away from anything related to Thomas Milner. I'm really good at my job, Andi, and I will find out who murdered him and their motive. So no more investigating. Do you understand? "

"But, what if you don't? The prosecution has enough evidence to convict me. There are plenty of people, like Thomas' ex-wife," Andi pointed to the building, "that believe I killed him. She even thinks it was a crime of passion."

Andi made a disgusted face then sighed and leaned against her car. In a softer voice, she said, "They broke into my house, detective." She folded her arms protectively around her midsection and looked down at the ground. "They didn't even take anything. They just smashed a few of my electronics and destroyed things that were important to me." She shivered.

His expression and voice softened, "I know. *Please*, trust me to find out who's behind this."

Hell, she looked so defenseless. Defeated. Even in this ridiculous disguise that she was wearing, he had a sudden urge to pull her into his arms and kiss her. His gaze drifted to her soft lips. *Unprofessional.* Instead, he lifted her chin with his finger, so she was looking into his eyes. In those sexy boots, she was practically eye level.

"I *will* find the people responsible and bring them to justice. The best way for you to help is by staying out of my investigation."

His face hardened to the bad cop expression that scared the shit out of the toughest criminals.

"I don't want your body to be the next homicide I have to investigate because you were trying to help."

He frowned at that thought.

"Go home, Andi."

Damn. Seemed like he was telling her that a lot.

She sighed, opened her door and sat in the driver's seat, staring out her front windshield, lost in thought.

He stood between her car and the car door and leaned in to tell her, "I *will* lock you in jail if it's the only way to keep you safe. Are we clear?"

She nodded without looking at him and started up her engine. He closed her door and watched her drive away.

Kendricks stood in place until her taillights disappeared into the darkness. Why did he get the feeling that he'd just encouraged her to investigate rather than scared her into backing down? He'd bet money that her nod was only an acknowledgment that she understood his threat, not that she was agreeing to anything. Andrea Sloan was going to do what she damn well pleased. *Hell.* He even admired her for it. It was exactly what he'd do in her situation. Kendricks rubbed his neck, sighed, and headed back to the funeral home to find that lead before Andi Sloan got herself killed.

***

After leaving Kendricks in the parking lot, Andi drove straight to the Star City Bar & Grill. Ben made her promise to come by directly after the memorial service to report on her progress. She walked up to the bar and waited to get Ben's attention. There were no empty stools, and these boots might look fabulous with her long legs and accent her short dress, but to spend even an hour standing in them was forty-five minutes too long.

She turned down three drink offers before Ben stopped in front of her and set his latest signature drink, Jail Break, in front of her. "I see your hair held in place."

Andi smiled. "It should. There are enough bobby pins in here to build The Eiffel Tower."

"You look fabulous. Can't wait to hear all the gory details of your evening. And given your track record, they *will* be gory." He grinned.

She stuck her tongue out at him and then looked around the restaurant. "It's busy tonight. Couldn't even find a seat." She took a sip of her drink. "You might not have time for my report."

Ben put his hand over his heart dramatically. "I'm never too busy for you, darlin'. The big crowd is here to listen to our boys. Isn't that great?"

He nodded his head towards the stage where they were setting up. Ben lit up every time he saw Daniel. So sweet. She spotted Cooper bending down to plug in equipment. Even from this distance, with his back to her, her heart sped up. It was irritating that her body betrayed her like this. Since her heartbreak, she usually enjoyed an immunity to men. Why did this one get under her skin so easily? She watched him stand up and turn around and quickly turned back to Ben.

"I've got a seat saved for you down at the other end of the bar for your debriefing." He pointed to the opposite end of the bar.

"Thanks," she said as she picked up her drink and started her trek to the end of the bar. Unfortunately, her new look was attracting more attention than usual. She turned down two more drink offers, an offer to dance, and some idiotic pickup line about a library card and checking her out. Her response to the last guy was just an eye roll and a pat on his chest as she said, "Sorry buddy, your card is as expired as that lame line."

She walked past him, her chin in the air, as his friends howled with laughter.

"Tiffany, we've saved you a seat!" Mrs. Harper motioned to an empty stool next to her. "Benny reserved this section for our meeting. He's such a thoughtful young man."

Andi should have known her neighborhood partners in crime would be here. "Thanks," she said smiling as she sat down and took another sip of her drink.

"This is way more fun than Monday night Bingo," Mrs. Barzetti said.

"Do you think I would look good with blond hair like yours?" Mrs. Davis reached out and gingerly touched Andi's wig.

"I'm sure Ben would let you try out this wig," Andi answered.

"And cover up that natural, gorgeous white hair. Never," Ben said.

Mrs. Davis pressed her hand on her chest. "Oh, Benny, you startled me."

"Sorry, darlin'. It's busy tonight, so I'll just be popping in and out all evening." Ben wiped their end of the bar with his towel and leaned forward with an excited expression. "So, what did I miss?"

***

Cooper felt a prickle on the back of his neck as he was squatting down to hook up the amplifiers. He plugged in the last wire and stood up, turned around and scanned the room for Andi. There was a pretty good crowd tonight, especially for a Monday night. Matt, the owner of the bar, said a few of his regulars had asked about their band and told him how much they enjoyed the entertainment. That's how they ended up scheduled tonight. It wasn't the sold out civic center, but at least they were building a fan base.

He didn't see her. *Dammit*, she should be here by now. He was hoping to get to talk to her before they began performing. He couldn't stop himself from thinking about her all day. He should have just taken off from work and helped her clean up that mess at her house. But no. She managed to convince him that she was fine and it was something she needed to do on her own. Why was it that the traits he admired in her also frustrated the hell out of him? He'd left her a text to which he'd just gotten a brief reply "I'm good, just busy." God, when had he become such a hapless sap? *Rhetorical question.*

He had asked Ben about her when they'd arrived to set up, and Ben had simply waved off his concern and said she was fine and that he'd see for himself because she was stopping by after completing her undercover assignment. What the hell did that even mean? Before he could ask for a clarification, Ben was off taking a drink order. Danny was right. Ben and Andi had their own coded language that no one else understood.

He took another look over at the bar. An extremely tall, leggy blond was attracting the attention of men like bears to honey. He was just thinking that he'd love to see Andi in boots and a dress like that when he took a second, closer look at the blond. *No fucking way.* Then he heard her voice over the crowd followed by hoots of male laughter. *Undercover Assignment. What the hell was she up to now?* He hopped off the stage and walked toward the bar.

***

"So, based on what Keith Marshall said, my guess is that Milner was in the very dangerous business of blackmail." Andi took another sip of her drink.

"And whoever he was blackmailing, thinks you have the goods on him," Mrs. Barzetti added.

"Probably on one of those gadgets his ex mentioned," Mrs. Harper chimed in.

"This is so exciting! It's like one of my mystery novels," Mrs. Davis grinned.

"But I don't have anything belonging to Milner," Andi said.

Ben sighed. "Guess that means we're back to square one."

"Before I could interview anyone else, I got busted by Detective Kendricks, so I had to leave Milner's memorial service a little sooner than I'd hoped." Andi frowned. "He confirmed my worst fear. They have no new leads in the investigation which leaves me as their primary suspect."

"Busted by Thor again? Some girls have all the luck," Ben sighed. "Did he show you his hammer?" Ben waggled his eyebrows.

"No," she grinned and punched Ben in the arm. "He tried to scare me off the investigation with his big bad cop routine. It didn't work. I'm not going to jail for a murder I didn't commit."

She blew out a breath and took another sip from her drink.

"No. I'm going to find the cretin who broke into my house because I'm certain it's the same guy who killed Milner. Then all I'll have to do is follow him around until I find the evidence I need to prove my innocence."

She shrugged and asked, "How hard can it really be?"

"If you find the guy, but don't get the evidence, just kill him since you're going to jail for murder anyway," Ben grinned at her. "As I always say, if you've got to do the time, you might as well do the crime."

She laughed, "Okay. Sounds like a solid plan B."

***

Cooper stood frozen in place. He originally planned to come over and hit on Andi, pretending he didn't recognize her. But he made the mistake of eavesdropping on their conversation, and that's when he realized that they were all *batshit crazy*. She, clearly, was insane. He should have suspected that from the start because normal, rational women didn't choose to repossess cars for a living. Sensible women, who innocently got embroiled in a murder and were the *goddamned prime suspect* in the case, didn't go *under-fucking-cover* to the victim's memorial service to interview his friends and family. So yeah, Andrea Sloan was certifiable. He ran his hand through his hair. But *Jesus*, they all were encouraging her madness, like it was some kind of game and joking about it like there wasn't a very likely chance her actions would get her killed. He was too furious to talk. How did you talk sense into someone who was deranged? He turned around and stomped back to the stage.

***

After performing their third song, Cooper caught Danny and Zach exchanging another apprehensive look. He knew they were worried about him. He was *fine, dammit*. Yeah, maybe he was a little tense, and his vocals might be a bit rough and hostile. And so what if he was directing that frustration towards the blond at the end of the bar. She must have picked up on it too because when they finally took a break after the sixth song, she was waiting backstage. *Shit.* He was still too angry to talk to her.

Zach and Danny gave her a quick hello and then disappeared. What kind of friends fled when you needed them to run interference?

"Hey Rock Star," her voice was soft and sexy and didn't sound the least bit like it came from the madwoman he'd observed earlier.

He didn't look at her, but instead grabbed his water bottle and took a couple big gulps.

She took a step forward and touched his arm, "What's wrong? Are you okay?"

He glared at her hand until she removed it.

"I'm fine," he said with an edge to his voice.

"Yeah. Sure you are," she held up her hands in surrender, "See you around."

She turned to leave.

With steel in his tone, he asked, "What's with the new look?"

She turned to look at him. *Damn.* She looked even better up close in that dress. He wanted to pull her into his arms and kiss the insanity out of her.

She glanced down at her dress and then reached up to touch her wig.

"I almost forgot I was wearing this. I went to Milner's memorial service tonight to see if I could get an idea what he got into that would get him killed."

Nothing like a little crazy to cool the libido.

"Yeah, I heard about that. Do you have a *death wish*?"

She stood straight. With those boots, she was so tall that he was eye level with her mouth—*hell if that wasn't hot.* He swallowed.

"No. I'm trying to stay out of prison."

She put her hands on her hips.

He ran his hand through his hair.

"No. You're going to end up dead like Milner. Why don't you just stay out of it, and let the police do their job?"

She raised her hands in the air in frustration.

"*Oh my god.* You sound just like Kendricks."

"Maybe that's because we're both smart and of sound mind," Cooper said.

"Well, it's not a smart plan if I want to stay out of jail. The police have no new leads. I'm their prime suspect" she pointed to herself, "and although Kendricks doesn't believe I killed Milner, there are plenty of people who do. I'm not leaving my fate in the hands of other people anymore."

"Andi, Milner is *dead,* and *your house* was broken into last night. The last thing you need to do is try to track down a killer. What, your life isn't exciting enough?"

"Oh, that's rich. Do you really think I'm doing this because I'm *bored?* God, you're such a *jerk.*"

She began pacing and then turned back to face him.

"I was the one who had the dead Milner drop in my lap. It was *my* home that was invaded. *My* irreplaceable things that were destroyed. Well, I am tired of being the victim. I'm fighting back. The killer already thinks I have something of value which is why he ransacked my house. I'm going to find out who's responsible."

She crossed her arms over her chest.

"Well, I'm not going to stand around and watch you provoke the killer. You are *crazy* if you think that's going to help anything."

"No. *Crazy* is sitting back and waiting for the killer to make the next move," Andi said.

"You're wrong," Cooper crossed his arms over his chest.

"No, you're wrong," Andi stood firm.

"Fine." Cooper unfolded his arms and threw both hands up in the air. "You're going to do what you want anyway. I just don't want to be around when it all blows up in your face."

She pushed her finger into his chest, and in a tone that matched his, said, "Fine because I don't need you to be around."

Then she turned on her heel and without stopping, walked straight out of the bar, into the parking lot, opened her car door, got in and slammed it shut. She gripped the steering wheel with her shaking hands and dropped her forehead on the top of the wheel. She would *not* cry. A sob escaped from her. She sat up and took a deep breath. A few tears trickled down her face, and she roughly brushed them away with the palms of her hands. The man didn't deserve a single teardrop. She took another deep breath and a few more insubordinate tears slipped out anyway. She started her car and began to drive home. *Stupid. Stupid. Stupid.* Lord, when would she learn?

Andi spent the rest of the night trying not to cry and mostly succeeded except for a sporadic sob that erupted from her chest without warning and an occasional discharge of tears. Not bad considering she felt like her heart had been ripped from her chest and run over by a convoy of 18 wheelers on Interstate 81. God, could she be any more pathetic?

Chapter Seven

The next morning, Andi woke up to a whine and then a lick on her face. *Ugh.* She opened an eye, and Dodger was staring at her, barked and then he closed in for another lick. *Ew.*

"Okay, I'm up boy."

Andi sat up, so she wouldn't get any more of those wake-up kisses. She glanced at her clock. Great. It was 6 am. That would have been fine, but she hadn't managed to fall asleep until after 3 am. She got up, let Dodger outside in the backyard, then grabbed a quick shower, got dressed and headed to the City Market to see Maggy.

"What the heck are you doing here so early?" Maggy asked, surprised to see her friend.

"I only got about 3 hours sleep, so I need your best wake me up juice. And a friend."

"You came to the right place. *For both,*" Maggy smiled and began preparing a juice, "So what happened?" she asked with an arched eyebrow.

"Oh Mags," Andi let out a long sigh, "I did it again. Why is it I'm attracted to the wrong kind of guy? When am I ever going to learn from my mistakes?"

"Wait, are you talking about Cooper? What did he do?"

"We got into this big argument last night because he was all upset that I went in disguise to Thomas Milner's funeral to try to figure out why someone would want to kill him and break into my house."

Maggy's mouth dropped open, "Disguise?"

192

"Yes—Ben helped me—skimpy dress, blond wig, and amazing makeup. I swear, my own Grams wouldn't have recognized me. Unfortunately, Detective Kendricks saw right through it," she frowned, "somehow."

Andi shook away the thought, "Anyway, I did find out from Kendricks that they've made no more headway on the case, which means I'm still their number one suspect."

She leaned in closer and said, "Plus, after talking to Milner's friends, I am more certain than ever that he blackmailed the killer. They must think I have whatever Milner used as blackmail, and that's why they destroyed my house while they were looking for it."

"*Oh. My. God.* Any idea what they're looking for?" Maggy asked, bringing the juice over and putting a lid on the plastic cup before passing it over to Andi.

"None—nada—zip. But whatever information Milner had was enough for him to be shot to death," Andi said.

"Thanks," Andi said and punched a straw through the top hole, took a sniff, and then a cautious suck through the straw.

"I don't even want to know what nutritious foods are in here, but it's delicious! Tastes like chocolate." She took another taste, "Mmm—and peanut butter."

"I added some peanut butter cups to cover up the kale," Maggy grinned.

Andi made a face and shook her head, "I *really* didn't want to know that."

Ignoring her, Maggy asked, "So, Cooper's mad because you were investigating?"

"Yes. We got into this argument about it, and he said he didn't want to be around when it all blew up in my face," Andi took another sip then said, "so I told him I didn't need him to be around."

"Oh, Andi," Maggy reached out and squeezed her hand over the counter.

"At first, I was really mad at him, but this morning I'm just mostly mad at myself. I mean, I get it, I guess. My life is always a mess, but especially right now. You know?" She took a deep breath and sighed, "Who would intentionally choose to stick around?"

Maggy gave her a smile and leaned over to give her a hug across the counter.

"Hey, he's an idiot. Your true friends aren't going anywhere."

Maggy glanced over at the empty hot dog station—speaking of idiots—Simon wouldn't be in for another two hours to prep for the lunch crowd.

"Who needs men anyway?" Maggy asked and then reached under the counter and grabbed two peanut butter cups, kept one and gave the other to Andi.

"I think this situation calls for the chocolate to be ingested directly, for maximum benefit," Maggy grinned.

Andi smiled, "Thanks, Mags, for staying."

"I wouldn't be anywhere else," Maggy said and smiled.

***

In downtown Roanoke, Cooper stepped into the office where Dr. Martin sat waiting for him in her usual spot, notebook at the ready, warm, welcoming smile in place. She was a beacon of light, guiding him to the safe harbor through the shit storm that was his life. After his disaster of a music performance last night and the argument with Andi, he'd called Dr. Martin's office first thing this morning and asked for her earliest available appointment.

He took a calming breath and sat down on the sofa which lasted for about five seconds and then he bolted up and began to pace, staring down at the floor, his hands clenched together behind his head. He stopped, looked at Dr. Martin, let his hands fall to his side, although they were now balled into fists, and said with barely controlled anger, "She is just so goddamned frustrating!"

"I assume we're talking about Andrea Sloan?" Dr. Martin said in her calm, soothing voice. The same tone she used when she volunteered once a month to answer calls on the suicide hotline.

Cooper stared at her like she had just dropped in from another planet. "Of course I'm talking about *Andi*. Who else makes me this crazy?"

He plopped down on the sofa, feeling exhausted. This was pretty much how the last sixteen hours had been. He experienced a surge of energy, usually in the form of rage and frustration, followed by a period of fatigue and irritability.

"Why don't you start by telling me why you're feeling so frustrated?" Dr. Martin suggested kindly.

Cooper leaned back against the sofa and rested his head back on the edge, so he was staring up at the smooth, cream-colored ceiling. He closed his eyes for a moment and then opened them again.

"We had an argument last night. I'm pretty sure we broke up," he sighed, "that is if this thing between us could even be called dating. I've never been in a relationship like this, so I have no freakin' clue."

He looked at Dr. Martin and tried to explain.

"It feels like a relationship. We had a connection, there was chemistry between us, we went out a couple times, she met my family, and we even got arrested together. Physically, we haven't done anything more than share some earth-shattering kisses."

He swallowed hard, remembering those kisses.

"It's not that I don't want to take it further. She's got trust issues, so I've been taking things really slow. Her last boyfriend was an asshole."

Cooper snorted and shook his head in disbelief, "Although I slept with her the other night. I've never done *that* before."

Dr. Martin tilted her head and stared at him in confusion. "But I thought you said..."

"I said we haven't had *sex*. Her house was vandalized while we were at my brother's wedding. We were both pretty shaken by that, so I invited her to spend the night at my place."

She lifted a brow.

Cooper clarified, "In my *guest* bedroom."

He placed his hand over his heart.

"Give me some credit. She was really distressed. I'm not a complete ass. But she knocked on my bedroom door, obviously still unsettled, and asked if she could just sleep with me, so of course, I said yes. And we slept. Nothing more."

When he closed his eyes, he could still feel her snuggled against his body, his arms wrapped around her. He shook his head trying to make sense out of it all.

"So it sounds like you really care for her," Dr. Martin observed.

"Yeah," Cooper nodded, "She's important."

She made a note on her pad.

"What did you argue about?" she asked.

Cooper frowned.

"I found out she's investigating the murder case on her own. It's too dangerous. She's going to get hurt or maybe even killed."

She nodded.

"Did you tell her how you felt?" she asked.

He gave her a "duh" look and then loosely described their heated conversation.

"But did you tell her how you *felt*?" she asked again, looking at him pointedly.

"What do you mean?" Cooper asked, confused.

He'd already answered her question.

"You told me she was *important* to you. Did you tell her that last night?" she asked quietly.

Shit.

"No."

He ran his hand through his hair.

"But I'm sure she knows."

"How is she supposed to know if you don't tell her?"

Dr. Martin wrote something in her notepad. She looked up at him.

"You said she had trust issues from a past relationship?"

He nodded.

"So you told her, more or less," she glanced at her notebook again and then looked directly into his eyes, "that you didn't want to be around when things got ugly."

Hell. Cooper dropped his head back against the couch and stared at the ceiling.

"What do you really want, Cooper?" Dr. Martin asked.

"I just want her to let the police handle the investigation."

"Why?"

"So she'll be safe."

He closed his eyes.

"Wasn't she already in danger before she started investigating? You said her home was ransacked."

Dr. Martin let that sink in a full minute and then she said, "It sounds like she might be in danger whether she investigates or not."

The last statement brought him sitting forward, his hands gripping the edge of the seat cushion, his chest filled with a helpless frustration.

"Clearly you have no control over her safety, so the real question is, do you still want to be in a relationship with Andrea Sloan?"

She looked at him thoughtfully.

Cooper sat in silence on the edge of the sofa.

"If your answer is no, then no further action is required. Between Andi's trust issues and the description of your argument, my guess is that the relationship is over."

"If, on the other hand, your answer is yes, then you've got your work cut out for you. You'll need to begin by rebuilding a strong foundation of trust."

***

Cooper left Dr. Martin's office, and as he walked to his car, he called Kelly to let her know he was taking the rest of the day off because he was sick. As a testament to his state of mind, Kelly didn't even tease him about it like she normally would. Probably because he sounded like shit. Taking a "sick day" wasn't too much of a stretch. He was nauseous, his skin felt clammy, and he had a headache. He took his tie off and unbuttoned the collar of his shirt. When he reached his car, he unlocked it, opened the door, sat down, leaned back and closed his eyes. *Damn.* His conversation with Dr. Martin made one thing very clear—he'd acted like an ass. He didn't cheat on her like the *calculus bastard,* but still, he freaked when she was just being her amazing, terrifying, brilliant self—the beautiful woman he really, really liked and lusted after.

So what had he done? He panicked like some little chicken-shit and then bailed on her—just another man she couldn't count on—*nice.* If he thought she was skittish before, how in the hell was he going to get through that fortress she hid behind now?

He opened his eyes, buckled his seat belt, started his engine and inhaled deeply. He positioned his left hand on the steering wheel and his right hand on the gear shift. He'd just have to storm the castle, wear her down by removing one stone block at a time, be there for her no matter what she catapulted at him. He nodded. Yes. That's exactly what he'd do. He'd start by finding her and helping her with her damn investigation, *and* he'd tell her how important, no, how *necessary* she was to him. He could do this. He could get her back, right? He had to.

***

After her talk with Maggy, Andi headed to the office, grabbed a couple repo folders and began her research. She decided to do a drive by and see if the Nissan Altima was conveniently parked at home in the driveway or on the street for an easy pickup. She was driving on Williamson Road looking for Lee Avenue when she spotted Under My Skin

Tattoo and Body Piercing Studio. No way. This must be where Liz, her cellmate, worked. On impulse, she whipped into the parking lot, parked her car, and walked in the front door. The shop walls were covered with artwork, some actual photos of tattoos on the skin, and other frames contained sketches of tattoo designs. There was a beefy, bald guy inking another man's bicep.

"Can I help you?" he asked.

"I was looking for Liz. Is she working today?" Andi asked.

"Liz! Customer up front," he hollered without looking up from his work.

Andi continued to look at the artwork displayed on the wall.

"Are you here for a tat or piercing?" she asked.

Andi turned around when she heard the familiar voice and smiled.

The blond's face split into a huge grin

"What the hell are you doing here, cellie?" she asked.

"I was driving by and remembered you worked here, so I thought I'd stop by to say hi," Andi said.

The guy working on the tattoo must have been the owner because he said, "You're on the clock, Liz."

Liz rolled her eyes and made a face and then said to Andi, "So, are you interested in a tattoo or a piercing?"

Andi said, "Actually, I am curious about a tattoo. I'm thinking about a specific design that I've seen, and I was wondering if it was a design you might have inked."

"What's it look like?" Liz asked.

"A dagger with a snake wrapped around it," Andi said.

"Black or Color?" Liz asked.

"Hmm. It was mostly black with some red on the dagger, I think." Andi said, trying to remember the unusual tattoo she'd seen on the Diamond Auto Body Shop guy. Then she remembered, "Oh, and there were two drops of red blood at the base of the dagger."

"Come back here. I've got a book we can look through, and we'll see if we can't find the one you're looking for," Liz winked and walked to a back room and whispered, "It's so good to see you! You obviously made bail. How are things going with clearing your name?"

Andi bit her lip, not sure how much to confide in Liz. Heck, she'd pretty much told her everything that night she'd spent in jail.

"Not that great, actually. The police still don't have any suspects other than me. I report back to court in a few weeks. I think this tattoo might help me get a step closer to clearing my name. I saw it on a guy that I believe is involved in the murder."

"What about you? How did things go for you?" Andi asked.

"Could be worse. I have been issued a restraining order, so I can't get anywhere near Axle for the next 12 months, but that's no biggie. I've moved on, and now I'm seeing a hot biker."

Liz opened a book with images of tattoos, sketches as well as photos, on laminated pages.

"Look through these, and let me know if anything looks familiar."

Andi turned the pages. Who knew there were so many designs with daggers and snakes? Then she spotted one that looked just like it. She pointed to the photo.

"Here. That's it," Andi said and looked up at Liz. "Have you ever done one of these?"

"*Damn girl,* you do like to keep things interesting. I've done more than one of those tattoos. It's a gang symbol for *The Sabers.* They are seriously bad news. They run one of the biggest drug and weapon rings in Roanoke."

Andi sighed. Well, at least she was on the right track.

Liz pointed to the drops of blood at the base of the dagger.

"You said your guy had two of these?" she asked.

"Yes, why?"

"Well, this designates their position in the gang, the higher the ranking, the more blood drops—each one usually represents a kill. I've added some blood drops to existing tattoos."

"I wish I could talk to one of the gang members. It just might fill in some of the missing pieces to this puzzle," Andi said.

Liz grinned.

"I can help you with that. This guy I'm into is in the gang, and many of these guys are regular customers, so I'm friendly with them, and I know where they hang out. Meet me tonight at The Last Call on Orange Avenue around 10 pm, and I'll introduce you to a couple of my customers."

"Liz, you're awesome. But I have to come in disguise since the guys I'm looking for won't want to talk to me, Andi Sloan. I'll come in a blond wig, and just call me Tiffany, okay?"

Liz looked at her and snorted, "You are so much fun, girl. I'm so glad we connected. We'll see if we can't get you the information you need. But, hey, I've got to get back out front unless you're really going to get a tattoo or a piercing."

Andi laughed, "Yeah, well I'm not that much fun. I've got to get back to work too. I'll see you tonight. Thanks again, Liz." She headed out the door to pick up her repo.

***

Downtown at the Star City Bar and Grill, Cooper sat next to Danny at the bar. They'd been there for about 30 minutes, and so far they had been ignored by Danny's boyfriend. Or at least, *he'd* been ignored. Without a word, Ben had placed a mug of Danny's favorite beer in front of him with a wink and blew right past Cooper without a glance in his direction. Cooper had tried to talk to Ben several times, but he was pretty much invisible to the bartender. Coop figured he had to wait it out. It wasn't a surprise—not really. He was *persona non grata* since the fight with Andi.

He needed to talk to her face to face, but finding her was a huge challenge. He'd gone to her house earlier, but she was already gone. He tried calling her and texting her and got no response. He even stopped by her office and was told, in no uncertain terms by her boss, that he better not find out she was being harassed in the slightest by Cooper or he'd have to deal with him directly. *Whatever the hell that was supposed to mean.* He was running out of options, so he recruited Danny as his wingman to solicit assistance from Ben.

Danny leaned next to Cooper and in a voice slightly above a whisper, said, "Listen, just some friendly advice. When Ben finally takes your order, you'd better only order something that comes in a bottle. He's obviously still furious with you, and he's likely to spit in it or *something worse* if you order from the tap."

"There's something worse than spit?" Cooper asked, alarmed.

"*Trust me,* you don't even want to know," he said as he patted Cooper on the back.

Ben came by, took Danny's empty mug and replaced it with a fresh drink.

Danny reached out and put his hand on Ben's arm. "Thanks, babe. Listen, Coop needs your help to fix the mess he made with Andi."

Ben stared at Cooper for the first time since they'd been sitting at the bar. He folded his arms across his chest and then shook his head. "No." He narrowed his eyes at Cooper and then slowly said, "Absolutely not."

Danny said, "Oh come on, Benji. They are both *too stupid* and *stubborn* for their own good. If we leave it up to them, they'll never work things out."

Ben looked back at Daniel, his gaze turned tender and said, "True," and put his hands on his hips after he turned to face Cooper, "I'm looking at *too Stupid*, right now." Ben pointed a finger at Cooper, "I used some of my best leverage with Andi to get her to go out with you." Ben shook his head in disgust, "What a waste."

Cooper leaned forward on his elbows, pleading with Ben, "I know I completely fucked up. Ben, I really like her. *A lot*. I'm trying to fix this—make things right."

Cooper swallowed. *Shit*. He didn't really want to talk about this with Ben and Danny. The person he needed to have this conversation with was Andi, and he needed Ben's help to be able to make that happen. He ran a hand through his hair.

"Here's the thing. I freaked out the other night. It's one thing to find a dead body in one of the cars she repoed. Don't get me wrong. It was seriously disturbing and getting arrested was surreal—but that was all because we were in the wrong place at the wrong time." Cooper nodded his head, "I could deal with that."

Then he exhaled and looked Ben directly in the eye, his voice dropped.

"When we walked into her house after my brother's wedding and everything was smashed and broken," Cooper shook his head and clenched his jaw, "that was just pure violence and it was personal—directed at Andi. When I think of what could have happened to her if she had been home," Cooper inhaled, "it scares the hell out of me."

Ben nodded, reached down below the bar, set out a long neck bottle of beer, popped the cap off and slid it in front of Cooper. Cooper looked at the bottle for a moment, glanced at Danny, and then cautiously lifted it to his lips for a sip.

"Hell, I just want to wrap her in my arms and keep her safely locked away at my condo until the police find out who's behind this."

This time, Cooper took a long swallow from the bottle then set it down on the bar.

"But no. Apparently, she's not the kind of woman who sits quietly by and lets the police solve the crime. So when I overheard her talking about how she went to Milner's funeral to do her own investigating, I lost it. I completely freaked out."

Cooper focused on the label on the bottle. He pulled at the corner with his thumb, loosening it from the brown glass.

"I just wanted to keep her safe, and when she refused to back off the investigation, instead of explaining how I felt, I pushed her away," Cooper said and looked up at Ben.

"Please help me, Ben. She won't answer my calls or texts. You were right. I was acting stupid. I need to tell her that I was terrified for her, and I was the one who acted crazy last night. I need to explain to her that I finally get why she can't just sit back and wait for the police. I want to do whatever I can to help her. I *need* to help her."

Ben sighed and wiped the already clean bar top and then looked at Cooper.

"Look, man, I want to help you. I really do. I just don't know what you think I can do. She was furious with you and the entire *straight* male population last night," Ben said and then glared pointedly at Cooper. "And very hurt when you bailed on her."

Cooper closed his eyes.

Ben continued, "I can't make any promises. Like I said, she's stubborn to a fault, but I'll see what I can do."

***

At 10 pm, Andi pulled her Honda into the parking lot of The Last Call. The place was so packed, and their parking lot so full that she had to park across the street. Music became louder as she approached the door. She touched her blond wig to make sure it was still in place and gently pulled the satin blue halter top down so that it reached the top of her distressed jeans.

When she walked inside, she spotted Liz almost immediately, laughing with two tough looking men at a tall round table. Andi glanced around the room. It was dim, loud, smelled like liquor and smoke, and had a very rough clientele. It made Star City Bar & Grill look like the country club. What did she expect? This is exactly the kind of place where gang members would hang. She took a breath, pulled her shoulders back, placed a smile on her face and headed towards Liz.

Liz's table was near a stage where a guy was singing karaoke—*Highway to Hell*—off key. Liz grinned as Andi approached and nodded.

"Hey guys, this is my friend *Tiffany*," Liz winked, "We met when we spent one glorious night together in the city jail."

Liz pointed to her right to a cute guy with a buzz cut, guyliner around his eyes, piercings in his eyebrows, nose, lip and large black gauges in his earlobes. He looked young, maybe 19 or 20. He must be one of Liz's frequent customers with all those piercings and tattoos. His arms were covered with tattoos making them look like long sleeves.

"This is Bowie," she said, and he nodded at Andi as he took his time looking her over before he returned his gaze to her eyes with a half-smile and raised eyebrows.

Liz pointed to her left and said, "And this is *Rapier*."

At first, Andi thought they just had weird names—then, she realized these were gang names representing different types of blades. The man on Liz's left had an arm casually draped over the back of Liz's chair. He wore his dark hair in a long braid down his back and a close-trimmed beard. One ear was pierced with a diamond stud, tattoos peaked from his black Harley Davidson t-shirt neck and short sleeves. No doubt one of the motorcycles she saw in the parking lot belonged to him. Rapier looked older, more like Jerry's age. *He must be Liz's hot biker boyfriend.* His hard gaze made her uncomfortable like he was seeing straight through her disguise. She touched a few strands of her wig to reassure herself it was still in place and then lifted her chin, giving both men her most dazzling, confident smile, and slid onto the stool.

"Hi, nice to meet you," she said.

Bowie gave Andi a wicked grin and asked, "So, why did you get busted?"

Andi's eyes widened and she glanced at Liz. *Oh shoot*— she couldn't say murder without revealing her true identity. *Stick as close to the truth as possible*—a policy she used when repossessing cars.

"Grand theft auto," she said with a cocky grin and lifted her chin, "Mercedes Benz, E-class sedan."

It was Russell Stewart's car, and Cooper had thought she was stealing it so that was pretty close to the truth.

Bowie let out a low whistle and said, "*Sweet.*"

Rapier was not impressed and with a raised eyebrow said, "Except you got caught."

"True. I did get caught *that* time," Andi said with a shrug, "How about you guys? Any jail time?"

"They haven't caught me yet," Bowie said as he leaned back in his chair, hands stretched behind his head, grinning at her. She turned to Rapier and felt a chill run down her spine. He was looking at her with such intensity, it freaked her out. He was dangerous, no doubt about it, and she wouldn't be surprised if he had killed someone. Still, she met his gaze head on and lifted her chin, refusing to back down. She swallowed as they held their own private staring contest. Thank goodness the waitress arrived with a drink tray, breaking the tension. She placed four shot glasses, a full bottle of Tequila and a bowl of lime slices in the center of the small table. *Tequila? Oh no.*

Rapier slid a glass in front of her and poured, staring at her, one eyebrow raised in a silent challenge. Was it her imagination or did her glass look bigger than the other three? As she was considering this, Rapier filled the rest of the glasses. While she watched Rapier closely, Bowie lifted her hand, licked the top of it—*what?*—and sprinkled the moist spot with table salt. He did the same with his own hand, winked at her and then passed the salt shaker to Liz who followed suit. When everyone had salted their hands, Liz held her glass up in the air and said, "To new friends!"

Liz and the guys licked the salt, swallowed the tequila in one gulp, and sucked on a piece of lime. Andi took a breath through her mouth, careful not to inhale through her nose, licked the salt, swallowed the tequila, and as she felt the burn down her throat, she grabbed a slice of lime and sucked on it. *This was going to be a problem.* She wouldn't be able to linger over a drink for an hour like she'd planned while her new "friends" were doing shots. A couple more of these and she'd be drunk. What was it that Ben said about tequila? *One shot, two shots, three shots, FLOOR*—and she was certain that was for regular shot glasses—not super-sized like the one she was drinking from. This was not the best way for her to question the gang members. Better work fast.

"So, I know Liz works at the Tattoo shop. Where do you guys work?" Andi asked as Bowie refilled her shot glass and winked.

Great—he was trying to get her drunk. She'd have to call a cab to get home because there was no way she was going to be able to drive if she had more than one shot. Good thing she had the yellow cab company on speed dial.

Bowie leaned in close to her ear, smelled her hair and said, "Rapier and I both work for Roanoke Mountain View Construction."

He lifted her hand again, but she took it back, gave him a smile and said, "Thanks, I've got it."

She salted her own hand and then passed the shaker back to Bowie.

This time, Rapier made the toast, raising his glass he said, "To avoiding jail."

The three of them drank the second shot. Andi followed a moment after. She felt the burn deep in her chest this time as she sucked on the lime. Okay, this wasn't working. Time to cut her losses and get the heck out of here while she could still walk.

Rapier poured another round of tequila. *Who was the patron saint of the inebriated because holy moly, she could use a little help.* She looked down at her shot glass and blinked until it was no longer blurry. *Uh oh.* Her response time was slower and it was getting harder to focus. It had been five hours since she'd eaten dinner, and the alcohol was hitting her bloodstream fast and hard. If these were double shots and she was pretty sure her glass was, then two glasses times two was...um...hmm. Her thinking was definitely impaired. She looked to Liz for help, but her cellmate was busy snuggling up to Rapier while tracing one of the tattoos on his arm.

There was no way Andi was going to drink that third shot.

"I want to sing!" she shouted.

Three pairs of eyes stared at her. *Oops, that was louder than she realized.* Bowie grinned at her.

"Come on Liz. Let's go pick out a song together," Andi said.

Andi stepped off the stool and the floor tilted. *Uh oh.* She placed her hand on the table for a second and her balance was restored. Definitely no more shots. Liz joined her, and they walked together to the karaoke table.

"Girl, don't tell me you're drunk already."

"I haven't eaten for hours, and I honestly was thinking I'd just sip on a beer or margarita. I didn't count on shots," Andi said and then she whispered, "I wasn't getting any information out of the guys, anyway."

"Well, they both are definitely members of *The Sabers.* Bowie's tat is on his back, and Rapier's is on his right butt cheek. He's got a great ass, don't you think?"

"I'll take your word for it," Andi said and bit her lip and frowned. She'd thought the gang tattoos would all be on the neck like the one she'd spotted at the body shop. It would make it a lot harder to identify gang members if the tats could be anywhere on the body. She could just imagine asking a gang member, *Excuse me, sir, can you strip, so I can check for a gang tattoo?* She snorted. *Oh man.* She was definitely drunk.

***

The first time Cooper drove past The Last Call, he didn't see Andi's car in the parking lot. He was relieved because honestly, the thought of her coming alone this late in this part of the city pissed him off. Then he spotted her Honda across the street. *Shit.* He found a parking spot, got out of his car, and took a deep calming breath. He reminded himself that he was here to support Andi, and he'd promised himself that he would do everything he could to help her with her investigation, but *dammit*, they were going to have a long talk about safety protocol. He ran a hand through his hair.

Ben had called him twenty minutes ago to tell him that Andi had just texted that she was undercover as *Tiffany* again and about to go to The Last Call. He said she was going to meet up with gang members that were friends of her former cellmate to get more information. Cooper had laughed and told Ben he had a whacked sense of humor. Ben then assured him he wasn't joking, and if Cooper was serious about getting back together with Andi, this was the time to "man-up" because Ben was stuck at Star City Bar & Grill until closing.

Jesus, the woman was going to be the death of him—literally— because he was probably going to be killed in a gang fight in the next ten minutes.

Cooper stepped into the bar. He wasn't entirely sure what he'd expected. Maybe a barroom brawl with Andi in the middle of it—bottles being thrown, chairs overturned, and knives flying through the air—probably gunshots too. Instead, everyone's attention was riveted to the stage where two women were dancing and singing—*badly*—but enthusiastically to Elvis Presley's Jailhouse Rock. His eyes were drawn to the sexy woman on stage shimmying for all she was worth in a silky blue halter top. *Oh hell*— he recognized that voice, and he knew that body. The crowd was cheering, most on their feet, holding their drinks, dancing and singing the chorus. Too bad Andi and her friend couldn't carry a tune—otherwise, this would be one a hell of a concert. This crowd didn't seem to mind.

He shook his head and grinned. *Unbelievable.* He thought he'd be coming to her rescue, but apparently, Andi had everything under control. He pushed his way through the crowd until he was closer to the stage. She was swiveling her hips, snarling her lips, all while singing and dancing across the stage. The song ended and the audience roared, demanding more.

Andi just smiled, took her friend's hand and they took a deep bow. Then, in what he could only guess was supposed to be an Elvis impression, she said, "Thank you. Thank you very much. Elvis has left the building," and waved to the crowd as she stumbled off stage.

She handed her microphone to the DJ and then her eyes widened in surprise when she spotted him.

"Cooper! I can't believe you're here!" she shouted, a huge smile spread across her face and then she wrapped her arms around him, pressing her body tight against him.

Well, this was promising—not at all the greeting he'd been expecting after their argument.

She stepped back, swayed and squinted at him.

"Wait," she said speaking slowly as she furrowed her brow and tilted her head, "I think I'm mad at you." .

Cooper narrowed his eyes and shook his head. She didn't have everything under control—*Jesus*—she was shit-faced.

He chuckled and said, "I came to give you a ride home, *Margarita.*"

He looked her over closely. She was drunk but otherwise appeared unharmed—*thank god.* Not able to help himself, he grabbed her by the waist and pulled her toward him to steal a quick kiss. As soon as their lips met, Andi caught his face with both hands, deepened their kiss and, for a moment, he was lost—forgetting everything but the amazing way she made him feel. She tasted like tequila and limes, but this time it appeared she drank the entire tray of margaritas instead of dropping them on the floor. He eased back from their kiss, smiled, and rested his forehead against hers, held her close to him with one arm and traced his thumb over her lips with his other hand.

"Who's *that?*" Liz asked Andi.

Andi tried to turn toward Liz and felt the room begin to spin.

With a huge grin, she said, "*My Rock Star.*"

She rolled her head back to face him again, her eyes unfocused, brows furrowed.

"Cooper? I don't feel so," she said and passed out before she could finish the sentence.

Luckily, she was already in his arms, so he was able to keep her from sliding to the floor. He bent his knees, lifted her up, draped her body over his shoulder so that her head hung down his back and carried her out of *The Last Call* to his car.

***

Damn. Rapier watched as that rich guy, Barnett—he recognized his mug shot from the front page, carried *Tiffany* out of the bar. If the boyfriend would have been ten minutes later, Rapier would have dragged her drunk ass back to one of the storage rooms until they figured out exactly what she knew, and what the hell she was up to. He wouldn't have recognized the repo girl if Liz hadn't told him she was coming tonight. He stepped outside the bar and watched as the boyfriend, with some difficulty, maneuvered her into his car. Then he heard an unmistakable retching sound followed by loud cursing and watched him get into his car and drive off. Rapier pulled out his phone and made the call.

"Boss, just wanted to let you know that the repo girl came in disguise to our bar tonight asking questions. She somehow linked Milner's death to The Sabers. We got her drunk, but her boyfriend came in and hauled her out before we could find out what she actually knew."

Moments passed and Rapier only heard silence. Had their call been dropped? He was about to say something when he heard a long sigh and then the boss spoke.

"I am so *fucking* tired of hearing about the damn repo girl. I don't think she has Milner's files or she doesn't realize she has them, otherwise, she would have contacted us or turned them over to the police by now. She is getting closer, and we don't need that kind of attention. Blade disappointed me from the beginning, first with the way he handled Milner and then by his messy search of the house. Just get rid of her. If you do it right, consider yourself promoted. Ideally, I'd like you to make it look like an accident, so there's no murder investigation, but at this point, I just want her gone. Preferably without bullets—they're too easy to identify and then that definitely involves the police. Whatever you do, don't fuck it up."

The boss disconnected the call, Rapier pocketed his phone and walked back into the bar.

Chapter Eight

The first thing Andi noticed was the pain. The worst of it was concentrated in her head, but as she focused on the rest of her body, she realized everything hurt, just not as much as her head. There was something over her face, so she carefully lifted her hands to remove it. A pillow. Oh my god, with the pillow gone, the light was blinding. *Was she dying? Wait, should she go towards the light? Definitely not because the light made her head hurt so much worse.* She groaned—*ouch*—it hurt to make any sound, so she gently returned the pillow to its resting place over her head. Maybe if she held it over her face tight enough, she could suffocate and end the misery.

"Good morning, *Sunshine*," Cooper said cheerfully as he walked in the room.

Andi peeked out from under the pillow and watched him sit on the bed next to her. She squinted in the bright light and saw that he was holding a glass of water.

"Here. Sip this water and take these two aspirins. There's also some hot tea over on the nightstand when you're ready for it."

"I can't. It's too bright," Andi said. *Ouch.*

Cooper got up, closed the blind and then gingerly sat back on the bed next to her and removed the pillow.

Andi slowly opened her eyes. *Okay, that was better.* Then she saw Cooper grinning at her. *The man was so annoying.* She pulled herself halfway up so that she was leaning back on her elbows. The pain remained, but it didn't seem any worse than lying flat, so she sat up the rest of the way, leaned her back against the headboard and placed the pillow on her lap. She took the aspirin and the glass from Cooper. God, the taste in her mouth was awful. *Had something furry crawled in there and died?* She put the aspirin under her tongue and swallowed a sip of water. *How could she feel this bad and still be alive?*

"As soon as you're feeling better, we really need to talk about last night," he said.

Talk about last night? She felt a sudden panic as she assessed her situation. She was in Cooper's bed. *Again.* She looked down—*not her shirt.* She ran her hands down her body, *um— no bra—yes she was wearing panties*—thank god. *Last night?* She remembered driving to the bar, meeting up with Liz and some guys from *The Sabers* gang—Bowie and Rapier. There were tequila shots—Jailhouse Rock karaoke—she kissed Cooper—and then nothing. She'd been so drunk she couldn't remember anything after kissing Cooper? Andi's forehead creased as she concentrated. Oh my god, did they have sex? She looked up at Cooper, eyes wide.

Cooper chuckled, easily reading her look of alarm and shook his head. He gently reached out to tuck a piece of her wild hair behind her ear.

"Nothing happened, Margarita. I'm zero for two in closing the deal with you. This is the second time I've had you in my bed and we've just slept. I must be losing my touch," he said with a half-smile. Then, his face turned serious.

"Listen, I hate to leave you like this, but I've got a meeting this morning that I can't cancel," he said, "and the taxi is already here."

She looked at him and noticed for the first time that he was impeccably dressed in a suit and tie, and of course she must look like a nightmare.

"I sent for your car," he glanced down at his watch, "The driver should drop it off in the condo garage within the hour and then he'll stop by to pick up my car to be detailed. I'd really appreciate it if you could give him my keys. They're on the kitchen table."

"Detailed?" Andi asked.

"Yes, well, you sort of vomited all over the passenger floor and my dashboard after I carried you out of the bar and placed you in the seat," he grimaced.

"Oh, and your clothes are in the dryer and should be ready in about 15 minutes."

Oh. My. God. Could this morning get any worse? She was mortified, and she could feel her face heat up. *Ouch*— blushing made her head hurt too.

She had to say something. She bit her lip.

"Cooper," she paused and looked him in the eyes, *ouch*.

"I just wanted to thank you for being there for me last night. *Again*. I was in way over my head and if you hadn't shown up when you did," she trailed off and studied the pillow on her lap.

She didn't really want to think about what could have happened to a passed out woman in a gang bar. God, she'd been so stupid and careless, and she was *never* drinking tequila again. *Ever*.

He leaned in and kissed her gently on the forehead which surprisingly didn't make her head hurt worse.

"We *really* need to talk—when you're feeling better and when I'm finished at the office. Meet me for dinner?" he asked.

Dinner? Her stomach revolted at the thought. Andi groaned. *Ouch*.

Cooper chuckled, "Maybe start with a piece of dry toast. Call me later, and let me know how you're feeling, okay? I'll see you tonight."

She nodded. *Ouch*.

***

Andi managed to drink three glasses of water and a cup of tea and was showered and dressed in her clean clothes from the night before when the driver came by to pick up Cooper's car. How was she ever going to pay him back? She was racking up a lot of IOUs with the man. And what price could she put on him rescuing her last night? There was no denying she'd needed help, and he'd swept in and carried her off. She'd repaid him by throwing up in his car—the very car he didn't even eat in because he didn't want to get it dirty. *Terrific.*

It was a stupid risk to go to the gang bar and even dumber to drink shots. What had she been thinking? She was making decisions based on desperation—a mistake she wouldn't repeat. And what information had she actually learned? Just that the gang tattoos could be anywhere on the body. The only other small piece of information was that two of the gang members worked for Roanoke Mountain View Construction. She didn't even get their real names. Somehow she doubted that Bowie and Rapier were the names printed on their driver's licenses.

By the time she locked up Cooper's condo, she was feeling more human, and her headache was a low hum in the background.

She sent Cooper a text that she was feeling better and thanked him again for his kindness, hospitality and informed him that she was definitely buying him dinner, even if she couldn't eat yet. Then, she called Ben for his bartender prescription for a hangover. He'd simply laughed and said that his job was to give people hangovers, not take them away; but if she drank plenty of water, that should help. Andi's last text was to Maggy, asking her if she had anything to help a hangover. Unlike this morning, she was able to move and talk without throbbing pain, but she was still very sensitive to light. She put on her sunglasses and drove to the City Market to see her friend.

It was too early for the lunch crowd, so there were plenty of parking spaces. She found a spot in the parking lot across from the market, paid for an hour, and walked across the street. The smells of lunch preparation weren't too awful, but she breathed through her mouth just to be safe. Andi said hi to Simon and went directly to Maggy's booth.

"Aw," Maggy said with sympathy as soon as she spotted Andi.

"I got your text, and I know just the smoothie for your hangover. Give me a minute to put it together, then I want details," Maggy said and began working quickly, dumping colorful ingredients into the blender.

Andi decided it would be better not to watch. She turned around and caught Simon watching Maggy. The look on the poor guy's face—he had it bad for her. Simon caught her watching him and his face turned a bright shade of red.

Quick to recover, he asked, "Interest you in your usual, chili dog with the works?"

Andi covered her mouth with her hand and abruptly turned back to face Maggy. She felt her stomach acids rise in her throat.

"*Idiot*," Maggy hollered over to Simon, "Are you trying to make her sick? She's hungover."

"Sorry Andi," Simon said while putting his hands up in the air in surrender and mouthed *I didn't know* to Maggy.

Maggy just rolled her eyes at him. *Men.*

She handed Andi the raspberry smoothie.

"So how did this," Maggy waved her hand in front of Andi, "happen without me?"

"It's not what you think. I was investigating Milner's murder and was attempting to interview some members of a gang at their bar—with Liz—you know, the woman I met from the night I spent in jail when I accidentally got drunk."

Maggy gaped at Andi.

"I know. It was the second dumbest idea I've ever had. The dumbest was when I thought I could drink shots with them."

Andi looked at her smoothie. *Why was it so red?* Best not to ask, so she took a sniff and a sip. It was cool and refreshing and didn't make her want to immediately throw up. *That was a good sign, right?*

"Thank god Cooper showed up before I passed out, and he carried me out of the bar."

Maggy, speechless, just stared.

"Oh, and apparently I threw up in his Porsche and then slept with him. *Again.*"

"Wait, you slept with him?" Maggy asked, eyebrows raised.

Andi rolled her eyes behind her sunglasses—*ouch*. She took another sip of her drink.

"After everything I just told you, that's the first question you have?" she asked and shook her head, "It's not like we *did* anything. I'm sure he found me very sexy after vomiting and passing out."

Jeez, she hoped she hadn't done or said anything more embarrassing. He was so insistent on talking to her about last night—she was worried.

"Mags, when did my life get so out of control?"

"Gee, let's see," Maggy pretended to think about it, "Hmm, probably the night you found the *naked, dead guy.*"

Andi stood up straighter, "You're right. I just need to stay focused on finding out who really killed Milner and things should return to normal."

She slumped just a little, "Of course, that would still leave the $35,000 in bail money I owe," then she shrugged and said, "I'll just have to worry about one thing at a time."

She tried to pay for her smoothie, and Maggy waved her away, "It's on the house. The story of your latest adventure was really payment enough," Maggy said as she winked and grinned.

Andi leaned in and gave her a hug and said, "Love you Mags. I always feel so much better after we talk."

"Love you too, Andi," Maggy smiled back at her friend.

Then Andi whispered, "Have you and Simon had a fight or something? He looks like his puppy died."

"Or something. Can't talk about it now," Maggy said and sent an annoyed glance over at Simon's booth.

Holding her smoothie with one hand, Andi waved goodbye to Mags and then Simon, walked out the doors of the City Market building and stepped onto the sidewalk. She looked both ways and seeing it was clear of cars, began to cross the street. That's when she heard the squealing wheels and a loud engine. A black car raced down the street, heading right for her! Andi didn't have time to think, she only reacted—running to the other side of the street to the sidewalk directly in front of the parking lot. Then she watched in horror as the car continued to head toward her on the sidewalk. *Oh my god*—she was going to be hit—*like Bambi*—she'd be smashed against the windshield—*I'm sorry Cooper*—he was going to be so mad that she got herself killed.

She dove on the hood of the first car parked in the lot and tucked her body and rolled across the top as the black car slammed into the parked car. She was just rolling off the hood when the impact of the collision threw her onto the asphalt where she landed on her knees and elbows then she tumbled onto her back. *Ouch.* She heard more squealing wheels and then the roar of the engine faded away.

People were yelling, and she opened her eyes, but it was so bright that she closed them immediately. Her sunglasses must have gone flying somewhere. She heard someone on the phone with 911 describing the accident and telling the operator that it looked like the victim was covered in blood. *Wait, covered in blood?* Another voice told her to stay still, help was on the way. She was sore all over but just her knees and elbows burned. She opened her eyes again and sat up. *Ouch.*

"Ma'am, you really need to stay still until the paramedics get here," the man said, concerned, "there's an awful lot of blood, and I'm not sure where it's coming from."

She looked down at her body, and he was right. There was red everywhere, her jeans were ripped, and her knees hurt like the dickens. She looked at the blood all over her shirt—weird that it didn't hurt there. *Must be shock—she'd read about that.* She reached down and wiped the blood and held it up to her nose and then put her finger in her mouth. *Raspberry.* She must be wearing her smoothie. She smiled and got up slowly. "I'm okay, thanks. It's just my smoothie."

The accident had attracted lots of attention. Maggy, Simon and many others had come out as soon as they heard the collision. The police came and took her statement. Apparently, someone had gotten the license of the black car that had tried to run her over, and it had been reported stolen that morning. She was tired, a little shaken, and she just wanted to go home and take a shower, and change her clothes. This was by far the unluckiest outfit she owned, and thanks to her fall on the asphalt, it was now ready for the trash.

After going home, taking a hot shower, bandaging up her knees and elbows, and drinking two cups of her hot tea, she dressed and headed for the office. She desperately needed some normalcy in her life. As she was driving to the repo office, she got a call from Detective Kendricks. *Terrific.*

"Good afternoon Detective," Andi said, "are you calling to tell me you've found the real killer on the Milner case?"

"No, but I just heard about the hit and run involving *you*. Are you okay? They said you refused to go to the hospital."

"I'm fine—really—just got a few scratches on my knees and elbows."

"It's statistically improbable that in a city with almost one hundred thousand people, *you* would be the one to be involved in a hit and run today."

"Well, technically, I didn't get hit."

"*Andi,*" Kendricks said in a low voice. She could imagine him rubbing the back of his neck in frustration.

"Why do I have the feeling that there's information you aren't sharing with me?" he asked.

"Why would I do that, detective? I'm sure if I had *innocently* stumbled across some information pertaining to the murder case, you would consider it interfering with your investigation and I would find myself sitting in a jail cell right now—for my own protection, of course."

"Andi, if you know something, you need to tell me right now," Kendricks said.

She interrupted him, "I'm sorry. I can't talk because I'm late for work, but thanks for checking on me."

"Don't you dare hang," Kendricks said in an angry voice before she disconnected the call.

He called back immediately and she let the call go to voice mail. When he called back again, she turned off her cell phone. *Please.* All she wanted was to pretend, just for the afternoon, that her life was somewhat normal.

When she walked into the office, Jerry looked up and said, "What the hell happened to you?"

She glanced down at her white bandages on her elbows.

"It looks worse than it is. Just got scraped up a bit when I fell. Scrapes are tricky to wrap, especially on elbows."

She gave him a big, bright, forced smile. It was the best she could do, given the morning she'd had.

"So, got any easy jobs for me today?" she asked.

"Take your pick," he said pointing to the full In-box and then he picked up the phone to make a call.

Andi grabbed up a couple repo jobs and did some quick research. *Bingo.* This could be an easy one. Alice Turley worked at Victoria's Secret at the mall and drove an orange Volkswagen Beetle—Andi had always wanted to drive one of those cars. She made a quick call to the store to see when Alice was working next, explaining that she was so helpful last time she purchased bras. *Perfect.* She was working now until close. Andi grabbed the VW key, waved to Jerry, and headed for the door. Finally, her day was beginning to turn around.

***

Over at Under Your Skin Tattoo and Piercing Studio, Liz had just finished up the tongue piercing on her last customer. She cleaned up, grabbed her purse, and told her boss she was taking her lunch break. Her next appointment wasn't until 2 pm. She got in her car and immediately sent a text to Rapier asking if he wanted to meet up for a *nooner.* She got his reply a few minutes later that he was on a job and couldn't get away, but maybe if the everything went well, they could *hookup* tonight to celebrate. Liz rolled her eyes and tossed her phone into the passenger seat. *What the fuck?* He was always up for sex in the middle of the day.

Rapier had been in a strange mood ever since meeting Andi last night. Even though he hadn't flirted with Andi, Liz couldn't help the feeling of jealousy that swept through her when Rapier and Andi had stared each other down—the tension was undeniable. *Had it been sexual?* The rest of the night, Rapier couldn't seem to keep his eyes off Andi—*which really pissed her off.*

Damn—she really liked Andi. She didn't bullshit her like most people. Plus, there was this weird connection they had made that night in jail – must be a result of coming down from the adrenaline rush they each had experienced earlier. Liz chuckled. Andi had turned out to be so much fun singing karaoke. She smiled remembering the provocative moves they'd both danced on stage and how they'd tried to keep up with the lyrics on the screen—*damn hilarious.* Liz shook her head—it had been so much fun, and the crowd went wild for them. At the end of the dance, did Rapier give her the lip lock like Andi got from her rock star? No. In fact, she watched Rapier follow Andi outside as she was being carried out of the bar to the parking lot. If that wasn't bad enough, Rapier left soon after saying he was tired and was going home to sleep—*like hell he was going to sleep.*

Liz found herself driving around the mall parking lot. She needed some fucking *Ben & Jerry's* ice cream to shake her foul mood. She picked the side of the mall that was closest to Victoria's Secret because she was going to treat herself to some hot lingerie while she was at it. That's when she spotted Rapier's motorcycle.

"On the job, my ass," she said as she parked her car a couple rows behind him.

He was just sitting on his bike, looking straight ahead. *Why?* Then she spotted Andi getting out of her car and looking around before walking up to a bright orange VW Beetle and inserting the key.

"She must be working a repo," Liz said to herself.

Andi looked around again and then got into the car and pulled out of the parking space. Once Andi was on the road in her newly acquired wheels, Liz frowned as she saw Rapier start his Harley. She thought for sure he was going to follow Andi and she was going to have to drive over to his house and trash it. Instead, he parked next to Andi's old Honda and used a Slim Jim to unlock her driver's side door. He walked back to his bike, pulled a cardboard box out of his saddlebag and carefully placed it on the front seat of the Honda. He knelt by the open driver's door for a moment doing something she couldn't quite see, and then carefully closed the driver's side door, climbed back on his bike and left.

Left her a fucking gift, did he? What could possibly be in there? There was only one way to find out.

Chapter Nine

Twenty minutes later, Detectives Kendricks and Richardson pulled up to the mall parking lot. There were five fire trucks, three ambulances, the state police bomb unit and about a dozen police cars—not to mention a large crowd of onlookers and reporters.

"It looks like a war zone," Detective Richardson said to Kendricks as they both got out of the car and walked toward the disaster. Several reporters swarmed and began firing questions at them.

Kendricks continued walking forward and said, "No comment."

When they approached the police barrier comprised of uniformed officers and yellow police tape, Kendricks nodded at Chris, one of the police officers, and ducked under the bright yellow tape. Even though everything was wet, there was still smoke coming from what was obviously a small compact car, although it was difficult to tell the make and model. Detective Anderson was talking with a firefighter when he spotted Kendricks and Richardson and waved them over.

"Hell of a mess," Kendricks said to Anderson.

"Yeah, I've never seen anything like this. Both the fire department and the bomb squad confirm a bomb caused the explosion that decimated the car as well as the victim. Looks like there was only one casualty although we've locked down the entire mall and secured the area to search for other explosive devices. Right now, we're not ruling out the possibility that this was a terrorist act."

"Have you been able to identify the victim or owner of the car?" Richardson asked.

"Apparently the vic was at ground zero when the bomb exploded, so the body is burned beyond recognition. Based on the skeletal structure, the coroner believes the victim was a young female. They are preparing to move the body now," Anderson said as he began walking toward the incinerated car.

"*Oh my God,*" Richardson whispered as they approached the body and car frame, and she briefly turned away from the scene, swallowed, then looked back, her best professional face forward.

"*Jesus,*" Kendricks said as he looked at the remains. Unlike a lot of the homicide victims they investigated, at least her death would have been instant—no suffering. "What do you know about the car?"

"We just found the plates over there," Anderson pointed to an area across the parking lot.

Then he pulled his notepad out of his front jacket pocket and glanced at it.

"It's a Honda Accord registered to Andrea Sloan – she lives right here in the city."

Richardson swore.

Kendricks closed his eyes and took a deep breath. Stomach acid burned the back of his throat. He opened his eyes and reached into his front pocket and put an antacid in his mouth. He slowly chewed it, swallowed, and took a deep breath. *Dammit*, he should have arrested her for interfering that first time he caught her at Diamond Auto Body.

"You know her?" Anderson asked.

"Yes," Richardson sighed, "she was the lead suspect in one of our homicides. You might have heard about her. She repossesses cars."

"Do you mean that Repo Girl? The one who just made the big drug bust in the ice cream truck?" Anderson asked with a faint grin, "That was quite a stint."

Richardson rolled her eyes.

Shit! Kendricks rubbed the back of his neck. There was a chance, although slim, that the victim wasn't Andi. He pulled out his phone and called her cell phone number. It went immediately to voice mail, *dammit.* He left a message.

"Andi, it's Kendricks. I have information to share with you about the investigation. It's critical that you call me immediately," and then disconnected. That was the only thing he could think of to get her to call him back. *If* she was still alive.

Was her cellphone nearby blown to smithereens or was she just being stubborn and ignoring his calls again? He called the department and requested they track her phone location. Someone sure was determined to kill her, and they weren't being subtle about it. She was in very real danger if she wasn't already dead. If this was her body, then he would track down her murderer and see that he spent the rest of his sad little life behind bars. Or if he got lucky, the killer would threaten his life, and he'd be forced to shoot him—fatally. He rubbed the back of his neck. *Shit—he wasn't thinking objectively.* He shook his head. He usually didn't *know,* much less actually *like* the homicide victim. He looked up as a helicopter from a local news station went overhead.

Kendricks sighed and said, "We'd better get started," and nodded to Richardson as he walked toward the crime scene. They had a lot of work to do.

After working the crime scene for over an hour, Kendricks was talking to one of the bomb experts when Detective Sanchez approached him.

"Thanks for your help, Tyler. Let me know if you learn anything else," Kendricks said and stepped towards Sanchez.

"Sanchez, what are you doing at my homicide scene?" Kendricks asked, one eyebrow raised. Seemed like Sanchez was always around lately and it was beginning to really annoy him.

"I heard that's Andrea Sloan's car," Sanchez said.

"And what does that have to do with *you* exactly?" Kendricks asked.

Sanchez smirked and shook his head.

"Did you forget already? She hauled in a couple hundred thousands of dollars in drugs with her ice cream truck repo. I can't think of a better motive for murder. And you have to admit, a car bomb isn't your typical murder weapon. I'm after the Big Fish – the man responsible for bringing the drugs into Roanoke. Let's just say that makes her a person of interest to me," he said as he pointed his thumb at his chest and then looked over at the mangled metal structure that was her car. "And apparently she was a person of interest to someone else too."

Kendricks narrowed his gaze, "We haven't ID'd the victim yet, so we're not certain it's her. And, as you can see, there are no drugs here, so I suggest you leave me to investigate *my* homicide scene. I'll be happy to let you read my report when it's completed."

Sanchez stared hard at Kendricks for a moment before a slow smile spread across his face.

"You can guarantee I'll be reading that report, Kendricks, and much more," he said as he walked away.

Kendricks glared at the back of Sanchez as he walked over to talk with Tyler.

***

A little while later, he heard someone holler his name.

He looked toward the police barrier. *Damn.* Two of Andi's friends, the bartender and the redhead from the bail hearing, were waving to get his attention. He sighed and walked over toward them, lifted the yellow tape, and let them step inside and moved them away from the reporters.

Ben spoke first, "We heard about it on the news but couldn't really believe it. Please tell us they made a mistake, and it's not Andi, right?"

Kendricks rubbed his neck. *Just great—somehow the information had already leaked to the press.*

"Look, we're still investigating. We're waiting to identify the body, but it was definitely Andi's car that exploded. Have either of you spoken to her in the last," he checked his watch, "hour?"

The redhead replied, "No. Last I saw her someone almost ran her over at the City Market about three hours ago. Andi brushed it off saying it was just some crazy driver, probably texting and driving. Do you think that was the same person that blew up her car?" Her eyes filled with tears.

Ben shook his head and folded his arms across his chest. "I bet it was one of the guys from the gang. I told her it was a stupid idea," Ben sighed and shook his head.

Kendricks looked at him and narrowed his eyes, "What stupid idea?"

Ben pressed his lips together for a moment and then unfolded his arms and once he began speaking, the words rushed out.

"Okay. She thinks someone from The Saber gang is Milner's killer. She saw a tattoo on the neck of the guy, you know, from the auto body shop the day after the murder. She asked her cellmate from prison about the tattoo, and she said it was a gang symbol and then invited her to a bar last night to meet some of the gang members."

Kendricks just stared at Ben like he had three heads.

"I know, right? Crazy. That's exactly what I told her, but Andi tends to get an idea in her head and then she runs with it before thinking it all the way through."

Kendricks pulled out his notepad and popped another antacid into his mouth.

"I need details. *Now.* Tell me everything you know."

Ben began to speak when he heard someone yell his name. The three of them turned toward the police barrier, and Kendricks sighed. It was the boyfriend and the other two guys from the band. *Great.* He waved to Chris and told him to let them through.

They ran over and Daniel embraced Ben in a hug and said, "I'm so sorry, Benji."

Cooper just stared at the burnt metal and shook his head. *No way in hell was this happening.* He ran his hand through his hair as he stared at the twisted frame. He called Andi's phone again, for the hundredth time since he'd first heard about the explosion, and whispered "Pickup. For once, please just answer your damn phone".

He got her voice mail again with her sassy voice on the outgoing message. Was this the only way he'd ever hear her voice again? His eyes stung, and he closed them briefly. Then he shoved his phone back into his pocket. *No.*

He was mad. Mad was better than the helpless/hopeless feeling that had consumed him since they got the call from Ben. He would NOT lose her this way. If she wanted to walk away from a relationship with him? Fine. Well, not really, but he'd eventually accept it. Probably. Eventually. But blown up? Dead? Not after she'd slammed into his life drenched in margaritas with her irresistible smile and soulful eyes changing his world irrevocably. *No.* He shook his head. *Sorry, but she wasn't getting out of this thing between them that easy.* He hadn't even talked to her yet. She didn't know how much she meant to him. Hangover or not, he should have never left her this morning without telling her how he felt. He dragged his hands over his face and looked back into the wreck before abruptly turning toward the BAD cop.

Cooper jabbed his finger into Kendricks' chest as he informed him, "It's not her."

Kendricks stared down at Cooper's finger on his chest and then looked hard into his eyes.

Cooper removed his finger from the bad cop's chest but continued talking to Kendricks with urgency, "Yes, I know it's her car, but that's *not* her body."

He said it with such conviction, such certainty, the tone and look he gave Kendricks dared him to say differently. Kendricks studied him. *Maybe Barnett had just talked to Andi.*

"You spoke to her?" he asked.

"No, but I *know* she's alive." Cooper placed his hand over his heart and gave Kendricks a look that dared him to challenge this statement.

It was in that moment that Kendricks realized the boyfriend was in denial. He wasn't going to inform him that it was likely that Andi died in the car bomb. *Shit*, he was starting to feel the stomach acid rise in his throat again. He popped another antacid and chewed. He'd been doing that a lot since meeting Andrea Sloan.

Anyway, there was no use in stating that awful likelihood until they knew for sure. He was a trained professional who apparently was suffering from a bit of denial himself. He wasn't accepting anything until he got the official coroner report. The next few hours were going to be pure hell. *Focus on the job.* He turned to Ben and began asking specific questions about Andi's stupid idea.

***

"Oh no. No, no, no, no, not my car!" Andi's voice had started as a whisper, but her volume increased with each word. She ducked under the police tape and ran towards the still smoking pile of metal.

"Ma'am, come back. No one is allowed beyond the yellow tape," the officer hollered and chased after her.

She stopped just before the pile of metal that used to be her car, dropped her purse on the ground, keys in hand, pointed to her car and clicked the keyless remote.

The officer caught up with her, grabbed her by the arm and turned her toward him and then gaped when he saw her face.

"Wait, I know you. You're that repo girl. The one everyone thought blew up with her car," the officer said slowly and then released her arm.

"This was your car, right?" he asked and turned toward the pile of metal.

Tears trickled down her cheeks. Looking up at the sky, she yelled, "Is this some sort of test because I'm not seeing the big picture? How am I supposed to work without a car?" she asked desperately. "When am I going to get a freaking break? H-e-l-l-o! I could really use a break!"

Someone screamed her name loud enough that she heard it over all the noise, and she turned toward the sound. Ben and Maggy came barreling towards her practically knocking her to the ground with a hug. They were both crying and laughing and talking to her at the same time. It was like her head was in a vice with each friend's head pressed against her cheeks, talking loudly in her ears.

"Guys, I can't breathe," she said as she stepped back and looked at them both, "What are you doing here anyway?"

Maggy wiped the tears from her eyes, "It's all over the news, you big goof," she couldn't help but put her arms around her dear friend for another hug. "They said a woman's body was found by your car and police assumed it was you." Maggy stepped back and pointed her finger at her. "Don't you ever do that to us again!"

Andi looked back at her car, confused. "A woman's body?"

Ben put his arm casually over her shoulder and said, "They've already removed it. *Damn girl,* you trying to give your friends heart failure? Someone is seriously trying to kill you. And I hadn't even heard about the hit and run until I talked to Maggy."

"After this, we can clearly conclude that was no accident, Andi," Maggy said, hands on her hips, the classic 'I told you so' look on her face.

Andi let out a breath as she let those words sink in.

***

Cooper stood frozen next to Kendricks as they both just stared at Andi, who was apparently alive and well. Even though Cooper had been certain in his heart that Andi was alive, he realized that was only because he couldn't handle the other possibility. He watched her standing next to the pile of metal that used to be her car, embracing her friends. The scene filled him with tremendous relief and terror. She was alive now, *thank God,* but someone had tried to blow her up. *Damn.* He ran his hand through his hair and blew out a breath. Then he straightened his shoulders and walked steadily toward her while reminding himself to play things cool.

By the time he finally reached her, his body completely ignored the command, and he pulled her tightly against him wrapping both arms around her in an embrace. *God, she felt so good in his arms.* He breathed in the familiar vanilla scent of her hair and let himself have just a minute of her body pressed against his, felt her breathing against him, reassured himself she was really okay—*she was alive.* Then he took a step back, so he could look into her eyes, eyes that were full of surprise and something else. He glanced down at her beautiful, tear-stained cheeks then to her slightly parted lips.

God, he had to kiss her. He would allow himself just one gentle, brief kiss. But when his lips touched hers, the thought was forgotten and replaced with an intense, passionate kiss that expressed all his longing, fear, relief, and love. *Love?* He tucked that thought away—he'd have to reexamine it later. After a full minute, he reluctantly pulled back from the kiss, his hands still holding her face, unwilling to let go of her.

He cleared his throat and swallowed hard as he looked into her beautiful eyes. *Keep it light or you'll scare her off.* He gave her his best cocky grin.

"I hope you don't think this is going to get you out of our dinner date tonight, *Margarita.* You *owe me* after last night alone. I'll have to think of a way for you to repay me for taking ten years off my life this afternoon when I heard about your car blowing up."

Just saying those words made Cooper's chest ache, but instead of pulling her back into his arms and losing himself in her kisses again, he brushed his thumb across her sexy bottom lip and grinned when he saw her face flush and felt her shiver.

Thank god he wasn't the only one affected by this thing that sizzled between them.

Kendricks watched as Barnett scooped Andi into his arms for a *welcome back from the dead* kiss. Before Andi made her appearance, Kendricks had been talking to Barnett, trying to handle the guy as gently as possible. The boyfriend had really looked like he'd wanted to take a swing at him. That's when Kendricks had spotted Chris chasing after a woman as she ran towards the pile of metal. When he'd realized it was Andi, he had sighed with relief. *Thank God.* Only Andrea Sloan would make an entrance like this at her own damn homicide scene. He grinned and shook his head. Anyone who got into a relationship with her was in for a wild, unpredictable ride. He almost felt sorry for Barnett. *Almost.* If he was honest with himself, he was maybe even just a little envious. Good thing he didn't have the time or energy for any sort of relationship, especially with someone like Andrea Sloan.

Even though Andi was alive and unharmed, some poor woman had been killed by that bomb, and he still had too many unanswered questions. Kendricks rubbed the back of his neck. *Who was the charred victim? Who set the car bomb, and why? How the hell was he going to keep Andi safe until they found and arrested the bomber?* He had to do something to protect her since someone seemed determined to kill her. The woman was a magnet for trouble. He spotted his partner staring at Andi like she was looking at a ghost. He walked over to her.

"Richardson, are you alright?"

Richardson shook her head in disbelief. She replied in a voice he could barely hear—like she was still in shock. "Yeah. It's just I thought for sure she was really dead this time. Her car, a burned female body at the scene about her size. I just *knew* the vic was Andrea Sloan."

Kendricks smiled. "There's no denying it, Andi's got unbelievable luck. Let's go see what we can do to protect her while we look for the bomber, so she won't have to rely completely on that luck to stay alive."

They were walking over to Andi and her posse when Kendricks stopped and narrowed his eyes.

"Sanchez? What the hell is *he* doing?" Kendricks asked more to himself than Richardson.

Richardson turned to study her partner and in her southern drawl, asked, "What is it about Detective Sanchez that you don't like?"

Kendricks rubbed his chin, "Everything," then he paused and said, "and nothing. Hell, I don't really know. Something just doesn't *feel* right about both of these cases – with Milner and the bomb victim. There's a common thread, and I just can't put my finger on it. As far as Sanchez? I just don't trust him. And I don't like him interfering in our investigation. Come on. Let's go remind him."

***

Andi stood staring into Cooper's amazing chocolate brown eyes trying to regain her senses. He had just *kissed* her again leaving her feeling boneless, breathless, and speechless. He had said some nonsense about dinner tonight—frankly, she was having a hard time focusing on his words while he was looking at her like she was a piece of Gram's double chocolate fudge cake that he was about to devour. Then, like a slap in the face, she returned to reality when she heard the distinctive voice of Detective Sanchez.

"I'm so glad to see you alive and well, Miss Sloan. We all thought it was *your* crispy remains in that parking space," Sanchez said.

She turned to look at Detective Sanchez. He was wearing another suit, smiling at her, but, like before, his smile didn't reach his eyes.

Cooper slung a protective arm over Andi's shoulder and pulled her to his side. He didn't recognize this guy, but it was obvious he knew Andi. The man was some sort of detective if the badge on his belt was an indication, but he obviously made Andi uncomfortable. She stood rigidly by his side.

Cooper reached out his right hand in greeting while holding Andi with his left.

"Hi. My name is Cooper Barnett. How is it you know Andi?"

Sanchez reached out to return Cooper's handshake, and that's when she spotted it. *No way.* Just above his wrist, where his sleeve had scooted up, was a tattoo that looked like a blade. Could it be the same blade as The Saber gang tattoo? She couldn't get a good look at it because the next moment, his hand was back at his side, and the tattoo was hidden from view. *Don't be paranoid. Liz said there were a lot of tattoo patterns of blades but only one specific design The Sabers used.*

"Detective Sanchez, Narcotics. I met Miss Sloan after her ice cream truck repo. I'm sure you read about it in the Roanoke Times," Sanchez replied smoothly.

Sanchez turned his attention back to Andi.

"Miss Sloan, do you have any idea who might have blown up your car?" Sanchez asked.

Andi was trying to decide how to answer when Kendricks walked up behind Sanchez.

Kendricks said, "Like I told you before, Sanchez, you can read about it in my report tomorrow morning. Back at the station. From your desk."

Sanchez turned with another one of his trademark smiles to face Kendricks.

"Ah, Detective Kendricks. I was just checking on the well-being of my favorite Good Samaritan. Miss Sloan is responsible for my biggest bust this year, and I'm sure the seller of those drugs was very unhappy to lose his inventory. When I heard she might have been killed by a car bomb, I was concerned. I just want to make sure this isn't a result of her involvement in *my* case. I'm sure you understand."

"What I *understand,* Sanchez, is that you are interviewing someone who may have information about my homicide before I've had a chance to speak to her."

Kendricks put his finger on Sanchez's chest. "You, Detective, are meddling with my crime scene and possible witnesses. I would hate to have to have a discussion about this encroachment on my case with the Chief." Kendricks removed his hand and stepped back, crossing his arms over his chest. He nodded back towards the police tape. "I'll be happy to answer any questions I can after I finish questioning Miss Sloan. Back at the station."

Sanchez narrowed his eyes at Kendricks and then spoke directly to Andi.

"You were very lucky not to have been killed this time, Miss Sloan. If I'm right, and the bomber was retaliating because of the drugs you took from him, your life is in danger. You have my card. Call me if you think of anyone that might be involved," Sanchez said before turning towards Kendricks, "and I suggest *you* put her under protective custody unless you are looking to open another homicide case, *detective.*"

They all watched Detective Sanchez walk under the yellow tape and then to his car.

***

Sitting on a bar stool at The Last Call, savoring his whiskey, Rapier watched the television screen with satisfaction. There was no need to go back to the mall to make sure the bomb detonated. He had the best view right here thanks to the helicopters that shot footage of the debris. It was beautiful. There was only one casualty, an unidentified female body. Oh, they'd eventually learn it was Andrea Sloan, the pain-in-the-ass repo agent. Sure, she might have evaded his attempt to plow her over at the market this morning, but what mattered were results, and he'd done it. He smiled into his glass and took another sip of his whiskey and then his phone vibrated. He looked at the screen. Yes, the boss was calling to congratulate him. He quickly answered.

"What the *hell* were you thinking? This is going to make the fucking national news."

"Hey Boss, you said you wanted her gone without a way to trace it back to us. I'm watching it on the news now, and

I can guarantee there's not much left of anything to trace. Plus, there were no other casualties. Just the target, like you requested."

There was silence on the other end. That was never good.

In a deadly, calm voice, the boss said, "You made this look like a god-damned war-zone and managed to blow up the wrong fucking person. Imbeciles. The whole lot of you."

"What do you mean I blew up the wrong person? I set the bomb to explode when the door was opened. No one else would open that junk car."

"Well somebody did because Andrea Sloan just made a grand entrance to the scene. She's very much alive and is at the station right now, being questioned. Consider yourself, at the very least, demoted. I'll handle this myself."

***

After spending several grueling hours at the police station and being questioned by Detective Kendricks, Andi was finally home, sitting on her comfy sofa with Dodger's head resting on her lap.

"This is not exactly how I imagined our dinner date tonight," Cooper said with a half-smile. "I was thinking more of a quiet, candlelit table at *Lorenzo's*, a bottle of Cabernet Sauvignon, a plate of Gemelli with shrimp, arugula, and feta."

Cooper sighed. Instead, he was sitting next to Andi on the couch, his bare feet propped up on her coffee table, jean-clad legs crossed at the ankles, a white carton of Szechuan shrimp with vegetables in his left hand, chopsticks in his right. He picked out a piece of shrimp and popped it in his mouth.

Andi smiled, "Well, at least you got the shrimp. You know, I've never learned to use those," she pointed to his chopsticks with her fork, then reached in her white carton for a piece of sweet and sour chicken. She glanced down at Dodger—he had that pitiful look down pat—so she tossed it to her loyal pup. He caught it mid-air.

"You know you're spoiling him, right?" Cooper asked.

"Maybe just a little," Andi said as she watched Dodger swallow the food in one gulp. He returned his head to her leg, his eyes looking at her with such adoration, silently begging for another piece. Andi patted Dodger on the head. The next piece was hers. She was starving. She hadn't had anything to eat since her raspberry smoothie earlier this morning, and she wore more of it than she got to drink. *Was that only this morning?* She bit off a piece of the chicken in a deep-fried batter covered in a yummy sweet, bright orange colored sauce.

"I know this isn't what you had in mind for dinner, but after the day I've had, this is pretty much perfect. Do you want a taste?" she asked as she offered her white carton to him.

Yes, he did, but not the food. And she was right. This was perfect. She was so adorable sitting next to him, *alive* and sexy, her feet tucked under her, orange sauce smudged on her upper lip. He wanted to kiss the sauce off her lip, but before he started any of that, they had to talk. So instead of leaning in like he wanted, he said, "You've got a little sauce just above your lip, right here." He pointed to his upper lip.

"Oops," Andi said and rather than using a napkin from the delivery bag on the coffee table, she swept her tongue over her lip.

"Did I get it?" she asked.

Jesus, she was killing him—and she wasn't even trying to be seductive.

He couldn't speak for a moment, so he just nodded then cleared his throat.

"I thought for sure Kendricks was going to throw you in jail after you refused to go to a safe house," Cooper said as he reached into Andi's carton and pulled out a piece of sweet and sour chicken with his chopsticks. It was amazing to him that her skin wasn't tinted orange with all the orange colored food she ate. He offered her his carton.

She just shook her head and stabbed another piece of chicken from her carton with her fork.

"I'm sure he would have if there was some legal way to detain me. Luckily we were able to come to a compromise with my babysitter out front," Andi said and bit into her chicken.

"That was nice of you to give the patrol officer *our* egg rolls," Cooper said and rolled his eyes.

"Well, it's got to be a boring job, sitting out there in his car, watching my house all night," Andi said after swallowing her food.

"Let's hope so," Cooper replied.

He set his carton down on the table, turned to face her, placing his right arm on the back of the sofa and his left hand on her knee. Dodger licked his fingers.

"Andi, I wanted to talk to you this morning, but you were so miserable with your hangover, and I had a meeting with an important client."

Cooper took a deep breath and exhaled slowly.

"After we had that big fight," he said and then ran a hand through his hair, "well, I realized I didn't really mean what I said to you that night. I was just terrified for you and mad that you were taking unnecessary risks."

"Cooper, I had to do *something*. The police had no new leads. I don't want to go to jail for murder and anyway, someone broke into my home and trashed the place. I was being threatened before I ever went to the funeral home," Andi said.

He raised his hands in surrender, "I know. I get it now. It's just that I freaked out because," he swallowed, "I really care a lot about you. The way I feel about you, well, I've never felt this way about anyone. That's why I followed you into the bar last night. I had to make sure you were okay even if it meant I was likely to get shot or stabbed to death by a couple of gangbangers."

Andi smiled. She couldn't help it. How was it possible that this incredibly hot, sexy, sensitive, frustrating, man cared for *her*? Her life was pure chaos, and she was a mess and yet, he always seemed to be there for her.

"Well, since we're sharing feelings and all, you should know that I really care about you too, *Rock Star*. When I was almost hit by the car today at the market, your face popped in my head, and all I could think was how mad you would be that I got myself killed before we had a chance to talk," she grinned at him.

Cooper grinned back at her.

Andi set down her empty carton and yawned.

"You must be exhausted," he said.

She yawned again.

"Yes, I think I'm finally crashing after my adrenaline filled day," she said and closed her eyes a moment.

"What time does Ben get off work?" Cooper asked.

Andi yawned then opened her eyes and said, "He's closing and then going to Daniel's for the night."

"Well then, you need to go to bed."

"I'll walk you out first," she said.

Cooper's mouth dropped open, "Andi, there's no way am I leaving you alone tonight."

When she just stared at him with her stubborn expression he said, "Look, it's no big deal. It's not like this is our first sleepover."

Andi raised her eyebrows and gave him her *I'm not budging on this* look.

"*Fine*. If you're uncomfortable with it, I'll just sleep out here on your couch."

"Cooper, I won't be able to sleep knowing you're out here on my sofa. You're too big for it. You'll be miserable." She stood, took hold of his hand and pulled him up. She reached down and picked up his shoes and walked him to the door.

"See. We agree," he said as he pulled her into his arms and cupped her face, "I'll sleep with you in your bed. That way everyone's happy."

Andi bit her lip and looked up at him, "That's a problem too. I don't think I'll be able to sleep with you in my bed either."

Cooper grinned and tilted his head, "I'm okay with that. I probably won't be able to sleep either, so we'll just have to find something else to do in your bed."

She pinched him on his waist.

"Ouch." He chuckled. "Seriously. I'm not comfortable leaving you here alone after there were two attempts on your life today."

"I'm perfectly safe. I've got my watchdog," they both glanced over to see Dodger eating the cartons left on the coffee table, "and Roanoke City's finest parked outside my house. Oh, and let's not forget about the neighborhood watch and Mrs. Barzetti's rifle."

"Mrs. Barzetti armed." He shook his head. "It's a terrifying thought."

"Believe me, Cooper, I'm perfectly safe here," she reached up and lightly kissed him on the lips.

He returned that light kiss with one filled with promises of boundless passion, a little frustration, and something else she couldn't quite identify. When he finally ended the kiss, they were both breathing hard.

"Andi, *please* let me stay. When I arrived at the mall today and saw the pile of metal that was your car," he sighed and shook off the memory. He hugged her tight. Thank god she was really here, alive and in his arms.

"Oh Cooper," she said as she hugged him back, "It's just that everything is so crazy, and I can't think clearly. Especially when you kiss me like that," she gave him a half smile and then looked away. "I guess I'm afraid. My feelings for you scare me," she said. "It's all overwhelming."

Cooper nodded. The last thing he wanted to do was make things harder for her.

"Fine," he sighed, resigned to his fate.

He put his fingers under her chin and lifted her face until she was looking at him again.

"Only if you promise me you'll be safe. If you have to leave the house for any reason, call me, and I'll come with you."

"Where am I going to go? I don't have a car anymore."

"You're resourceful. Promise me," he cupped her face with both hands, "We're in this together, okay?"

She smiled and said, "Okay," and she set his shoes down.

Cooper slid them on and then turned to face Andi. He gently kissed her forehead because he was afraid he'd renege on his promise to leave if he got anywhere near those amazing lips again.

"Good night, Andi. Sweet dreams," he said as he turned and stepped out on the porch, "Lock up, okay? If you change your mind about being alone, call me?"

"I will. Good night, Cooper," she said and watched him walk down to his car.

Chapter Ten

Andi didn't sleep well, despite being exhausted. She got up early, showered and dressed, fed Dodger and let him outside before sitting down to eat a bowl of cereal. She had just finished eating when her cell phone rang. She glanced at the screen—Detective Kendricks.

"Good morning, Detective. You're up nice and early," Andi said.

"Actually, I'm just getting ready to go to bed. I've been working on the case all night and have just finished up my report. I wanted to let you know that we've identified the body."

Oh no. She was glad that she wasn't incinerated in the explosion, but she still felt responsible for the woman who was killed. The bomb was meant for her and instead, some poor woman, who just happened to be in the wrong place at the wrong time, paid with her life.

"Who was she?" Andi asked in a whispered voice.

"I'm sorry, Andi," he said softly, "It was your friend Liz."

"What?" Andi asked. She thought it must have been some random mall shopper that bumped into her car or something. She never imagined it was someone she knew.

"What was Liz doing at my car?" she asked.

"I was hoping you could answer that question," he said, "When was the last time you talked to her?"

243

"The last time I saw her was at *The Last Call*. We sang karaoke and then Cooper took me home. Poor Liz," she said as her eyes filled with tears.

"Do you have any reason to believe Liz could have set the bomb for you? Maybe it went off early?"

"No," Andi shook her head, "I didn't really know her very well, but she seemed like a good person, you know? She had bad taste in men and anger management issues, but I can't imagine she'd ever try to blow someone up. No, Detective. She didn't plant a bomb. If she was going to damage a car, she'd use a brick or tire iron."

"I don't really think it was her either," Kendricks said, "What about her boyfriend?"

"I only met him briefly that night, but I didn't like him. He had a hard look about him. Dangerous. I think he's capable of killing someone. I have no idea why he'd want to blow me up unless he recognized me in my disguise and there's no way he could have."

"*I* recognized you," Kendricks said.

"*You* only recognized my voice. Rapier has never heard my voice."

"Maybe Liz told him who you were," he said.

"That's possible. She had a blind spot where men were concerned. It would explain why he stared at me all night like he knew I wasn't who I was pretending to be. *Poor Liz*. I just can't believe she's dead."

"Andi, plan on working from home today, okay?" Kendricks said.

"Am I under house arrest?"

"No, but you're safer if you stay at home. If you're not worried about your own safety, at least consider the safety of the police officer that has to guard you. Whoever is out to get you is very determined. I'm tired, and I don't need any new homicides."

"Fine. I've got some files here that I can work on. Please let me know when you learn anything new. Go get some sleep, detective."

"I will. Stay put, Andi," Kendricks said.

After she hung up, she pulled out her notebook, a repo file folder and looked in her kitchen drawer for a pen. Was Dodger eating them? She reached into her purse to find one. Why did everything always sink to the bottom of her purse? With a sigh, she dumped the contents out onto her kitchen table and spotted five pens. She shouldn't have blamed the poor dog.

That's weird. She saw the silver pen and picked it up, looking at it closely. It wasn't one of her dollar store black pens. This one was a more expensive looking metal pen—her heart rate accelerated—*like the one Keith had at the memorial service.*

"*No way,*" Andi whispered.

She carefully held the pen with a hand on each end and gently pulled it apart. It was one of Thomas' gadgets! A flash-drive. In her purse. Must have gotten mixed up with the stuff that went flying in the car the night of the accident and since it just looked like a pen, it got sorted with her stuff.

What were you involved in Milner?

She inserted the flash-drive into her laptop and saw there were three files stored on it. She opened the first file.

It was a porn video of a couple having sex on—was that a trapeze?

"Classy, Milner," Andi said and tilted her head, "I didn't know that was physically possible."

She quickly closed the file and shook her head to erase the scene from her mind.

Andi opened the second file and squinted her eyes, afraid to look. She really had no desire to see anyone else having sex. Unfortunately, she didn't get a vote because there was a naked man standing directly in front of the camera—*yikes*—saying something about charging the camera for hours yesterday, so there would be plenty of battery life. *Holy Mary, Mother of God.* The camera was at waist height, so she didn't see his face but saw everything else. This must have been some sort of homemade sex tape. She was about to close the file when she heard a second, familiar male voice in the background. He was also naked—great—and she could see his face. He was asking the first guy if the camera was pointed at a good angle. She didn't recognize his face, but she knew that voice—*The Broker*. Now she definitely knew what he looked like. Really more than she ever wanted to see. The first guy stepped back to stand next to The Broker, and she finally could see his face. That was a face she recognized. It was Councilman Felix Evans. No wonder The Broker said this would cover the $35,000 Andi owed him. She slid her chair back and stood up.

"YES!" she shouted and raised her hands over her head. What a relief!

She sat back down in front of her laptop and rubbed her hands together. There was one file left. Could this be what Milner had used to blackmail the Diamond Auto Body guys? Andi double clicked the file and looked at it. It looked like some sort of delivery schedule spreadsheet. There were columns with dates, addresses, and packages measured in grams. That's odd – grams were used for small weights which wouldn't be practical unless the packages—were filled with drugs!

She scanned down the business names and saw Diamond Auto Body Shop listed multiple times and the home address of James Foley—the ice cream truck driver! Yes! This must be it! From her laptop, she sent the file to her phone. She called Detective Kendricks, but it went immediately to voice mail, so she left a message.

"Detective, I took your advice and worked from home today and I found it! The men who ransacked my house were looking for a flash drive that contained the delivery schedule for what I believe are drugs, being trafficked into Roanoke. The list of businesses includes Diamond Auto Body Shop and James Foley—my ice cream truck repo. I bet Thomas was blackmailing the Diamond Auto Body guys and they killed him. When they couldn't find the file on him, they assumed I had it, which I did, I just didn't realize it. I know this doesn't tell you specifically who killed Milner, but it should be a huge lead in the investigation and at least take me off the top of the list of suspects. As soon as I hang up, I'll send the file to you via text. Oh, and it looks like there's a delivery scheduled for today at a warehouse on 12th Street. I'm staying put like you requested. Sleep well."

She hung up and forwarded the file to Kendricks. Then, she rummaged through her purse until she found the business card from Detective Sanchez. The man made her nervous, so instead of calling him, she just sent a text and attached the file to it.

> I found a file that might be a delivery
> schedule for drugs being trafficked
> into Roanoke. The list of businesses
> includes Diamond Auto Body Shop and
> James Foley. Big delivery scheduled for
> today at a warehouse on 12th Street.
> Hope this helps with your
> investigation. - Andi Sloan

She saved the sex movie onto an empty flash-drive and then dropped it in her purse—she'd deliver it to The Broker later today. She called the number she'd programmed in her phone for him under Bail Bondsman.

"Hello, this is Andrea Sloan. I'm trying to reach The Broker. He said I could reach him at this number."

A man with a deep voice answered, "He's unavailable. Give me your message, and I'll see that he gets it."

Andi wondered if this was the same guy that had shoved her in the back of the car the night she met The Broker.

"Please tell him that I found what he was looking for, and I'm ready to exchange it as payment for my bond. He can reach me at this number I'm calling you from."

Now, what to do with the evidence. She'd sent the police the information they needed. She knew enough about computers to know that any deleted files could be recovered which meant she wasn't going to be able to turn over the silver pen without risking the discovery of The Broker's sex file. *Hmm*, it was probably illegal to tamper with evidence, but, she shrugged, she was between a rock and a hard place. With that thought, she got a hammer out of her kitchen drawer and smashed Milner's silver pen flash-drive with a couple quick whacks. No one would be recovering that data. She swept the mess into the trash.

There was a knock on her door. She peeked out the window and saw it was a police officer. She read his name tag, Mike Herrick, unlocked the door and opened it.

"Good morning Miss Sloan. Detective Kendricks wants me to drive you over to the station. He's got some new information and a bunch of questions he wants to ask you."

"Must be about the file I just sent to him. Just let me just grab my purse and lock up. I'll be right out."

When she walked out to the patrol car a few minutes later, Officer Mike Herrick opened the back car door for her.

"Sorry. It's policy that only officers can ride in the front seat. Don't worry, it's a short drive."

"That's okay. This isn't my first time riding in the back of a police car. As long as I'm not handcuffed, I don't mind," Andi smiled up at him as he closed the door and then he got in the driver's seat.

"You've had quite a time of it. In all my years on the force, we've never dealt with a car bomb before. That was something else, huh?"

Andi said, "Yes. I was very lucky," and frowned as she thought about Liz. She was looking out the side window when she noticed they weren't headed to the police station but driving down Campbell Avenue. *This wasn't right.* They turned onto 12th Street into a warehouse parking lot. There was a large white truck and several men were unloading boxes.

"Mike, what are we doing *here*?" Andi asked.

Mike looked at her in the rearview mirror and grinned.

"I thought you wanted to find out who was responsible for killing Thomas Milner and blowing up your car. Well, here we are. The person responsible is anxious to talk to you."

Andi glanced at the door—no handles—she was trapped. *Stay calm.* Of course, that became even more difficult when Mike opened her back door, his revolver pointed at her.

"Come on," he said, "we're going inside."

The men unloading boxes ignored them completely. The warehouse was a huge, metal building. Large windows, at least 12 feet from the ground level, provided lots of natural lighting but no means of escape. *Don't panic.* The inside of the warehouse was filled with huge boxes of different sizes and shapes that were stacked neatly in rows. Mike pushed her toward the center of the building where there was a break in the rows of boxes. Smaller boxes were scattered throughout the open space and two men stood talking to each other.

"The boss' special package is here," Mike said, and the two men turned around to face them.

It was Rapier and Bowie, from the bar the other night.

Rapier stepped forward, "You *bitch*," he spat as he pulled out a rather large knife and moved toward her.

Jesus, Mary, and Joseph

Rapier, with lightning speed, held the blade to within an inch of Andi's neck and said, "It's your fault Liz is dead. The bomb was meant for *you,* not her."

He narrowed his eyes and his lips curved up just a bit, "I'm going to enjoy slicing you until you beg me to kill you."

Mike pointed the gun at Rapier, "Put the *damn* knife down before I shoot your sorry ass. The boss wants to take care of her. You've already had your chance."

He waited until Rapier put his blade away and stepped back from Andi.

Mike said, "Bowie, tie her up."

Bowie approached her with that same flirty grin from the other night at the bar, pulled zip ties from his pocket and then pulled her arms behind her back. *Don't panic.* Andi bunched her forearms toward her chest as Bowie tied her hands behind her back. After her meeting with The Broker, she'd used the internet to look up how to escape such a situation. Who knew she'd be testing out this knowledge so soon.

Bowie whispered in her ear, "You left early the other night before you and I could have some fun, *Tiffany*. I think I like you better as a blond."

"*Please* Bowie. Don't do this," Andi pleaded, quietly so that Mike couldn't hear her.

He tugged on the ties until they were tight around her wrist.

"Sorry babe. You shouldn't have come snooping around the bar."

Well, she wouldn't be getting any help from him.

Bowie pushed her back until she was sitting on one of the boxes then he stepped away.

He snickered and turned to Mike, "The boss' present is all tied up and ready."

Andi glared at the two gang members.

With a superior tone, she said, "I'm not surprised you two *scumbags* are involved in drugs and murder," then she turned to look at Mike with disgust, "but you? On the gang payroll Officer Herrick? How cliché."

Mike sneered back at her, "Shut up or I'll let Rapier sharpen his knife on you."

Andi looked at Rapier and said, "Liz was a good person. She didn't deserve to die like that," and she blinked back the tears that filled her eyes.

Rapier clenched his teeth, stepped forward and punched Andi in the face.

The force of the impact knocked Andi to the floor on her side. She felt numbness on the right side of her face, dazed from the punch, and then she became aware of the cold concrete floor on her side. From the floor, she had a clear view of everyone's shoes. *Huh, not helpful.* She began to wonder if she had a concussion. There wasn't time to ponder that too much because Rapier was hovering over her in a full rage. He yanked her up by the arms and began shaking her.

Andi heard a couple of loud noises from outside, and then someone yelled, "POLICE, drop your weapons, and put your hands in the air!"

She knew that angry voice. Turning her head towards the sound, she saw Detectives Kendricks and Richardson, armed and pointing their weapons at Mike and Rapier. *Thank heavens!*

"Slowly step away from Andi," Kendricks growled.

Rapier looked at both Kendricks and then Richardson before he stepped away from Andi, his hands raised high in the air.

"Are you alright, Andi?" Kendricks asked from the other side of the room.

"Yes," she said, softer than she intended. Now that the cavalry was here, she was starting to feel a little shaky. *Hold it together. Just a little longer.*

That's when Detective Richardson turned toward Kendricks and fired her weapon.

"*No!*" Andi yelled.

Kendricks dropped behind a crate. Did he fall because he was dead or did he dive behind there to take cover? *Please be alive.*

With everyone's attention on Kendricks, Andi plopped down on the floor behind the box where she'd been sitting. She rolled onto her back and lifting her legs straight up in the air, tried to scoot her butt through her arms, so she could get her hands in front of her. She wiggled and squirmed. The guy on the YouTube video made this look a lot easier than it was. He probably didn't enjoy a regular diet of M&Ms and Cheese Curls like she did. *Just relax and slide through.* If she lived through this, she was going to eat healthier and have a more toned skinny butt. Maybe even take a yoga class.

"You two," Richardson looked at Mike and Rapier, "go make sure he's dead."

The two men ran behind the crate, and Andi heard another gunshot.

No. Andi closed her eyes and swallowed back tears. *Kendricks couldn't be dead. He was her Thor, right?* She couldn't focus on that now – she had to get herself free. She wasn't going to be any use to anyone if she was dead. She inhaled and then slowly exhaled like she had all the time in the world. Then she tried once again, and this time, her butt slid through her arms. She wiggled some more so that her legs followed and then—*YES*—her hands were in front of her.

"Looks like he's been hit. There's blood on the floor, but Kendricks is gone," Mike hollered from behind the crate.

Richardson yelled, "Find him and kill him!"

Andi placed her palms together like she was praying; she really should. She could use all the help she could get. Using her palms as leverage, she pulled her wrists apart with all her might and *snap* – the plastic ties broke and her hands were free.

Richardson told Bowie, "You go help them. I've got this."

Andi was sitting on the floor, hands behind her back planning to push herself up off the floor and take off running for the other end of the building when she saw Richardson standing in front of her, gun pointed at her head, looking at Andi with such loathing. Andi slid her hands together, behind her back, like she was still cuffed.

"It's *you*? *You're* the Boss?" Andi asked.

Richardson frowned and in her southern drawl said, "Now, look what you made me do. I've had to go and kill my partner, and he was so easy on the eyes."

The detective sighed impatiently.

"Oh, don't look at me like I'm some sort of monster. This is all your fault, after all. I wouldn't have had to shoot Detective Dreamboat if you had just simply *died* like a normal person. You had plenty of opportunities. A quick and easy hit and run? A car bomb? But then you are a very lucky and smart woman, aren't you? Men always underestimate us. Just like me, you're working in a traditionally male-dominated career. Women have to work twice as hard as men and still get paid less and passed over for promotions. Ah, but a clever woman, now she'll use that to her advantage. Especially if she's the head of a billion-dollar drug empire. What better place to hide than in plain sight as a detective? What better place to track your competitors and remove them from the game board than by arresting them? Yes. Being a detective has its benefits, although the paperwork's a bitch."

While Richardson was talking, Andi glanced around the warehouse looking for some kind of weapon she could use. There wasn't much there—only lots of boxes and crates. Plus, what could she use against a gun, anyway? The only thing she saw was her purse. It had fallen on the floor next to the boxes when Bowie had tied her up. She didn't have any weapons in there anyway. The only useful items in there were her phone and Gram's binoculars, and neither of those items were much good in a gunfight. Plus, it wasn't like she could reach over and grab it without Richardson shooting her first.

The detective saw her looking around the room.

"Aw, darlin', nobody's going to be coming to your rescue. Your champion, Detective Dreamboat, is probably bleeding out somewhere in the warehouse. If he doesn't die from that, one of my boys will find him and finish him off."

Richardson smiled.

"And no one knows you're here. I switched the patrol officers this morning, so my very own pawn, Officer Herrick, could bring you to me. I was planning to come here to kill you all by myself, but you had to go and send Kendricks that schedule this morning. Very inconvenient. He called the officer who was supposed to be on duty, found out there was a change, and because he's a suspicious bastard, he tracked your location from your phone and followed you here."

The detective rolled her eyes, "Oh, let me tell you, he was furious." Richardson leaned forward and in an exaggerated whisper, said, "Between us girls, I think he really likes you."

There were more gunshots outside. Andi winced.

"Yes, that's probably my boys taking out Kendricks now. As for you, Andrea Sloan, I'm going to kill you myself. I've had two of my top gang members try to take you out," she shrugged, "but like my momma always said, if you want something done right, you've just got to do it yourself. Bye-bye, Andi. It's just business. Nothing personal, sugar."

"POLICE, drop your weapon, and put your hands in the air where I can see them," Detective Sanchez said from behind the box where Kendricks had been shot.

Richardson glanced over her shoulder and then turned back to Andi.

"Oh, for the love of God," she whispered in frustration.

In a louder voice, Richardson said, "Detective Sanchez, I've got the situation under control."

She continued pointing the gun at Andi as she spoke more lies to Sanchez.

"This girl shot and killed my partner and was one of the key players in that drug ring you've been trying to tear down. I've already cuffed her, and I was just about to read her rights."

"Detective Richardson, I need you to slowly place your gun on the ground, and put your hands in the air where I can see them. I will *not* ask you again."

Richardson bit her lip for a couple seconds, then spun around to fire at Sanchez. In one quick motion, Andi jumped up, grabbed her purse and swung it hard at Richardson's head, knocking her off balance, making the bullet Richardson fired at Sanchez go wide. Then, Sanchez fired off three rapid shots, and Richardson dropped to the floor. Andi dropped her purse and raised her hands in the air. She did not want to get shot today.

Sanchez walked over to Richardson, knelt down next to her body, and checked her pulse. Andi stared down at the detective's chest that had three red circles that looked like red roses blooming on her pale pink silk blouse. A pool of blood was forming beneath her body. Then Andi looked at her eyes, still open, staring blankly up at her.

Detective Sanchez looked up at Andi and said, "She's dead."

He stood and looked Andi over, from her head to toes and back into her eyes. "Are you all right?"

Andi nodded yes, but she wasn't really sure that was the truth.

Then, as if suddenly awake, she asked, "Have you seen Detective Kendricks? Richardson shot him right over there, and then he ran off, and she sent two other gang members after him. Oh, and Officer Mike Herrick is working for her too. He's the one who brought me here."

Andi grabbed a hold of Sanchez's sleeve, "You've got to find Detective Kendricks! They were trying to kill him, and I'm afraid he might already be dead!"

Sanchez nodded, "Come with me." He gently took her by the arm, and they walked back outside to the parking lot.

There were police officers all over the place, about a half dozen men in handcuffs, and a couple ambulances. Andi *heard* Kendricks before she saw him.

"I'll get the damned treatment *after* I apprehend all the suspects! You've got to let me up, so I can do my job!" Kendricks yelled.

She spotted him, lying on a gurney, shirtless, as one paramedic was hooking up an IV in his right arm, and the other one was attempting to get an oxygen mask on him. He kept waving the medic away with his good arm. His shoulder was wrapped in a large white bandage.

She stopped at the foot of the stretcher and just stared. *Kendricks was alive—thank goodness.* He'd been shot by his partner, chased by a bad cop and members of a gang, and yet here he was, injured yes, but alive. *Huh, maybe he really was Thor after all.*

Sanchez spoke to another paramedic, "I need someone to check this woman out to make sure she's alright."

Kendricks stopped yelling, looked over at Sanchez and that's when he saw Andi. *Jesus.* She had blood splattered over her clothes, an abrasion on her temple, and the right side of her face was a yellowish-purple color. She looked like she'd been to hell and back, but she was alive. He felt a wave of relief rush over him.

Kendricks looked back at Sanchez and asked, "Richardson?"

"She's dead. It would have been me lying dead on the warehouse floor if it weren't for Miss Sloan."

Kendricks nodded at Sanchez and then looked at Andi with a half-smile.

He turned his attention back to Sanchez.

"How did you know to come here?" Kendricks asked.

"Again, we have Miss Sloan to thank," Sanchez said and glanced over at Andi with a genuine smile. "She sent me a text with a spreadsheet attachment and pointed out this address and today's scheduled delivery. Thanks to her, I was able to make another huge drug bust, even bigger than the ice cream truck, and finally find the person behind the drug trafficking ring."

Kendricks started to get up and was immediately held down by both paramedics. The medics raised the gurney and lifted him into the ambulance.

"I can't leave now. I've got lots of work still left to do here!" he yelled to both paramedics.

Sanchez smiled and said, "No, detective. You need to go to the hospital and get that bullet removed. As you can see, this is *my* narcotics investigation. There are drugs involved, and I need to question my witness down at the station, once the paramedics attend to her injuries. *You* can read my report tomorrow. Back at the station. From your desk."

Kendricks grumbled and Sanchez smiled—a real smile that lit up his whole face.

Chapter Eleven

The rest of the day was exhausting. Andi spent most of it at the police station answering all of Sanchez's questions the best she could. Of course, she omitted details about destroying Tommy's fake pen and the file on The Broker. He thanked her again for saving his life, and she thanked him for saving hers. If he hadn't arrived exactly when he did, she'd have a bullet in her brain—no question about that.

Sanchez was much less intimidating when he smiled, and he was doing that a lot. Collecting all those illegal drugs, arresting the bad cop and the punks from the gang, and taking out the head of the organization, made him a *very* happy cop. Later in the afternoon, they got word that Detective Kendricks was out of surgery and doing well. Apparently, he was throwing a fit about not being released from the hospital until tomorrow.

Andi had called Cooper and her friends after she was safely back at the station and told them all about her adventure. She assured them all that she was alright and, honestly, she really was. Sure, she'd probably have nightmares for the next few weeks about Detective Richardson's dead eyes staring at her and having guns and knives pointed at her in a threatening way, but she was okay.

She took a taxi home, walked up the porch steps and unlocked her door. She could hear Dodger barking like crazy and scratching at a door. *Huh.* She must have accidentally closed him up in a room before she left with Officer Herrick this morning. She stepped into the living room, dropped her keys back in her purse, and set her purse on the table near the door.

"Poor boy," she said in that playful voice she used whenever she talked to him, "have you spent all day locked up in my bedroom?"

She took a couple steps toward the hallway when Rapier stepped out of the kitchen, his long knife pointed at her. She screamed, at first startled and that was quickly replaced by terror.

"I've come to finish what we started at the warehouse," he said.

He was dirty, bloody, and pointing that knife at her again. He wasn't as close to her this time, but his face was more terrifying. His eyes had a wild, crazed look. She was in big trouble.

Andi began backing up slowly, back towards the living room. *Oh. My. God.* She was shaking all over, and her heart was pounding in her chest. *She'd survived the warehouse horror only to be killed in her home. Now. By this homicidal maniac.* She began pleading with him.

"Rapier, you don't need to do this. Listen, your boss is dead, your gang has been arrested. Leave here, get out of town before someone comes over, sees and arrests you too. I've got very nosy neighbors. I'm surprised they aren't here already."

He kept walking towards her, that crazy expression fixed on his face. Andi's eyes filled with tears. *This was it.* She shook her head. *She didn't want to die.* A sob escaped from her.

Rapier's eyes narrowed, his brows furrowed, and his lip curled. "There's no place for me to go. You took *everything* from me: my girlfriend, my job, my gang. I'm going to make you pay, repo girl. Just like I promised."

Then he stopped suddenly, his eyes changed from crazed to startled, and he dropped face down onto the floor in front of Andi. *What?* She looked down, and there was a knife sticking out of his back. *How?* She looked up again and standing in the arch between her kitchen and living room was the big bald guy that had shoved her into The Broker's car.

He said, "Live by the knife, die by the knife."

The Broker stepped around him and walked toward Andi.

"Throw him in the trunk," The Broker told his big friend and then turned to Andi. "We'll dispose of him for you."

The bald guy bent over the body, pulled his knife out of Rapier's back, and wiped the blood on the dead man's pants before sheathing it. He lifted the body, as easily as he might carry Dodger's 40-pound bag of kibble, and carried him out her kitchen door.

"I've been trying to reach you since I got your message this morning," The Broker said with a slight grin, "You've been busy today. I didn't expect you to be entertaining anyone after spending most of the day at the police station."

Andi, who had been standing in one place, mouth hanging open in surprise since Rapier dropped to the floor, finally spoke.

"Thank you," she said with a squeak.

Her voice was wobbly, so she cleared her throat and squared her shoulders.

"Thank you for saving my life just now."

Then she remembered.

"Oh, I have something for you," she said and then turned abruptly to her table by the front door and grabbed her purse. Her hands were shaking, but she somehow managed to open her purse and fumbled inside until she found the flash-drive. She quickly handed it to The Broker.

"I trust the contents of this file will remain confidential," he said with a raised eyebrow.

"Absolutely," Andi said firmly and nodded vigorously, "I fully understand the devastating effects this would have if this was ever leaked. I don't want to see anyone hurt."

The Broker studied her for a moment and then nodded. He extended his hand, and Andi quickly reached out and shook it.

"Andrea Sloan, I consider your debt paid in full."

He released her hand and began walking towards the kitchen.

He suddenly turned around and said, "You're a woman with an interesting skill set. If you ever get tired of working for Jerry, give me a call. I'd be happy to have someone like you in my employ."

Then he turned back and walked out the kitchen door.

Sweet Baby Jesus. She leaned her back against her front door and slid down until she was sitting on the floor. She needed a drink—and a security system for her house.

Chapter Twelve

Later that night, Andi was sitting at a table at Star City Bar and Grill, surrounded by her friends—friends that were really more like family. She grinned as she looked around the table. Maggy and Simon were arguing about the dangers of nitrates. Mrs. Davis and Mrs. Barzetti were discussing the best way to make chili-cheese fries, as they sampled the fries from the center of the table. Next to them, Jerry had a pained expression on his face as his grandmother, Mrs. Harper, told him about a nice girl named Beth that he absolutely had to meet. Her newest friends, Daniel and Zach, were talking with Cooper about their upcoming gig at Virginia Tech's Lane Stadium. Cooper's hand was resting on her knee. He was talking excitedly with the guys about how many seats they were likely to fill at their first big concert.

Cooper. He'd arrived on her doorstep less than ten minutes after she'd called him, just after The Broker had left, and the last of her adrenaline had finally fizzled out. He just held her on the sofa while she cried—tears for Liz, tears for Detective Kendricks when she thought he was dead, and even tears for Detective Richardson and crazy Rapier. When she finally stopped crying, she took two ibuprofen, washed away the trauma from her day in the shower, and got dressed. Cooper informed her they were going to Star City Bar & Grill to celebrate. When they arrived, everyone was already there, waiting for them. They exchanged hugs, she told them all an abbreviated version of her day, brushing over some of the more scary and gruesome parts.

Ben came back from the bar carrying a tray full of bright blue drinks. He passed one out to everyone and then held his up in a toast.

"This is my latest creation because," he looked at Andi, "*damn girl*, your life is an inspiration for drinking."

Everyone at the table laughed.

"Since I created the *jailbird* when you got arrested, I decided you deserved a drink for being cleared of your murder charges. This is the *freebird*. Let's toast to our dearest friend, Andi Sloan, Repo-Girl Extraordinaire; we love you. Cheers!"

Everyone said, "Cheers!" and took a sip.

Andi stood up, held her glass up and said, "Before she was shot to death, Detective Richardson said I was a very lucky woman, and she was right. I have the *best* friends in the world. I could not survive this crazy life of mine without each and every one of you," she looked at each of her dear friends and smiled, "I love you guys. Cheers!"

Everyone said, "Cheers!" and took another drink.

The rest of the evening was filled with laughter, silliness, and dancing. She was on the dance floor with Cooper during a slow song, her arms were around his neck, his arms were wrapped around her waist, and their foreheads were touching. This felt so right. *He felt so right.*

Cooper smiled at her, "This is nice."

Andi smiled back, "Yes."

"You know, I'm beginning to realize that this is probably the new norm for us."

Andi pulled her head back in alarm, "I hope not!" Then she relaxed and rested her forehead back on his and said, "But if it is, there's no one else I'd rather have by my side."

"I knew my life would never be the same that first night I met you." Cooper shook his head.

Andi smiled. "You know, almost dying multiple times in less than eight hours has really brought clarity to my life."

Cooper pulled her closer just to reassure himself she was really alive and in his arms.

"Really?" he asked, "Please don't feel you need to go to such extremes next time you're feeling unsure about something, okay?"

"I promise not to make a habit of it," she grinned, "but it did clear up something I'd been worried about."

"What's that?" he asked.

"I think I'm finally ready for that sleepover you've been promising me."

He stopped moving and held her back, so he could look into her eyes.

"You're sure?"

She gave him a slow, seductive smile and whispered, "Yes."

He gently kissed her and then took her hand and pulled her off the dance floor.

"What are you doing?" she asked as he dragged her towards the doors.

"Taking you home. *Right now*," he pulled her in for another kiss.

"But I have to pay for dinner," she said, looking back at the table.

"I already took care of it. Now let me take care of you."

"Hey, we're in this together," she said as she brushed her lips against his. "We'll take care of each other."

Thanks for reading Repo Girl!

If you enjoyed this book and would like to read more adventures with Andi and her friends, check out the fun sequel—A Repo Girl Christmas. Also, you can head over to my website www.JaneFenton.org to sign-up for my newsletter to find out about the latest books, contests, and giveaways.

Acknowledgements

This book is about learning to trust in love, and I wouldn't have been able to write it without the tremendous love, support, and encouragement from my amazing family and friends.

First, I'd like to thank the brilliant, meticulous editors that proofed my final draft and provided valuable insight; Candy Andrzejewski, Sue Quaintance, Julie Vice, and Debbie Teeple.

Second, I'm very grateful for my creative home team— Andy, Emma, & Peyton—for providing tons of suggestions for evil characters and terrible catastrophes—*it's really quite scary that these ideas came so easily to you.*

Third, I have to give special thanks to my sister and publicist, Amy Rider, for telling complete strangers that I was a best-selling author and writing *Repo Girl* before I had even completed the rough outline.

Special thanks to my Mom, for giving me a lifetime of unconditional love and always nudging me in the direction of my dreams.

A big thank you goes out to Emma Fenton, for embarking on this exciting adventure in writing with me, reading through *all* the versions of this book, and encouraging me to "expand" the story in just the right places.

Finally, thank you, Peyton—my best-friend, husband and love of my life—for helping me realize my dreams and sharing this incredible life adventure.

About the Author

Jane Fenton is an avid reader of books that combine romance, mystery, and laughter because they're as satisfying as a triple fudge sundae — without the calories. Although she shares her heroine's love of Roanoke City, good friends, junk food, stray dogs, and Jeep Wranglers, she's quite happy to create these fun misadventures from the comfort of her quiet farmhouse in the foothills of the Blue Ridge Mountains in Virginia where she lives with her family.

61764863R00148

Made in the USA
Columbia, SC
26 June 2019